VALOR WINGS

SAM SUBITY

SCHOLASTIC PRESS · NEW YORK

All rights reserved. Published by Scholastic Press, an imprint
of Scholastic Inc., *Publishers since 1920.* SCHOLASTIC, SCHOLASTIC
PRESS, and associated logos are trademarks and/or registered
trademarks of Scholastic Inc.

The publisher does not have any control over and does not
assume any responsibility for author or third-party websites
or their content.

While inspired by real events and historical characters, this
is a work of fiction and does not claim to be historically
accurate or portray factual events or relationships. Please
keep in mind that references to actual persons, living or dead,
business establishments, events, or locales may not be factually
accurate, but rather fictionalized by the author.

Library of Congress Cataloging-in-Publication Data available

ISBN 978-1-338-88503-3

10 9 8 7 6 5 4 3 2 1   24 25 26 27 28
Printed in Italy   183

First edition, September 2024

Book design by Christopher Stengel

For my grandfather, who taught me
you don't need wings to soar

CHAPTER ONE

IRIS

England, May 1940

Each day Iris woke before dawn to milk the cows, feed the chickens, and leave breakfast for the dragon. A half dozen fresh eggs—or sometimes a couple more if she thought they wouldn't be missed—placed on a tree stump near the edge of the forest. Iris liked to save this task for last so that she could lie in the tall grass and watch. Because oh, what a thrill it was to watch!

The dark wood bordering her family's farm would fall silent as if the whole world had frozen in hushed anticipation. Even the fog that silently crept in each night from the sea appeared to cease curling lazily through the trees.

Today was no different. Iris held her breath, not wanting to break the spell.

Everything watching. Waiting.

Something stirred in the grass nearby. As Iris turned toward the noise, a huge form loomed out of the grass and barreled into her from the other direction. Iris tumbled over and found her shoulders pinned to the ground. A pair of large golden eyes stared down at her.

The eyes of a dragon.

Iris exploded in a fit of laughter. "Galahad! Get off me, you big brute!"

The dragon snorted puffs of smoke in a harrumph of protest.

Iris wrinkled her nose and waved her hand in front of her face. "Ugh, what in the world did you eat for breakfast?"

The dragon made a small rumble in the back of his throat.

"Fine. You're a glorious creature of unmatched beauty and odor," she deadpanned. "Now get off me."

Satisfied, Galahad shifted his horse-sized bulk. Iris got to her feet and brushed herself off. The dragon curled his body around hers and gently nudged her toward the stump, gesturing with his snout at the eggs.

"Oh," Iris said, "you want *me* to eat them?" She lifted her nose snootily in the air. "Well, sir, ladies prefer our eggs cooked."

Galahad spat a small fireball. The eggs instantly burst into flame.

"Galahad!" she chided playfully, and hurried to put out the flames. Shaking her head, she stared down skeptically at the charred lumps. "A little too well done for my taste, I'm afraid."

Then, becoming more serious, she stepped toward the dragon. "What would you think about another flying lesson today?" Galahad started to turn his head away, but Iris gently reached out and guided his snout back so that their eyes met. "You can do it. I'm sure of it. You're only . . . a little afraid. I know. I am too."

She suspected that Galahad's fear largely stemmed from being orphaned at an early age and having no older dragons to teach him dragonish things. His body already bore a few bumps and bruises from his previous unsuccessful attempts at flight.

But Iris refused to give up. As Galahad had grown older,

she'd observed him watching other creatures with wistful interest. Ducks flocking together. A herd of sheep grazing in quiet community. She sensed that he longed to be among his own kind. Which was why she continued to gently persist in their lessons. She realized she was a poor substitute for another dragon to teach him. But that was just the problem. There *were* no other dragons.

For centuries, a herd of dragons had lived in the forest near her village. However, conflicts with humans had forced them to gradually depart for the wilds somewhere far to the north. By the time Iris had been born nearly fourteen years ago, all the dragons were gone. All except for Galahad. Iris believed that teaching him to fly was the key to his following the dragons one day and reuniting with his herd.

The creaking of an approaching wagon pulled her out of her thoughts.

"Galahad, quickly!" she said. By the time she turned around, the dragon had already disappeared into the forest with barely a rustle of leaves.

"Ah, there you are!"

Iris's shoulders relaxed. It was only her older brother, Jamie. He and her father were probably the only ones who didn't think she was crazy for befriending a dragon. Most everyone in their village had enthusiastically bid good riddance to the dragon herd. As well as blaming dragons for the occasional goat or sheep that went missing, dragons were widely considered to harbor disease, and worse, foul magic.

Iris had her doubts about the former, but she knew the latter to be utter nonsense.

The rising sun framed her brother's strong form as he approached in a rickety hay wagon pulled by their mare, Juniper. The horse neighed warily as they drew near, scenting the dragon.

"Easy, girl," Iris said, running a hand along the horse's neck.

"Been playing with your dragon again?" Jamie asked. He looked her over closely as if expecting to find her missing a limb.

"He's not *my* dragon," Iris protested. "Galahad belongs to no one but himself. And besides, he's perfectly harmless."

"Well, in case it's escaped your attention, your once-little hatchling is now a beast as big as a horse. With sharp claws as long as a man's fingers. Oh, and he breathes fire. So forgive me for—"

"Your extreme pigheadedness?" Iris knew her brother adored her, but even so she felt it to be her sisterly obligation to point out his lack of reason where her safety was concerned.

Jamie cocked an eyebrow at her. "If you're done pouting, Dad's asked me to go down to the village to pick up a few things. Thought you might want to join me."

Iris's face lit up. "Oh, can I?" She scrambled onto the wagon, letting her feet dangle off the back. The village was one of her favorite places, with all its little shops and wonderful smells. It all held precious memories of her mother and the hours Iris had spent exploring its delights with her. It was almost as if her mother's gentle spirit still wandered those cobbled streets.

Soon they were winding down a lane lined with trees blooming in the late spring. After a long gray winter, the whole world seemed to burst with hope in greens and pinks. So it felt strangely out of place when a regiment of British soldiers marched by in their plain brown uniforms.

Her heart squeezed with worry when she noticed Jamie's head turn to watch the troops. "Remember, you promised me you'd stay to help with the farm," she reminded him.

"I remember," he said, nodding slowly. "It's only, I can't help but feel that I have a duty to help our country too."

Something in her brother's voice made Iris's heart pinch, but her thoughts were soon interrupted by the clack of their wagon's wheels on the cobblestoned lanes as they entered the village. The tightly clustered shops and buildings with their shaggy thatched roofs always reminded her of squat old men sitting shoulder to shoulder. Eventually, they neared the central square and came to a stop. Iris hopped down from her perch and turned in a slow circle, trying to decide where to go first.

She felt her brother's hand on her shoulder. "Try not to cause too much trouble this time?"

"I'm sure I don't know *what* you're talking about."

"Oh, so you're already forgetting what everyone called the Great Pig Parade last spring?"

"Those pigs were being treated unfairly."

"It's a butcher's shop. That's . . . kind of the way it works." He turned and strode toward the feed store on the corner, calling over his shoulder. "Maybe try avoiding the butcher's this time? And meet me back here in an hour?"

Iris nodded, then quickly crossed the street, already enraptured by the smells wafting toward her from the bakery. She stared into the window at the rows of warm bread and sweet rolls. The shelves weren't even half-full. It was a sight that had become all too familiar with the war rationing.

She continued down the street, ignoring the "dragon girl" a few villagers muttered under their breath as she passed. At last Iris arrived at her favorite store: Pickwick's Fine Books. When she stepped inside, the store's owner, Mrs. Pickwick, turned from where she was shelving a book and smiled.

"Hello there, Miss Iris!" she said cheerfully.

"Hello, Mrs. Pickwick!" Iris replied, relieved to find a friendly face at last. She paused and breathed in the aroma of old books. The small store was stuffed practically floor to ceiling with them. Her skin tingled with excitement as she thought of the adventures waiting within their pages.

"I just happened to receive a new shipment this morning," said the bookseller, pointing to the box she had been in the process of shelving. "You're welcome to take a look if you like."

"Oh, if you don't mind?" Iris said, crossing toward the box.

"Not at all. In fact, I imagine the water is nearly ready for my tea. Would you like some?"

"Yes, thank you," Iris mumbled, already lost in studying the spines. She caught the word *Dragons* on one and quickly slipped it out of the pile. Opening it, she saw that it was a children's book. Page after page was filled with illustrations of dragons soaring through the air, carrying riders on amazing quests far away. *Maybe,* she thought, *if I showed Galahad some pictures of dragons flying—*

Suddenly, a loud clanging noise broke the morning quiet. Iris jerked her head up in surprise. She recognized the sound. It was the church bell by the village square. But it shouldn't be ringing at this time.

Something was wrong.

Racing out the bookstore's front door, she could clearly hear another noise mingling with the gonging bell: a dragon's scream.

A flame of fear ignited in Iris's chest.

Galahad was in trouble.

CHAPTER TWO

MAX

Belgium, May 1940

Five times. That was how many times the hour hand had to go around before school let out. Five whole times. The day had barely started, and already Max was itching for it to end.

This was bad.

His gaze shifted to the window of the one-room schoolhouse. Just beyond the glass, a redbud's pink blossoms promised the coming of spring. Normally, Max would have been excited at the prospect of warmer weather. But his village had spent the entire winter under the threat of a possible German invasion. Would the thaw bring enemy soldiers flooding over their border like a river swollen with melting snow?

"Eyes on your papers, children." The voice of his teacher cut into his thoughts. Max blinked and pulled his eyes away from the window. What was he supposed to be doing again? Oh yes, underlining nouns and circling verbs. And there was some bit about prepositions too.

He knew perfectly well how to construct a sentence. After all, he was going to be a writer. Just like his father. Although maybe a fiction writer rather than a journalist. He had put plenty of sentences together. He didn't understand why teachers were always so keen on having students tear them apart again. And anyway, this felt like kid stuff. Max was thirteen, not a child anymore.

The door to the schoolhouse banged open. Max's head joined twenty others that swung toward the noise. The headmaster strode in and stopped beside their teacher. As the two adults spoke in hushed tones, their teacher paled and put her hands to her mouth in surprise. Max felt worry drop like a lead ball into his stomach.

The Germans had come. He wasn't sure how he knew, but somehow, he was certain of it.

The headmaster turned toward the class, raising his arms into the air for silence. Max's father had taught him that a writer's sharp observational skills were what brought a story to life. What Max observed now was that the headmaster's hands were trembling. That made Max even more nervous. This was a man known for making others quake with fear.

"Children," he said, "I'm afraid we will have to release you from your studies for the rest of the day."

The announcement was greeted with a roar of voices, everyone asking questions and more than a few cheering the news. Max leaned back in his seat in surprise at their reaction. Had they not guessed what had happened? Or could he be wrong? He prayed with all his might that he was.

He looked across at his best friend Peter's desk. It was empty. That wasn't unusual. While Max spent most school days lost in his thoughts, Peter chose to while away the hours in the toilet. He claimed he suffered from the frequent urge to vomit. Max knew it was actually just schoolwork that made him ill.

"You are to go straight home." The headmaster spoke above the clamor. "That means no lingering in the schoolyard for games or idle gossip. Directly to your homes until you receive further instructions."

Max wasted no time in collecting his things and filing out of the room with his fellow students.

"Max!" someone called as soon as he stepped outside.

Max turned toward the voice. Peter was weaving through the crowd toward him, his face tight with tension.

"What do you think is—" Max started.

"Germans!" Peter cut in breathlessly.

Max felt like an electric shock had coursed through his body at hearing his fears confirmed. "What?! How do you know?"

Peter waited for a pair of younger kids to run past before continuing. "I was in the toilet and, well, I overheard the headmaster talking with another man."

Max slipped into his jacket as they left the schoolyard. "Who was it?"

"I didn't recognize his voice," Peter said. "They were talking about the fort. It sounded as if it might have been . . . captured."

"Captured? How? And in one day?" Max had seen some of the fort's soldiers in their village just the previous day. It wasn't an unusual sight, with the fort situated only about a mile away.

"Well, the Germans took Poland in barely more than a month," Peter said, shaking his head as he stared anxiously in the direction of the fort. "And that's a whole country!" Max knew his friend worried every day about his aunts, uncles, and cousins who still lived in Poland.

"But that seems impossible!" Max said. "Especially since there was that terrible thunderstorm last night."

"I know! I barely slept all night, the way it seemed to go on for hours."

Max studied the ground, his brain spinning as they continued walking. For the first time, he noticed the dirt lane was perfectly dry. There had clearly been no rain. His heart thudded a double beat. The rumbling that had woken him hadn't been thunder after all.

"Whatever's happening right now," Peter said, "I can't imagine simply waiting at home."

The school was out of sight now. Most of the other kids had split off in separate directions, each making their way home. Peter was right. Their village needed to know. Needed to be able to prepare if what his friend had overheard was true. He stared down the road in the direction of the fort. The road disappeared around a curve ahead, and his imagination easily supplied all sorts of dangers that loomed around the bend. Worst of all, a horde of gray-clad soldiers bristling with weapons marching their way.

His heart knocked loudly in his ears as the next thought entered his head. "What if . . ." He swallowed nervously. "What if we went to the fort ourselves to find out?"

CHAPTER THREE

IRIS

England

Iris raced through the village toward the sound of Galahad's shrieks. The narrow lanes seemed to close in around her as fear for her best friend swelled in her chest.

Her mind flashed back to the first time she'd heard that shriek, a little more than five years ago. She'd been scared then too. She was exploring the forest despite the faded wooden signs warning that dragons lived there. As she plunged deeper and deeper into the tall, dark trees, the nervous fluttering of her heart grew worse.

Peering around in the gloom, she whispered, "I'm not—"

Afraid, was how she meant to finish. But she always felt it was important to be honest with herself. And honestly, she was very much afraid.

However, she was also extremely curious. If there really *were* dragons, she desperately wanted to meet one. Even if it would be terrifying.

Iris remembered hearing the muffled crack of a gun in the distance. She stopped as the forest fell silent around her. The noises of birds chirping and tiny creatures scurrying all ceased abruptly like someone had switched off a radio. Then, into the stillness, came a low, soft shriek. The sound was unlike anything she'd ever heard, but the fear and deep loss in that single cry nearly broke her heart. Her legs trembled as she silently crept toward it. Then there he was. His golden eyes were wild and round with fear.

A baby dragon.

Iris must have made a noise because the dragon suddenly turned his huge eyes directly toward her. Iris froze, her eyes nearly as wide as his. Then, as she remembered a bit of biscuit she had in her skirt, she slowly extracted it and held it out toward the dragon. He shambled cautiously forward and sniffed at the morsel. Finally, deciding it was safe, the dragon snatched the biscuit from her palm and gulped it down whole. The girl and dragon looked at each other. Then the dragon burped, tiny tendrils of smoke trailing from his nose. Iris giggled. The dragon's mouth curled up in what seemed to be unmistakably a smile.

The two had been best friends ever since. She'd named him Galahad after the noblest of King Arthur's knights. They'd been like two lost souls. But then they'd found each other.

Another scream from Galahad tore Iris back to the present.

Arriving at the village green at last, she shoved through the mob of people that had gathered there. Everyone was yelling and talking excitedly. When Iris saw the cause of the commotion, her heart fell into her stomach. At the center of the crowd, a creature twisted and writhed against the ropes tied around his neck and legs.

Galahad.

It felt like a crime against nature itself for such a majestic spirit to be tethered there like he was nothing more than a common animal. His dull brown, mud-caked scales looked nothing like those of the beautiful dragons she had just seen in the children's book. Still, she saw echoes of nobility in the graceful curve of his long neck and the powerful wings that lay pinned against his sides. If only he could spread those wings and launch himself into the sky to safety.

"Stop!" Iris shouted, and pushed through the throng.

Suddenly, a leg shot out, and she tripped headlong onto her hands and knees. She looked back over her shoulder. It was Tommy, one of the boys from the village. *Dragon girl*, he mouthed with a sneer.

A girl standing next to him gave Tommy a sharp elbow to the ribs. He flinched and shot her a hard look, but otherwise did nothing to retaliate. The girl's name was Margaret, or Maud, as Iris had heard most people call her. Maud was the sort-of unofficial leader of the village children. As usual, she was dressed in pants and a loose-fitting shirt. Combined with her short bob haircut, the outfit made her look more like a boy than a teenage girl.

Another scream from the dragon pierced the morning air. Iris quickly pushed herself back to her feet and shouldered the rest of the way to the front of the crowd. When he saw her, Galahad made a soft, pitiful mewling noise.

Please.

It broke her heart to pieces just like it had that day so many years ago.

"Let him go!" she cried to the men struggling to hold Galahad down. "You're hurting him!"

"This dragon's a menace to our village!" shouted an older woman, pointing an accusing figure.

"It'll murder our children!" called another voice.

"But dragons are gentle!" Iris insisted, feeling like a lone voice in a hurricane. She knew Galahad could easily free himself with a swipe of his claws or a blast of his fiery breath. But she knew with just as much certainty that he would never strike out against a human, even to defend himself. "He would never hurt anyone!"

One of the men restraining the dragon glowered at Iris. "There's a sheep o' mine in its belly as would beg to differ with you." He tugged harder on the rope, pinning the dragon against the ground, and Galahad yelped in pain. "And a little wisp of a girl like you? Well, he'd gobble you right up."

Galahad, no! Iris groaned inwardly. She could almost feel the hurricane swirling faster. Ripping her breath away. So that explained why he hadn't been hungry earlier. *Never go near the villagers' livestock*, she had warned him time and again. But he was a growing dragon, and her meager offering of eggs wasn't enough to satisfy his appetite anymore.

"W-what are you going to do with him?" she asked.

"The only sensible thing," said a cold voice. Major Stevenson, the steely-eyed leader of their local regiment, stepped out of the crowd with his rifle at the ready. "Kill it."

The shock of his pronouncement made Iris's head swim. But then she collected herself and ran forward, stopping just short of the major. "You . . . you can't! I won't—"

"The beast is eating livestock that's sorely needed for our country's war effort. I'm invoking my powers as a military officer to eliminate this threat to our national security."

"That's ridiculous!" she exploded. "Galahad's no threat to anyone!"

"Oh, Galahad, is it? And I suppose that'd make you Lady Guinevere then?"

A murmur of laughter rose from the crowd, along with more mutterings of "dragon girl."

Galahad twisted in his chains and shrieked again. *Help me! Please!*

I'm trying! Iris thought. *I'm trying!* "You don't have to hurt him! There's got to be another way."

The village blacksmith raised a huge fist above his head. "I'm with the major! And I say we shoot it here and now!"

The crowd cheered.

Galahad's large, terrified eyes met Iris's. Never had her entire body ached with such fear, grief, and helplessness.

"Iris!" She felt strong arms gently wrap around her. Jamie was there at her side. She buried her face in her brother's shoulder as she burst into tears. She felt powerless. Was there nothing she could do? The jeers of the crowd filled her ears, mixed with the terrified screams of the dragon. Nearby, she heard the click of the rifle as the major took aim.

Then, before she could think better of it, Iris spun out of her brother's arms and rushed toward the major.

"NO!"

The word exploded out of her mouth as she threw herself into the line of fire.

The major's eyes went wide. At the last second, he jerked the gun's muzzle upward. With a deafening *CRACK*, it fired harmlessly into the sky. Iris felt her legs turn to water at her near brush with death. She squeezed her eyes shut and willed herself not to faint. When she opened them again, Major Stevenson was standing over her. His eyes blazed.

Jamie raised one hand placatingly. "Sir, she . . . she was only trying to help her—"

"Help her dragon?" the major spat out. "What about her countrymen? The entire German army is marching across Europe. Dark days lie ahead bleaker than any of us have ever witnessed. We are at war, and she's worried about a filthy beast?"

Iris saw the faintest glimmer of hope. "But maybe Galahad could help with the war!"

The major laughed bitterly. "Help how, exactly? The beast is so skittish the barest snap of a twig would send him running for his mother."

"He could . . ." Iris trailed off, looking around desperately for inspiration. It was hard to think straight with all the faces of the crowd turned toward her. There had to be some way Galahad could help that wouldn't put him in danger. She spotted their mare, Juniper, across the common waiting patiently with the cart. "Well, he could help transport supplies, for one."

The major frowned, so she added, "Or . . . or deliver messages."

He considered this for a long moment. "Now that's interesting. Our communications are constantly breaking down. Which makes it nearly impossible to coordinate troop movements. Can the brute fly?"

"Yes," she said quickly. "That is, well, he's only a little . . . out of practice, you see. And . . . and may need a week, or maybe two, before he's fully ready."

The officer looked from Iris to Galahad. "Very well, then. But I'll need to see proof. Today is Wednesday. I will be detained in London Thursday and Friday, so you will demonstrate his flying abilities at sunrise on Saturday. Or I won't hesitate to shoot the beast."

"That's impossible!" Iris exclaimed. "Why—"

"In the meantime, we will keep the creature under lock and key where it belongs, outside the village to prevent any further danger to the public." He looked at her pointedly. "Or its escape." Then he turned and strode off, motioning for his soldiers to bring the dragon with them.

Galahad's claws scrabbled frantically at the cobbled streets as he was dragged away, still shrieking. Iris helplessly held one hand out toward him before letting it fall to her side.

Jamie sighed and looked at Iris. "I hope you know what you're doing. This is far more serious than setting a few pigs free in the streets."

Iris's legs finally gave out, and she collapsed to her knees, burying her face in her hands.

CHAPTER FOUR

MAX

Belgium

"What?!" Peter said, eyes wide. "Go to the fort ourselves? What if it's crawling with Germans?"

"Would you rather wait at home, not knowing if the entire German army is lurking right there practically on our doorstep?" Max shivered, picturing his grandmother opening their door and finding a squad of Nazis waiting there.

"But . . . but what if we stumble right into them and are captured ourselves?"

"We won't," Max said with more confidence than he felt. "We'll cut through the woods. No one will even know we're there."

Peter hesitated, looking back and forth from the direction of the fort to the route home.

"I'd feel better if you were there with me," Max said. Then, jabbing him lightly with his elbow, he added, "Plus, you're slower than me, so the Germans will catch you instead."

Peter's mouth gaped open like a fish's before his lips slowly curled into a grin. "I clearly beat you only yesterday."

Max knew his friend was in, if just barely. Before either of them had the chance to change their minds, he tore off in the direction of the fort. "See if you can keep up then!" he called back over his shoulder.

The two boys raced down the road together before turning onto a trail on the outskirts of their village. The path snaked through the woods, rising higher as it neared the fort. After several minutes of climbing steadily uphill, the boys slowed as they approached the hilltop.

Max panted heavily, both from the exertion and fear. "Quiet now," he whispered. "We can't risk making any noise." He cautiously made his way up the final feet. It was nearly impossible to hear any sound from their movements over the thundering of his heart in his head. The flicker of courage that had burned in his chest when they were a safe distance from the fort seemed to have fizzled out now that they were close.

He glanced back at Peter. The boy's face looked nearly green. Maybe it wasn't only schoolwork that made him sick.

When he reached the top of the hill, Max ducked low beside a giant oak tree. Peter joined him, and both boys peered out across the sweeping view of the rolling countryside. An expanse of treetops stretched as far as their eyes could see. It was broken only by a thin ribbon of water where their country met the Netherlands and then Germany beyond.

And my mother and father, Max thought to himself. Early in the war, his parents had left Max in the care of his grandmother when they returned to Germany to join the underground resistance against the Nazis. He understood why they had done it. It was more than simply helping their friends and family there escape danger. They were fighting against the extermination of the entire

Jewish race at the hands of the Nazis. But their capture would almost certainly mean execution.

Max worried about them constantly, but his parents had managed to get messages out to him regularly. That is, until all communications abruptly cut off. That had been two months ago. Max's heart ached, wondering what had happened. Were they captured? Lying hidden somewhere? Were they even still alive?

He shifted his eyes to the squat fort that guarded Belgium's eastern border. Although there was no sign of trouble, he could sense a wrongness to the scene. He knew there should have at least been sentries visible walking its walls. But everything was still.

Beside him, Peter shifted nervously. "The men I overheard earlier"—the boy's voice trembled as he whispered—"I just remembered they also mentioned something else."

The tone of Peter's voice sent a chill down Max's spine. "What was it?"

"A German general who's rumored to be nearly seven feet tall. And . . . and with a black cane they say was carved by the devil himself. They said he's called . . . the Dragon."

Max shivered. Part of him wanted to turn and flee back down the hill. This general sounded like a creature from one of the fairy tales his grandmother used to tell him years ago. But now that he was older, monsters and goblins didn't scare him half as much as real, flesh-and-blood German soldiers.

"I'm sure it can't be true," Max said.

"Oh, of course," Peter agreed quickly, adding a nervous laugh. "Probably just—" Max's cry cut off the rest of his words. He gripped the tree tighter to steady himself. "The flagpole! The one over the main gate."

Peter's face turned a deeper shade of green. "The Belgian flag," he gasped. "It's . . . gone!"

At that moment, a large military truck rumbled toward the gates of the Belgian fort. On its side was a large swastika, the symbol of the German Nazis.

So it was true—the Germans had invaded Belgium.

The stories that children in Max's school whispered about the Nazis' earlier conquests of Poland and Denmark had haunted his dreams for months. Stories of destruction. Families torn apart. Men, women, and children murdered for any reason, or none at all.

Max felt as if he had climbed the hill to find himself directly in the path of a swirling black tornado. He had dreaded this day's coming for so long, but all the while never fully believing it would happen. Not to Belgium. Not to him. But he couldn't deny what he saw with his own eyes. And he knew that he and his entire village were in terrible danger.

He was torn from his thoughts by the feel of someone tugging on his arm.

"Come on!" Peter urged. "We need to go. Now! For all we know, this area may already be crawling with German scouts."

Max was on his feet in an instant. "We need to warn everyone!"

"First, we need to escape before we're captured too!" Peter said, plunging back down the trail.

Max raced after him. With every step, he imagined the thump of a seven-foot German general's boots closing in on them. He was soon out of breath, but fear propelled him onward. It was up to them to warn their village. The Germans were coming!

Just when Max thought his legs would give out, the boys arrived at a split in the trail. One direction curved south toward Peter's farm. The other led west toward the village and Max's farm beyond. Peter slowed and looked toward Max uncertainly. Max understood the reason for his hesitation—the fear that if they separated, they might never see each other again.

"Go!" Max urged his friend. "We'll meet here again after dark to share what we've learned."

Peter wavered a moment, then grasped Max's hand. "Until tonight," he said, and sprinted away.

Max raced off on the second trail with a feeling of dread steadily building in his chest. Was he already too late? The stories of the Germans' atrocities were so grim and terrifying that he didn't know what to expect. Would he arrive to find his village ablaze and bodies scattered in the street? The bodies of people he had known his entire life and . . .

. . . he stumbled and nearly lost his balance . . .

. . . his grandmother.

Max forced himself to run faster.

Soon, however, a wave of relief washed over him as the village came into sight. The forest merged into a soft green meadow that rose to a knoll where a squat brown church sat unharmed among a grove of stately maples.

"Germans!" Max began to shout as he drew nearer. "They've taken the fort!" He came around the rear of the church into the heart of his village. "The Germans are—"

Max recoiled in confusion and horror. Soldiers in the gray uniform of the German army seemed to be everywhere. One of them turned his rifle toward Max, pinning him to the spot. Among the soldiers, a dozen or so men from his village lay face down on the ground in a row. Max looked closer and was relieved to find that they were still alive. At least, for now.

At the sound of Max's shout, a giant of a man slowly turned toward him. In one hand he held a thick black cane. It had to be the German general Peter had told him about.

The Dragon.

"I am afraid you are too late, my boy," the giant said. "The Germans are already here. Your village has fallen. And soon all the West will follow."

Max's blood turned to ice. Behind the man's pale gray irises seemed to rage a soulless fire that would consume everything in his path.

Max knew at that moment that he was going to die.

CHAPTER FIVE

IRIS

England

When Iris lifted her head again, the crowd had cleared from the village green. All except her brother, Jamie, who knelt beside her with his forehead creased in worry.

"I've seen that look of yours before," he said. He held out a hand to help her up. "What are you thinking?"

All the fear, helplessness, and anger that Iris had felt at Galahad's capture had burned away, leaving her with only this single ember of determination smoldering hot and bright: She would save her friend. No matter what it took.

She took Jamie's hand and stood, brushing off her clothes. "That I've only got till Saturday morning to teach Galahad to fly, so I'd better get started."

"Well, I have an idea of something that may help with that. But I'll need some supplies from home." Jamie rested his hands on her shoulders. "Can I trust you to avoid causing more trouble?"

"That depends entirely on Major Stevenson," Iris said darkly.

"Then I'd better get to work." He squeezed her shoulders. "Galahad will be okay. We'll figure something out."

Iris watched him climb into their wagon and ride out of

sight. However, her mind was elsewhere, already busily planning Galahad's flying lessons. She knew that what little time they had was precious indeed if they were to succeed. She had read no leniency in the major's eyes. No sympathy for the life of her best friend.

But could she really teach Galahad to fly in barely three days? Iris squared her shoulders and began her march resolutely back across town toward the barracks. Passing the bookstore again, a flash of inspiration came to her. She quickly ducked inside to buy a small present to lift Galahad's spirits, then continued on her way.

As she hurried along, she replayed their previous failed flying lessons in her mind. What was she missing? There was nothing wrong with his huge, leathery wings as far as she could tell. However, he had always seemed afraid to use them, preferring to amble on the ground alongside Iris instead of taking to the sky.

Except . . . she remembered now there was a handful of times when she had observed Galahad stare up at the birds wheeling through the sky, then flex his own wings once or twice before becoming distracted by a particularly pretty flower or a mouse scurrying along the forest floor. So there was at the very least a seed of curiosity there. A seed that she might be able to nurture into something more provided the right motivation.

If not, they were doomed.

The barracks soon came into view on the western edge of the village. It was a plain, low-slung building surrounded by parade grounds stamped hard and barren by centuries of marching feet. Iris stopped short of the entry gate, wondering how she would gain admission to speak to the major. However, this was easily resolved when the man himself pulled up in his military vehicle just as she arrived.

"You can't be here," Major Stevenson growled as he climbed out of his car. "This is a military facility. It's no place for a child."

"I'm very sorry, sir," Iris said, standing her ground. "It's only, I'm here to begin Galahad's preparations."

The man stared at her blankly.

"As I mentioned earlier," she continued, "Galahad needs a little practice before his demonstration on Saturday. I'm here to help him."

"I see," he said. "And did you expect that I would simply hand the dragon over to you, therefore presenting you with the perfect opportunity to make the beast disappear into thin air?"

That was, in fact, Iris's fallback if all else failed. But she planned to do everything she could to take the honorable route first. "Oh, well, perhaps you expected one of the dragon experts on your *own* staff to handle his training, then?"

Iris thought she saw the faintest hint of amusement in the major's eyes. Then, turning his head toward the gate, he shouted, "Boone!"

A soldier who looked barely old enough to wear a uniform emerged from the nearby guard shack. "Sir!" he said, saluting and standing stiffly at attention.

"This girl wishes to prepare the dragon for its upcoming demonstration. She is permitted to remove it from captivity to do so, but you will accompany them wherever they go. At the first sign of any trickery, you are to shoot the thing on the spot. Am I understood?"

Iris felt her breath catch in her chest at these last words.

"Yes, sir," Boone said.

"Understood?" the major repeated, inclining his head slightly toward Iris.

"Yes, sir," she said.

The soldier named Boone ushered Iris into a military jeep and drove her to an old barn not far away. *So this is where they've decided to keep Galahad,* Iris thought, sizing up the structure.

Boone climbed out and unlocked the heavy padlock on the barn's broad doors. As soon as he'd slid the heavy door aside, Iris burst into the building. She stood for a moment, letting her eyes adjust to the dim light, before she spotted a large form curled forlornly in one corner.

"Galahad!" she cried, and ran toward him.

The dragon's eyes opened. Iris's heart sank as she saw the once-bright shine of those golden eyes dimmed in defeat. Galahad let out the most miserable sigh she'd ever heard and closed his eyes again.

Iris knelt and gently took his head in her hands, stroking his forehead and down the side of his neck. "There now. Everything's going to be alright. I promise." She glanced over her shoulder at the soldier who was staring cautiously from the doorway. He clearly had no interest in coming any closer to the dragon. Lowering her voice, she said, "I always come up with a plan, don't I? And I will now! A very good one too."

Galahad harrumphed sullenly.

Iris put her hands on her hips, pretending to be insulted. "I know we don't have a lot of time, but I believe . . . yes, I *know* you can learn to fly."

Galahad's eyes slid open again and peered at her through the gloom. Iris thought she saw the tiniest glimmer of hope.

"You'll see. We'll do it together. You just have to try."

Then, remembering the small package under her arm, she set it down on the ground and pulled the brown paper wrapping open. "I almost forgot. I stopped at the bookstore and got you a little gift."

It was the picture book about dragons that she'd been admiring earlier in the day. Galahad lifted his head curiously and studied its illustrations.

"Just look at all the wonderful dragons here," she said, slowly flipping through the pages. "See how they all seem so free—so alive—soaring through the sky?" Iris pointed at one of the pictures. "Why, this one looks a lot like you, doesn't it?"

Galahad snorted.

"Well, obviously you'll look *much* more fearsome and majestic." She threw her arms around the dragon's neck. "Does this mean you'll try?"

In response, the dragon slowly shifted his bulk and rose to his feet. The soldier Boone clutched his rifle and backed away as Galahad began to move toward the open door. After a few paces, the dragon arched his neck around in nearly the shape of a question mark as if asking, *Are you coming or not?*

Iris felt like she could finally breathe again.

"I know just the spot for your lessons," she said, leading the way toward the nearby forest.

Their military chaperone trailed behind at a cautious distance. But when they reached the edge of the trees, he stopped and looked around nervously. "You're not . . . not planning on going in *there*, are you?"

Iris's heart thumped a little faster with excitement. She'd been worried that the soldier would see right away that Galahad couldn't fly. But the forest's reputation as a haven for dragons meant most people steered clear of it. Even though the dragons were long gone, rumors abounded that their spirits lurked within the trees, waiting to feast on any who ventured into their domain. Iris knew this was perfectly ridiculous, but she figured there was no need to enlighten the soldier.

"We're only going a little way in. There's a sunny hilltop that I think will be ideal for Galahad's training." She paused, then added casually, "It was once a favorite spot for dragons to sun themselves." It wasn't exactly a lie, she told herself. Galahad did, in fact, enjoy lying there on his back with his belly toward the sun on lazy summer afternoons. "I promise to bring him back as soon as we're done."

Boone stared up at the trees nervously. "Alright then," he said with a brisk nod. "But don't forget. You gave me your word."

Iris nodded solemnly before turning and leading Galahad farther into the trees. The pair picked their way through the underbrush like they had many times before. At one point, Iris heard the loud snap of a twig behind them and whirled around, half expecting to find the soldier had changed his mind and followed them after all. But there was no one.

A few minutes later, they arrived at the top of the hill she'd had in mind for Galahad's flying lessons. Its gentle, grassy slope was free of trees and other impediments.

Now came the hard part. Not being able to fly herself, Iris had already failed numerous times in trying to teach Galahad. She thought of how her brother, Jamie, had taught her to ride a bike. He'd run alongside her using a contraption he'd designed to help her balance. Maybe if she helped Galahad hold his wings in flight-ready position while he ran, this would help him too.

"Okay, are you ready?" she asked. "Let's start by spreading your wings to their fullest. Then run, like this." She demonstrated by putting her arms out to both sides and bounding down the hillside a ways before turning and climbing back up to where he stood.

While the dragon watched her curiously, she slid underneath his right wing. "I suspect that if you can gather enough speed . . ." She grunted as she gently hefted the wing up onto her shoulders. It was heavier than she'd remembered. "Then the wind might do the rest."

It occurred to her that she would only be able to support one wing, but there was nothing else for it. There was only one of her, after all.

"Ready?" she asked. "On three. One . . . two . . ."

At the count of three, the pair barreled down the hill at top speed. About halfway down, Iris ducked out from underneath her friend's wing to see if he could do it on his own. However, instead of continuing down the hill, Galahad spun and tackled her. They rolled the rest of the way down the hill until reaching the bottom in a tangle of arms and legs.

"Are you sure you're taking this seriously?" Iris asked, spitting out bits of grass in frustration.

An hour passed. Then another. And another still. They had made no progress.

Iris eventually found herself lying again at the bottom of the hill after yet another failed attempt. A pair of clouds overhead seemed to resemble a long rifle chasing a dragon as they scudded across the sky. As she watched the pursuit, her heart started thudding faster. And faster.

"I'd say he's a little more than out of practice," said a voice behind her.

Iris sprang to her feet. A girl sat on the ground ten yards away, reclining against the trunk of an old beech tree with her hands behind her head. It was Maud. The same girl she'd seen in the crowd before Major Stevenson nearly murdered Galahad. Also, she knew, Maud was the major's granddaughter.

Panic bubbled up from Iris's chest. What if Maud ran back to the barracks and told the major what she'd seen? "W-what are you doing here?" Iris stammered.

"I'm simply observing," Maud said.

"You can't tell your grandfather," Iris pleaded. "I *know* I can have Galahad ready. We just need a little time to—"

"Don't worry," Maud interrupted her. "He didn't send me to spy on you. And I don't see any reason he needs to know about any of this."

Iris exhaled with relief. "Then why are you here, exactly?"

"Call it curiosity, maybe? Everyone seems to be terrified of dragons. And then there's you. Throwing yourself in front of a loaded rifle to save a dragon's life. I mean, either you're crackers, or there's another side to the story."

Iris stared at her suspiciously. "What about you? You're not afraid of dragons?"

"Should I be?" Maud asked, watching Galahad dozing peacefully in a patch of sun nearby.

"It's just, your grandfather—or really anyone else, for that matter—refuses to listen to reason on the subject."

"Well, I'm not my grandfather," Maud said matter-of-factly.

Iris weighed the girl's words. Maud seemed open, at least, to making up her own mind about dragons. Was there any harm in letting her continue watching their lessons? Maud had already seen the true state of Galahad's flying skills, and yet had not run off to report to her grandfather.

"I suppose it's okay, then, if you wanted to stay," Iris said at last. "I was hoping to try the lessons a little longer."

"Oh, of course. Don't let me keep you." Maud stood and walked a few paces toward Iris. "But in the end, my grandfather is going to do what he wants. The strong make the rules, and the rest of us have to learn to live with them or suffer the consequences."

"So might makes right?" Iris said a little heatedly. "Is that it? And I should just give up and let whatever happens happen?"

"I didn't say it was fair," Maud said, shrugging. "But that's the way the world works."

Iris spun around and steamed off back up the hill. "Come on, Galahad," she called over her shoulder.

The dragon rambled back up the hill after her. They spent the rest of the afternoon running down again. And climbing up again. And down again. With each repetition, Iris could feel the panic and frustration swelling larger and larger in her chest until she was sure she would burst.

Galahad was trying his best, but something was wrong. And

that something, Iris feared, might be her. She was a poor substitute for a mother dragon. Still, she refused to quit. Her best friend's life quite literally depended on their success.

Iris and Galahad collapsed on the grassy peak together as dusk gathered. Her hand automatically went out to caress his weary head. "I think that's enough for today." She blew out an exasperated sigh. "All we can do is try again tomorrow, I suppose."

Staring down the hill, Iris saw that Maud had disappeared. She shifted her gaze farther beyond the treetops to the sun as it slipped below the horizon and plunged the world into darkness. And her heart ached to think of how dark indeed the world would feel without Galahad's gentle spirit in it.

CHAPTER SIX

MAX

Belgium

The German general slowly raised his heavy cane into the air.

Max cowered away from it, unable to breathe as he waited for the blow that would end his life. He knew instinctively that if he ran now, he would be shot instantly. So he remained where he was and clenched his teeth tightly to stop his chin from trembling. No matter how scared he was, he refused to cry. He hadn't cried for a long time. Not even when his parents had left. And he wouldn't now.

But instead of striking Max to the ground, the giant merely brought the large red stone on the end of his walking stick closer to his face and stared into it for an agonizingly long time.

"Mueller!" the German barked.

Max flinched.

The general's eyes shifted from the stone to Max, and he smiled cruelly as if acknowledging that he'd been toying with the boy.

A soldier appeared at the man's side and saluted. "General Wyvern, sir!"

"See that this boy is escorted home," Wyvern said. "If you

encounter any others, you will deal with them similarly. All are to remain confined to their homes until further notice."

Max's parents spoke multiple languages at home, so he knew enough German to catch the word that Wyvern had used for him. It didn't mean "boy" exactly. More like "infant." He wondered if his life had been spared only because the general viewed him as no threat to the invading Germans.

"And if any refuse?" the soldier asked.

"They are to be shot as an example to the rest."

Max's heart thumped. Whether he was a threat or not, he realized the consequence for disobedience was death.

A strong hand grabbed his shoulder and roughly spun him around. He found himself staring into the face of a German soldier.

"Where do you live, boy?" the soldier demanded.

"I . . ." Max said, his mind suddenly going blank in his panic. He pictured his grandmother's face. For a brief moment, he thought of lying. Of leading the soldiers away from her so that she would have a chance to escape. But then he realized she would never leave without him. And by misleading the Germans, he might only guarantee a death sentence for both his grandmother and himself.

"To the west," he finally managed, nodding in the direction of his farm.

The soldier grabbed him by the arm and shoved him in that direction, motioning for another soldier nearby to join them. "Then you will lead the way."

As they started toward Max's home, Max glanced sidelong at the line of men still lying face down on the village green. Among them he spotted his school's headmaster. Seeing a man of such authority being forced to cower on the ground like a dog made Max realize his worst fears were coming true. Again, he pictured his village being destroyed in flames. People he had laughed with, who had shared meals at his family's table, murdered by the Germans.

If he had been able to warn everyone in time, could he have made a difference? How many lives could have been spared if he had only acted more quickly? And would he be here now, leading the Germans right to his very doorstep?

The small but solid-looking farmhouse where Max lived came into view. Every board and shingle had been nailed into place with pride by several generations of his family. Now his brain struggled to reconcile the sturdy sense of safety it always gave him with the feel of the rifle muzzles that he knew were trained on his back.

With his father gone, Max was the man of the house now. It was his responsibility to keep it safe. To keep his grandmother safe. He silently prayed that she was not home, though the cozy trail of smoke rising from the chimney made that unlikely.

A cold fear settled into the pit of his stomach. A fear that, in the moment his grandmother opened the door, his German captors would recognize her for what she was. Would somehow detect her Jewish blood. And would not hesitate to murder the both of them right there in their doorway and stain it with that same blood.

Max slowed as he climbed the porch stairs. He aimed his feet for every loose section of board, willing each shriek of wood to cry out a warning to his grandmother: *Run! Hide!* Though, in his heart, he knew she never would.

His grandmother pulled the door open when he was halfway across the porch. Though her face was calm, her eyes shone with terror. Behind him, the steps groaned, and the two German soldiers seemed to loom up behind him. Their stink of motor oil and death filled his nose. His heart thundered as he walked forward, waiting for the crack of gunfire.

When he reached her, his grandmother pulled Max into an embrace, while at the same time discreetly moving him past and behind her into the house. He kept his face turned into the house as if the soldiers might read his secret on his face.

"Does this boy belong to you?" one of the soldiers asked in a broken combination of Dutch and German.

"He does," she replied simply. Max sensed she was attempting to hide the tremor in her voice.

"Very well. Be certain that he does not wander off again. All are ordered to remain at their homes. On penalty of death."

"Danke," she replied in German. *Thank you.*

Max's mind spun as he waited for the moment of revelation. The instant when their lives would come to an end.

He started at the sound of a sharp click behind him. But then he felt a gentle touch on his shoulder and realized the sound had only been the click of the door closing.

The soldiers were gone.

The quaking started in Max's legs. Then moved up into his torso. Soon, he was shaking all over. All the fear, shame, and guilt bursting like a dam from every part of his body.

"I'm sorry," he said. "I tried to warn . . . but I couldn't . . ."

"Oh, Max," his grandmother said, coming around in front of him. "None of this is your fault. You are so much like your father. Always carrying the weight of the world on your shoulders."

She reached out and put her hand on the back of his head, gently drawing his forehead to hers before wrapping her arms around him. He huffed in and out between clenched teeth, again fighting back tears. He finally steadied himself by focusing on the feel of her soft, worn shawl against his cheek. The familiar, heady scent of pumpernickel bread that enveloped her.

Finally, embarrassed, he pulled away and dragged a sleeve across his nose. "Thank you?" he said. "How could you thank"—he gestured angrily toward the door where the soldiers had just been—"*them?*"

"My dear, you must learn that with such men, you must appear to be meek even though a fire burns in your heart."

He sighed and looked up at her, registering for the first time that she was dressed in her heavy shawl and cloak. "Were you about to go somewhere?"

"I was," she said, and brushed a leaf from his hair. "I was preparing to come rescue you from the Germans, of course."

Max blinked, then laughed out loud as he imagined the tiny woman staring down a squad of German soldiers. The unexpected moment of humor helped ease the fear that seemed to grip his chest like a vise.

"Oh, you think that's funny, do you? I'll have you know my generation taught the Germans a lesson or two they won't soon forget in the Great War. And I'd have those young lads over my knee if they'd harmed even a hair on your head." She started to remove her shawl and cloak. "Peter's father was here not long before you arrived and—"

"Peter?!" Max exclaimed, suddenly remembering his friend as if their parting had occurred days ago, though it had probably been less than an hour. "Is he . . . ?"

"He is well and at home with his family. When you didn't appear, I began to fear the worst. You are unharmed, yes?"

"Yes, I'm fine," Max said. And at least outwardly, he was. However, his insides were in turmoil. He told her about his journey to the fort, and the run-in with the German general. As he spoke, he saw fear spread across her face. Whatever flash of humor he'd felt evaporated from his body like steam from a teapot.

"My dear Max," she said when he had finished. "Do you understand the terrible danger you put yourself in? What the Nazis might do if they discovered that your parents are part of the resistance?"

Max's face burned with shame, and he could no longer meet her eyes. "I only wanted to help. Somehow."

"But your mother and father . . . They have put their lives in danger in the hope that many others won't have to take such risks. Most of all you, my dear." She sighed.

"I'm so sorry," he whispered, speaking to his parents as if they might have heard him.

His grandmother's hand clutched his. "We must continue to hope that we will all be reunited. And for now, that means we must be sure of your safety."

Max's chest tightened. "We're . . . leaving, then?"

He knew what had happened to Jews like himself in every country the Nazis invaded. Some had been executed on the spot. Others were rounded up and herded like cattle onto trains heading east toward Germany, never to be heard from again.

"I am afraid so, my dear," his grandmother replied. "We will depart shortly after nightfall."

Max had known this day would come. The small bundles secreted around their home were evidence of their months of preparation for it. Each bundle contained the essential possessions that they felt they could carry. However, nothing could have prepared him for the stark reality of that moment.

The Germans had come. And now he would abandon the only home he'd ever known and flee for his life.

Max felt his heart seize in panic as he voiced the question that sprang to his mind: "But how will Mother and Father find us?"

"They know to look for us in France where we are headed." She moved across the kitchen and slid the teapot onto the stove before lighting a burner. "As for the present, Peter's father will take us part of the way in his wagon. Then we will continue to France on foot. If all goes well, then we will slip away without the Germans noticing."

"And if they do?" Max asked, nervously looking toward the window.

She lifted a rolling pin from the counter and twirled it menacingly in the air. "Then they will find more trouble than they bargained for." With a thump, she brought the rolling pin down on a lump of dough and began to knead it vigorously. "Now slice yourself some bread and help me prepare. We have much to do before we leave." She raised her rolling pin again and pointed toward the rear of the house. "You might start by freeing Plum."

For the first time, Max became aware of a scratching noise coming from the direction she had indicated.

"When I saw you being escorted home earlier," she explained, anticipating his question, "I assumed she would not be so polite to your German captors. Therefore, she is currently confined to your room."

Max stuffed a slice of warm bread into his mouth and headed toward his bedroom. He wasn't the least bit hungry, with his stomach tied up in knots. But he knew he needed to eat to give him strength for the journey ahead. The scratching noise grew louder and more frantic as he approached. When he had barely opened the door a crack, a tiny ball of fur burst through the gap and danced around his legs, barking furiously.

He knelt and lifted her to his eye level. "I'm okay, Plum!" he assured the dog as her tiny wet tongue attacked his nose and cheeks.

When a local farmer had given Max the pick of his litter a year ago, he had immediately been drawn to the tiniest red-black pup. Back then, her entire body fit into the palm of one of his hands like a small, wrinkly plum. Even now, Plum was still hardly bigger than her namesake, but she was usually bursting with the energy of a dog five times her size.

Max set her down and stepped through the door. He wanted to soak in every detail of his room. The way the light fell across the small desk where he'd spent hours writing his stories. The faint smell of peppermint from the candies his grandmother knew he loved. He shivered, picturing men in gray uniforms lying on his bed and thumbing through his favorite book, or even worse, smashing his things just for fun.

"It's too hard, Plum!" he said, grasping a carved wooden dragon from his shelf and sinking to the floor. "I know I haven't really even played with this for years, but what if I never see it again?"

Max set the dragon aside and reached under the bed, pulling out a small sack his mother had knit for him. It held the few things he'd decided, after an agonizing process, to take with him if this day ever came. As he settled the sack into his lap, three wooden arrows inside it rattled together with a sound like his mother's knitting needles. Max pulled out the bow his father had carved for him and plucked its string. In its faint vibration, he thought he could hear his father's quiet hum as he worked his tools patiently along the grain of the wood.

The last item inside the sack was an old, tattered journal where Max recorded his thoughts, wrote stories, and even made the occasional drawing. He wished he could spill out all his fear and frustration onto its pages now, but guessed he would need many more volumes.

Plum nudged something against his foot. He looked down to see her small, thoroughly chewed ball. Max smiled and added it to his collection. "Definitely an essential item," he said, and ruffled the dog's coat.

A shadow passed across his floor. Max jerked his head toward the window, half expecting to see the huge German general standing there peering in. It was only a cloud passing across the late afternoon sun. He quickly got to his feet. How long had he been sitting there? Time was quickly running out.

He hurried out of his room and spent the next hours helping his grandmother with chores like polishing silverware, washing windows, and sweeping the back stairs. He suspected that she was merely giving him tasks to help keep his mind off their coming departure, as well as the worry that the Germans might discover who they were at any moment. So he was grateful for the busy-work, even if that's all it was. As dusk gathered at last, he was just finishing piling wood they might never use beside the fireplace.

"Max, it is time!" his grandmother called from the back of the house. He could hear the edge in her voice urging him to hurry.

A bolt of nervous energy coursed through him. "I'll be right there!" he replied.

His grandmother met Max and Plum at the open back door and laid her hand gently on his shoulder. Neither of them found themselves able to form words around the lumps in their throats. She handed him the bag from his mother and a few other small parcels to carry. Even the familiar juddering of the door closing stiffly behind her in its frame made his chest ache with all the memories they were leaving behind.

His grandmother crooked her finger toward the orchards behind their farm, and they stole off silently into the night. Max's pulse raced. Would they be discovered at the last moment and stopped before they could escape?

But all remained quiet. When they had gone a short distance into the trees, Max saw Peter's father waiting there as planned with his horse-drawn cart. Peter, as well, stood by the horse's side with a hand on the reins.

"It's not safe for you to be here," Max chided Peter lightly, though he was deeply grateful that his friend had come to see them off.

Peter shrugged. "I'm faster than those Germans."

"But I'm still faster."

"I guess we'll have to see once you come back. So just make sure you do."

"I will." Max pulled his friend into a tight hug. "Until then."

"Until then," Peter echoed.

Then Max turned and helped his grandmother and Plum onto the back of the cart. At a command from Peter's father and a soft nicker from the horse, they started off. Max strained his eyes in the dark, not wanting to miss what might be his last view of his best friend and the wide valley he called home. At last, everything melted into the night. Their journey into the unknown had begun.

CHAPTER SEVEN

IRIS

England

"Once more, then we'll take a break for a bit," Iris said wearily.

Galahad sighed but bravely headed back up the hill again. It was already late afternoon on Thursday, and every part of Iris's body ached from their flying lessons. Their deadline was sunrise on Saturday. That left them only one more day of training after today. And Iris wasn't sure if either of them could do this for another day.

"After tumbling down this hill so many times, I believe I know how Jack and Jill from the nursery rhyme felt," she said, hoping to lighten the mood. But it did little to soothe the growing panic that drove her relentlessly onward.

As they marched upward again, Iris's mind spun with frenetic activity, rapidly coming up with plans and just as quickly discarding them. Her original plan to teach Galahad to fly was destined to fail miserably. That much was obvious. But she refused to let her friend die.

Perhaps Galahad could overpower the guard tonight, and steal off in the dark? But Iris quailed at the idea of resorting to violence, even to save the dragon's life. And she was sure Galahad felt the same. Slip away during their training, then? No, that was unlikely to work. Not with the major's granddaughter observing them. Still, there had to be some other way he could escape. She just didn't know what that was yet.

Later, as the last light bled out of another day, the soldier Boone met them at the edge of the trees and escorted them back to Galahad's prison. Outwardly, Iris put on a show of being exhausted. Which, admittedly, wasn't very hard. But inwardly her mind was practically bubbling like a cookpot plotting the dragon's escape.

Whatever they did, she knew she had to make it look as if Galahad had gotten free on his own. Otherwise, there would likely be consequences for her and even her family. And with a creature of Galahad's size, the only way he had a chance of escaping undetected was at night. From there, her thoughts turned to the old barn where he was being kept. With a building that old, there had to be some structural weaknesses—a rotted section of wood, perhaps. Or somewhere animals had burrowed under the foundation to make the beginnings of a possible getaway route. If she could create a large opening somewhere, then maybe Galahad could sneak out.

But then . . . where could he possibly go where he would be safe?

"Alright, Harry?" she heard Boone say.

Iris startled out of her thoughts and looked up to realize they had arrived at the barn already. Another soldier waited for them there.

"The major's asked me to join you in guarding the dragon tonight," Harry said, eyeing Galahad.

Iris led Galahad into the barn, feeling like every muscle in her body was tensed with worry. Had the major somehow read her mind and seen her desperation? Did he sense that she was plotting Galahad's escape?

It didn't matter if he was onto her though. She needed to try anyway.

While the dragon settled with a sigh onto his bed of dry straw, Iris paced inside the barn. When she reached its back corner, she nearly stepped on a few rusty nails before catching herself just in time. Her gaze rose from the nails to the wall above them. It appeared that some of the boards were loose there. This might be just the place she was looking for.

She wriggled her fingers into the gap between two boards and pulled. The wood shifted slightly but held. Looking around the barn, she spotted a small metal shovel leaning against a support beam nearby. Galahad's head rose to watch her with curiosity. She retrieved the shovel and wedged its spade into the gap, then leaned against the handle with all her weight. At last, the board came away with a loud protest of wood and nails.

Iris winced and looked toward the barn's entrance. The guards apparently hadn't heard. Good. More carefully, she went to work on the next board. It came free more easily. She wasn't as lucky with the third one. It popped free with an earsplitting creak.

"Oi! What's going on in there?"

Iris spun around, quickly hiding the shovel behind her back. Boone stood in the open doorway holding up a lantern. Before Iris could respond, Galahad opened his mouth and emitted a shriek that mimicked the sound of the creaking board so well that even she was fooled.

Boone eyed them both for a couple of moments longer. "Keep him quiet in there," he said at last. He started to turn away, then added, "Visiting hours are over for today. I'll give you a minute to say your goodnights, then I'm locking 'er up."

After he had left, Iris turned back to the hole she'd started. It wasn't anywhere close to large enough for a dragon to slip through yet, so she would have to finish the job tomorrow. Her stomach roiled with worrying about all the things that remained to be done.

Glancing over to find Galahad watching her, she forced an encouraging smile onto her face. She carefully fitted the boards loosely into their original positions. Then, giving Galahad a kiss goodnight, she headed out into the dusk.

By the time Iris arrived home, it was already well past sunset. She was both mentally and physically exhausted, but not yet ready to sleep. Because that would bring her to Friday. And that could be the last full day of her friend's life before their deadline of Saturday at daybreak.

"Dad?" she called as she entered their dark kitchen through the back door. "Jamie?" A plate of food sat in her place at the table, but the sight of it made her stomach churn. How could she eat with her best friend's execution looming so near?

"In here," came her father's voice.

She found him seated on the sofa in the living room. He lowered the newspaper he was reading as she came into the room.

"Flying lessons still not going well?" he asked, reading the expression on her face.

Iris grabbed a throw pillow and collapsed on the cushions beside him with her head tucked against his side. "I don't understand it! I've tried everything I can think of, but we've made no progress whatsoever."

Her father stroked her hair. They sat in silence, listening to the sound of the fireplace crackling in the hearth.

"These honey-colored locks of yours," he said after a while. "Sometimes I catch my breath, thinking I'm seeing your mother when I look at you. You know, she was the only one I ever knew who loved dragons as much as you do. Enough, even, to travel for days to visit them after their herd left our village."

"Wait," Iris said, turning her face toward him. "Are you saying she knew where the dragons went?"

"Oh, yes. That was a long time ago, of course. Before you were born. I know she hoped to take you one day." He rose to his feet and walked over to the cabinet. There he removed a small stack of papers from a drawer and walked them across to Iris.

Iris flipped through the papers, confused. They were her mother's drawings of dragons in flight, of every size and color. They were beautiful, but she'd seen them all before. How did this—

She froze when she arrived at the last page. It was a simple sketch of a jagged opening in a cliff face above a rocky beach.

"She described it as one of the loneliest coastlines you'll ever see," Iris's father said. "With sharp rocks that look almost like dragons' teeth jutting out of the sea. There aren't any roads up that way, but it's a few days north of here on foot. After she died, I thought I might take you and Jamie there someday when you were old enough."

Iris couldn't believe how blind she'd been. She'd looked at these papers at least a hundred times without registering what they were: sketches of the lost dragon herd. And not only that, their new home. Like a thunderbolt hitting her, she knew she had her answer to where Galahad could go after his escape. Surely he would be safe from the major far away and among his own kind.

She barely noticed her father go to bed a little while later, or the fire slowly dying in the hearth. She was too busy plotting Galahad's escape.

The next thing Iris knew, she woke up curled on the living room sofa surrounded by her mother's sketches. She lay there for a moment, listening to the silent house, then rose to her feet to start her chores. It was the murky hour between night and daybreak when she slipped out her kitchen door. The familiar rituals— filling a trough with fresh water for the goats, rubbing a brush rhythmically over their horse Juniper's coat—soothed her frayed nerves even if they didn't completely distract her from the all-too-heavy burden of saving her friend's life. Still, her discovery of the previous night gave her the smallest bit of new hope.

"Iris!"

She looked up from her brushing to see her father striding toward her across the yard holding a small slip of paper in his hand.

"What's happened?" she asked, seeing his furrowed brow.

"We've just received a message from the military base," he said. "It seems the major is back from London early."

Iris felt her heart freeze. She already sensed what was coming next.

"And he expects to see Galahad fly at the parade ground"—he hesitated as if unwilling to deliver the final bit of news—"at noon today."

Iris didn't even realize she'd collapsed until she found herself lying on the ground with her head resting in her father's lap. Just when she had allowed herself to feel the littlest bit of optimism, she had been dealt this crushing blow. Not only would it be impossible for Galahad to learn to fly by noon, but the news had dashed her plans for escape. Now there was nothing whatsoever she could do. Her best friend was going to die.

"Is she okay?" Iris heard Jamie's voice say.

She turned her head to see her brother peering down at her, holding a strange-looking tangle of ropes and pulleys.

"I'll be fine," she said, though that was far from the truth. She sat up and pressed her fingertips to her head, still feeling woozy. She peered between her fingers at the thing in Jamie's hands. "What in the world is that?"

"I'm sorry it took me so long, but it's a sort of harness for Galahad," Jamie said. "I don't have his exact dimensions, but see here"—he tugged on one of the ropes—"you can adjust it to fit just right. We figured when you teach him how to fly, then he's probably going to need a pilot."

"We . . . ?" she asked.

Her father nodded. "I admit I don't love the idea, but I've always encouraged both of you to dream big and aim for the skies.

I suppose literally, in this case. Jamie convinced me we could at least do our best to keep you from falling off."

Jamie started to give her a quick demonstration of how the harness worked using their mare, Juniper, as a stand-in for Galahad, but Iris waved him off.

"I truly appreciate all the time you put into this," she said. "But the fact is, there's no way to save Galahad now. It's too late."

"Why?" Jamie asked. "What do you mean?"

"You heard the news, right?" she replied, trying not to let her exasperation creep into her voice. "The major moved the demonstration to today. At noon."

"Which means you have a little more than four hours to get Galahad in the air. So what are you doing still sitting here moping?"

Iris stared at him. With anyone else, she might have been offended. But coming from her brother, it was just the sort of thing she needed to jolt her back to her senses.

"Your brother has a point, you know," her father added. "The Iris I know wouldn't give up on her friend if there's still even the slightest chance of success. Maybe there's something different you can try today?"

"Something different," Iris said slowly. She rose to her feet, feeling her spirits rally a little. "Yes, there still is a little time. And I'm going to do whatever it takes in these last few hours to save Galahad's life."

Jamie held out the harness toward her, and she gathered it in her arms. Then she turned and sprinted toward the barn where

Galahad was being kept, her feet driven by desperation, fear, and just the tiniest bit of hope.

Twenty minutes later, she burst into the barn.

"Galahad!"

The dragon's head lifted sleepily from the ground. Iris noticed the book with pictures of dragons lay open beside him as if he'd been studying it.

"Galahad! Come on! I think we could both use a change of scenery."

The rest of him reluctantly uncurled to follow her out of the barn. Iris led the dragon in the opposite direction from the forest, through a field of tall grass. Spring wildflowers bobbed in the brisk wind off the ocean as they passed. At last, they arrived at a bluff overlooking the water. Overhead, dozens of seagulls circled and dove through the sky, greeting the morning with their calls. A hundred feet below, the surf pounded noisily against the white limestone cliff.

Iris looked behind them and spotted the two soldiers of their military escort settling in to watch a safe distance away. It didn't matter. She would put them out of her mind and focus on the task at hand.

"First of all," Iris said to Galahad, holding up the harness, "I have something for you. Or for both of us, I suppose. Jamie made it."

The dragon nudged his snout curiously against the ropes while Iris tried to remember exactly how the contraption worked.

"This goes across here," she said, draping the harness across his back. "Then this part"—Galahad snorted as she scrambled under his neck and cinched the ropes around his shoulders—"Oh, I know it may take some getting used to, but think of what fun it will be to fly together!"

In her head, her voice sounded almost giddy, and she worried that all the strain of the past few days was making her lose her mind. Choosing to ignore it, she tugged on one side to fasten it a little tighter, then stood back to inspect her work. The dragon craned his neck around, clearly still unsure of this new business with the ropes crisscrossing his back.

"I do believe we've got it," Iris said. Then, pressing her hands together as if she was praying, she added, "And now, let's see if we can get you in the air."

She led Galahad to an open section of ground and pointed at the seagulls. "Like this, I think." She studied one of the birds and flapped her arms like wings, then leapt into the air.

"See how they do a sort of run and hop while furiously flapping their wings?" she asked the dragon. "Maybe that's what we were missing."

Galahad eyed the birds with interest, a low rumble in his throat.

"No, don't eat them, silly," she chided. "I know you haven't had breakfast yet, but this is important. Watch them and see if you can copy what they're doing."

Iris mimicked their movement again in slow motion, nodding toward Galahad for him to try. The dragon unfolded his wings and stretched his neck around to watch uncertainly as he flapped them up and down.

"That's it!" Iris said encouragingly. "And now a little hop and flap and let the wind do the rest."

Galahad obediently jumped into the air, beating his leathery wings, but he only thumped back down to the ground.

"Almost . . . maybe?" Iris said. "But now take a few steps to gain momentum before you leap."

The dragon moved back several steps, then lumbered forward. He surged into the air with powerful strokes of his wings. For a few seconds he hovered there on a particularly strong gust of wind off the ocean.

"Yes! That's it!" Iris shouted encouragingly.

Galahad thudded to the earth and skidded to a stop right at the edge of the cliff. Looking down with terror as a rock tumbled into the water far below, he quickly scrambled back to safety.

"Hmm, I think that was it . . . sort of . . . maybe? Ooooh, why must this be so frustrating?"

Iris climbed onto a large rock at the cliff's edge and stared at the gulls. Her hair whipped in the wind while her skirts billowed around her legs. Behind her, some loose stones clattered to the ground. Surprised, Iris spun toward the noise. Maud crouched there, peering out from behind a rock where she had apparently been spying on them.

Iris opened her mouth to speak, only to find the words oddly sucked out of her lungs. Her body went weightless, almost like she was flying. Only, she quickly realized it was quite the opposite. With a scream, she lost her footing and plunged off the side of the cliff.

CHAPTER EIGHT
MAX'S JOURNAL

Belgium

Morning

I awake before sunrise with the echo of bombs in my ears and fear in my heart. We walk endless miles, yet the Germans draw always closer. Peter's father turned back at dawn the first day. I must return to my family, he said. That was only two days ago. Can that be right? It feels like years. It is hard to tell when each mile is the same as the last. Only endless walking, walking, walking. France is surely on the other side of the world. Grandmother begins to hum as she gathers our belongings. Plum snuffles nearby after something only she can smell. Then I hear the sounds of others stirring. Hundreds (thousands?) of refugees like us coming awake in the field where each person collapsed and slept wherever they could find an empty bit of ground. The sound of their waking reminds me of the ocean surf. We are like a wave of displaced people seeking some safer shore. Yes, I think Father would be proud of that description. There are old men and women, fathers, mothers, and children like me. Most are on foot. One was on a unicycle. For a moment, I imagined we were only visiting the circus and not fleeing for our lives. The bombs rumble again in the distance. A boy younger than me stands and looks toward the horizon with wide eyes.

From a simple thread around his neck, the six-pointed Star of David peeks out. He sees me staring and tucks the star beneath his collar. I slide my own star out of my pocket and show it to him. We are brothers, I say. And we are both brave, like David. He shakes his head. The Nazis came to where we were hiding, he says. They almost found me. They were right on top of me. Then my father burst from where he was hidden and drew them away. I watched them beat him and drag him off while I hid under the stairs and did nothing. I am not brave. There is a bright flash on the horizon. Then another boom that makes the ground shake. I squeeze the star in my hand. Will I be brave when the time comes? The sound of the bomb echoes in my ears. The fear curls tighter around my heart.

CHAPTER NINE

IRIS

England

Iris threw her arms out, grasping for anything that could stop her fall. Her fingertips found a tree root that had grown right through the cliff face and instinctively closed around it. As her body jerked to a stop, her palm ignited in pain. But she held on anyway for dear life, her legs cycling uselessly in midair.

Galahad's panicked face appeared over the cliff's edge. Above the sound of her heart thudding in her ears, she could hear him roaring in terror as he raced back and forth along the ledge, unsure what to do.

Maud's face came into view next. "Hold on! I'll . . . I'll find something to lower down to you!"

Iris felt the cliff face slowly crumbling and giving way around the exposed root. "Hurry! I don't have very—"

Snap!

The weakened root split in two and suddenly Iris was falling. A thousand thoughts collided in her mind as she fell toward her certain death. She had failed Galahad and he would surely be killed. Would she be able to see him after she died? Would she get to see her mother?

She closed her eyes to focus on her mother's face, almost feeling herself falling gently into her warm embrace. Then her mother raising her up and—

Roaaarrrrr!

Iris's eyes snapped open. Confused, she blinked, then looked down and found that she lay on a bed of tough, dirty-brown scales. Scales that she would recognize anywhere. Because they were the scales on Galahad's back. And he was—

"Galahad!" she cried with delight, hugging her arms around his neck. "You're . . . flying!"

The dragon roared happily and banked downward through a veil of ocean mist to glide just out of reach of the white froth of the tossing waves before soaring back upward toward the sun. As he leveled off, Iris stared in wonder at his huge wings, then down at the ocean sparkling far below them. A series of musical bellows and shrieks emanated from her friend's jaws. It was something she'd never heard him do before.

Wait, was he . . . singing? The sounds made her heart swell with love for this beautiful and complex creature.

Iris rose to her knees and stretched her arms wide as if to embrace the sky. The sensation of flying felt delicious and exhilarating and frightening all at once. The cool wind sliding through her fingers and tossing her hair wildly. The smell of the clean ocean air and its salty tang on her tongue. Her stomach gently rising and falling in rhythm with Galahad's easy climbs and dips through the sky. And as her body soared, her spirit soared with it. She never wanted it to end.

Then the realization hit her: Galahad was saved! Assuming,

of course, the major kept his end of the bargain and spared his life. But she had no reason to believe he wouldn't.

At last, Galahad banked again, and Iris threw herself down on his back, grasping the ropes of Jamie's harness. "Okay, maybe I'll just hold on for a bit after all," she said to herself with a nervous tremble in her voice.

They flew in a smooth arc, heading back toward the cliff where Iris had fallen. She smiled so wide it made her cheeks ache. The dragon gently drifted downward to meet the ground. But when his feet made contact, the speed of the landing caused him to stumble, sending the pair rolling headlong across the ground. Galahad caught Iris protectively in his wings until they finally tumbled to a stop.

Iris sat up laughing and pulling dandelion seeds from her hair. "Okay, maybe the landing part can still use a little work. I think—"

She never got to complete her sentence.

From behind them came a loud shout. Before she knew what was happening, a half dozen ropes lassoed around Galahad's neck and legs. The dragon roared in fear as brown-uniformed British soldiers emerged from all sides, dragging him to the ground.

"Stop!" Iris cried. She spotted Maud nearby and turned to her pleadingly. "Can't you do anything?"

Maud shook her head. "I tried to warn you this would happen."

Iris launched herself at one of the soldiers, uselessly trying to pull him away. "What are you doing? You're hurting him!"

"I would advise you not to interfere this time," came a voice from behind her.

Iris spun around, coming face-to-face with the steely-eyed army major.

Galahad shrieked again. Rage and terror for her friend's life whirled like a hurricane building inside her chest. "You . . . you can't do this! You promised you'd spare him!"

"This was our bargain," Major Stevenson said. "I'll spare the beast's life if he can prove himself useful."

"Am I at least permitted to continue visiting him?" Iris asked.

Galahad had stopped struggling. His head hung low in defeat as the soldiers led him back toward the barn.

"You may say your final goodbyes tonight," Major Stevenson said. Then, starting after his men, he added, "We deploy for France in the morning."

Iris staggered backward as if he'd struck her. They were leaving that soon? She recovered and stood glowering at the major's back as he walked away. From a distance, she could still hear Galahad's mournful roars. They were soon lost beneath the hollow sound of the waves breaking against the unflinching cliff face nearby. The man thought he had won. Well, she was not done fighting yet. Even if it took her all night, she would free Galahad.

She spun toward home but stopped short.

Maud was still standing there. "I'm sorry," the girl said. "I tried to talk to him earlier. Really. But Galahad is alive. That's what matters, right?"

Without a word, Iris quickly hurried past Maud, then dashed toward home. *And I plan to make sure he stays that way.*

It was barely ten minutes later when Iris sprinted up the lane to her house. She lifted the hem of her skirt a few inches to avoid tripping on it as she ran. *Maybe Maud has it right with her boy's clothing,* she considered. Skirts were completely unsuitable for running about, and certainly for riding dragons.

She paused in the barnyard to catch her breath, but her brain kept moving at full speed. Where to begin? Escape was Galahad's only option now. And it had to happen tonight. One of her gardening tools might do just the trick to score the barn wood to look like claw marks. And then—

The kitchen door creaked open, and Iris glanced toward it. Her father's anguished expression as he stood there in the open door caused her to turn fully toward him. Every part of her tensed with worry.

"Dad?" she asked. "What's . . . what's happened?"

"Can you come inside for a moment?" he asked.

Iris quickly closed the distance between them and stopped, staring up into her father's face where he held the door open for her. "What is it?"

Instead of answering, he turned to look inside the kitchen. Following his gaze, she gasped. She would have collapsed if her father had not slipped his strong arm around her waist.

Jamie sat at the kitchen table with a brown military uniform folded neatly in front of him. Iris instantly grasped what had happened.

Her brother had enlisted in the British army.

Jamie was going to war.

CHAPTER TEN

MAX

Belgium

The afternoon sun shone down mercilessly on Max's neck as he plodded along the road. They had been walking for nearly a week. The heat combined with the low murmur of voices from the crowd of refugees around him lulled Max's brain into a daze.

He might have even fallen asleep on his feet except for one thing: the stink. Somehow, with each passing mile, the throng of unwashed bodies moving westward seemed to swell larger. And as their numbers grew, so did the smell. Everyone badly needed a bath, himself included. The odor assaulted his nose and made his eyes sting. Eventually, Max imagined he could even taste it on his tongue. Now he understood why those who had been traveling even longer than him mostly kept their mouths closed and walked in grim silence.

They were constantly dogged by the ever-nearing sounds of battle at their heels. Tension seemed to prowl among the crowd like a hungry animal. Nearby, a man accidentally stumbled into another man as they walked.

The first man spun around angrily, shouting, "Watch where you're going!"

"Maybe you should try walking faster!" said the second man.

It wasn't the first time an argument over something so minor had broken out. Everyone was on edge.

"Here, my dear," Max's grandmother said beside him. She held the remnants of a stale loaf of bread toward him. "I suppose it is past time for lunch. You can eat as we walk?"

Max and his grandmother had begun rationing the last of the food they had brought with them. At some point, they had stopped resting for meals, instead preferring to keep moving as much as possible. He nodded, taking the loaf and breaking off a small piece. This he broke even further, taking some for himself while bending over to offer the rest to Plum.

He waited until his grandmother was distracted and quickly slipped the larger piece back into her woven basket. It was a game that had started between them over their journey. She would pretend not to be hungry while giving him all their food. And Max would find a way to sneak the food back into their supply when she wasn't looking.

He hoped she might eat some of their extra bread later. She was tired, he could tell. While her feet had not yet slowed from the days on the road, the endless walking seemed to be sapping her normally resilient spirits.

"What is France like?" Max asked with forced cheerfulness, hoping to distract his grandmother from her road weariness. "And our family there—I want to know more about them too. Do they have a French château? Maybe even a swimming pool, and horses, and—"

"My dear Max!" she said finally, throwing up her hands and

chuckling. "Sometimes you are like the birds that *chitter chitter chatter* all day—your imagination soars on the wind, but your beak, it rarely ceases moving!" She was silent for a few moments. "I had originally planned for us to stay with a cousin of mine just over the French border. However, given how quickly the war has moved westward, I fear it may not be long before the Germans arrive there. Fortunately, we have some distant relatives in the city of Dunkirk."

"Dunkirk?" Max asked. "But isn't that all the way on the French coast?"

"It is, but I believe we should be safe from the Germans there. Now listen carefully. If along the way we are to become separated, I need you to promise me something: that you will not put yourself in danger from the Germans by searching for me. Instead, make your way as best you can to Dunkirk, and we will meet there."

"But . . . but why would I lose you?" Max sputtered. "And how will I know you are there?"

"I promise you this," she said, extending her hand toward him and the papery skin of her palm finding his cheek, "if I know you are waiting at Dunkirk, then not even the entire German army could stand in the way of my reaching you."

Max studied her eyes for a moment. "Okay. Then I promise. Only, how will I know which direction to go?"

Her eyebrows knitted together for a moment, then she smiled. "I believe I may have a solution for that. Please show me the star your mother gave you."

Confused, he slid it out of his pocket and offered it to her.

"Ah," she said, and lifted it out of his palm. Then, holding it out at arm's length, she nodded toward it. "As you know, we are currently traveling west. If you should ever be in doubt as to which way Dunkirk lies, you have only to aim the star's topmost point toward the north. The point just to the left of that will guide your way to Dunkirk."

She handed the star back to Max and they continued in silence for a while. He felt as if each step was now heavier somehow.

Soon, Max noticed a plume of dust approaching from ahead in the distance. His heart fluttered with fear, thinking maybe the Germans had managed to get ahead of them and were now hemming them in from both sides.

"That will be the French and British, I suspect," said his grandmother as if reading his mind. "When they join up with our boys, they'll surely give Les Boches second thoughts about moving any farther west."

"Les Boches?" Max asked.

"It means roughly 'Cabbage Heads.'"

Their eyes met and they shared a grin.

"Cabbage Heads, Jerry, Fritz—there are many others," his grandmother continued, turning up her palms. "Silly nicknames we give to the Germans. Perhaps it is to make them seem not quite so scary."

Up ahead along the side of the road, Max spotted what looked like an empty can someone had left sitting on a fence post. He decided maybe it would be useful to start practicing his archery skills. It had been a couple of years since he'd used the bow.

"I'll be right back," he told his grandmother.

She nodded. "Don't wander too far."

He slid his bow and an arrow out of his quiver and wormed

his way to the edge of the crowd with Plum at his heels. Then he carefully took aim, centering the tip of the arrow on the can. However, when he let the arrow fly, it zinged sideways instead of straight. The arrow plucked the hat right off the head of a man walking not far ahead. The man whirled around, his eyes darting through the crowd until they found Max standing there guiltily holding his bow.

"I'm so sorry—" Max started to say.

"What sort of irresponsible, worthless brat—" the man steamed. He stooped to pick up the hat. Carefully separating it from the arrow, he snapped Max's arrow across his knee and threw the two halves to the ground. Still not satisfied, he stomped toward Max. "What are you trying to do? Kill someone?"

"Sorry! Sorry! Sorry!" Max exclaimed while backpedaling away from the red-faced man.

Another man stepped between them. "Leave the kid alone," he said. "It was clearly an accident."

Unable to adjust his momentum in time, the first man barreled into the second. To Max, the result seemed almost like a powder keg igniting. Both men began shoving each other and then pummeling each other with their fists. Their scuffle soon carried them into the surrounding onlookers. Max watched in terror as the fighting spread quickly through the mob like fire across a field of dry grass.

Then he heard a familiar cry and whirled toward it, his heart skipping a beat at what he saw. His grandmother was jostled by the flailing bodies and stumbled forward. For an agonizingly long moment, he lost sight of her as the crowd shifted around her. At his feet, Plum barked furiously.

Max's heart nearly stopped altogether when his grandmother flashed back into view, just in time to see her stumble again. What was left of their meager rations were knocked from her grasp. The hard bread and a little cheese toppled to the ground, where they were immediately trampled into the dust.

If Max didn't do something, the same thing might happen to his grandmother!

CHAPTER ELEVEN

IRIS

England

Iris drew in a shaky breath and waited for the sight of her brother to swim back into focus. The kitchen held the familiar scents of coffee and bacon. And the sunlight splashed across Jamie's calm face. As if it was a completely normal day and the uniform on the table in front of him didn't mean all their lives were about to be turned upside down.

She finally shook off her shock and marched across the room toward him. "You promised!" she cried. Jamie rose to meet her, and she softly pummeled his chest with her fists as tears sprang to her eyes. "You said you wouldn't leave us!"

He enfolded her in his arms and pulled her close. "I know. I'm so sorry. But I . . . I just can't ignore the duty I have to our country."

Iris felt her knees get weak again. Jamie pulled out a chair for her, and she collapsed into it, staring dejectedly at the uniform on the table.

"Don't worry," he continued. "I doubt I'll see action. I'm going to request to be Galahad's handler. I figured the major hasn't got anyone else who isn't afraid of dragons. I'll look after him for you and make sure he's treated well." He paused. "I hear congratulations are in order on a successful flight, by the way."

Iris wasn't surprised he'd already heard. Theirs was a small village, after all. She went back to staring at the uniform, directing all her anger, frustration, and fear at the stiff brown fabric. Obviously, she couldn't rescue Galahad now. His usefulness to the major as a message courier was the best way to keep Jamie safe. Or, at least, safer than being on the front lines.

"How much longer do we have with you?" Iris asked.

"I ship out for France tomorrow morning."

She buried her head in her arms and wept.

Early the next morning, Iris stood at the water's edge with her father and brother. A large steamer ship floated in the harbor, being prepared for the soldiers to board.

Jamie's smart new uniform made him look so strong and brave. Braver than she felt, with her stomach tied up in knots at the thought of both Jamie and Galahad—her brother and her best friend—on the verge of leaving for war.

She inhaled deeply, hoping the salty air would help revive her sluggish brain. After staying up half the night talking with her father and brother by the crackling fire, she felt that she had barely slept at all. None of them had wanted to go to bed. Although no one said it aloud, Iris had sensed they were all thinking the same thing—it could be the last night they would ever have together.

Iris turned her attention to the dozens of other families there with them. Everyone's shoulders sagged under the weight of the war. Like her, they would stay to soak in every second before their brothers, sons, and fathers left for Dover. And from there, across the English Channel to Europe and the battles raging there.

For at least the hundredth time, Iris's eyes scanned the road approaching the harbor for any sign of Galahad. For at least the thousandth time, she chided herself that she should have gone to ensure his safe arrival at the port.

"He's likely already been boarded and moved belowdecks before we arrived," Jamie said, reading her mind.

Iris's heart squeezed painfully at the thought of not even being able to say goodbye to her friend.

Her father sighed loudly and turned toward Jamie. "Son," he said. He grasped Jamie's hand and placed his other hand on his son's shoulder. Iris knew that her father struggled to show emotions, but she could see the pain in his eyes. He nodded quickly and said, "Go show those Germans what British boys are made of."

Nearby, a small group of other fathers were disguising their worry behind a bluster of bravado about the military feats their sons would surely accomplish in the coming days.

"Let me tell you," one of them was saying, "my son can stop one of those German Panzers with his bare hands and not even blink an eye."

"Well, *my* son," said another, "he'll top that and bring down five Stukas during breakfast without even setting down his marmalade spoon."

Iris turned back to Jamie. "The way they're talking, you'd think this will all be over by dinnertime."

A wry smile crept across his face. "I think it's the British *girls* they need to worry about. Send them into France, and it'll all be over by afternoon tea."

"Do you think they stop all that nasty war business for tea?" she teased. "Imagine being so uncivilized as to not set down your guns long enough for a companionable bite of cucumber sandwiches before going back to blasting away at one another."

Jamie's gentle laughter trailed off as his eyes drifted back toward the slate-gray ocean. Overhead, the sun shone warm in the clear blue sky, a perfect spring day if not for the distant booms that might be thunder beyond the horizon toward France. But Iris knew it wasn't thunder. It was the boom of guns. Big guns. And bombs. Men killing one another and being killed.

She studied her brother, wanting to preserve this image of him standing so tall and strong in the brown uniform of the British Expeditionary Force. On his shoulder was stitched the emblem of their local unit—a golden dragon with its wings spread wide. A reminder of a time long gone.

Past Jamie's shoulder, Iris spotted Maud standing with her brother, Jack, a solidly built young man with the same shade of dark, nearly black hair and blue eyes as Maud. Jack's uniform bore the golden dragon as well. The girls exchanged wordless looks of sympathy and understanding.

A horn blasted from the waiting steamer. Other men in uniform hugged their loved ones and started moving toward the pier.

"Hold out your hands," Jamie said. "I have something for you." He fished a few fingers into his breast pocket.

Iris dutifully extended her cupped hands. "What is it?"

Jamie carefully placed a delicate silver chain in her hands. Threaded onto the chain was a brilliant blue stone that lay in sharp contrast to the pinkness of her palms.

Iris's eyes widened. "But this is . . . I can't . . . I mean, Mum gave you this just before she—"

"I know," Jamie said, closing her fingers over the necklace. "I can't risk losing it while I'm traipsing all over Europe. And in any case, I think she'd want you to have it. I'm too old for all that dragon stuff anyway. You remember the legend she used to tell about it, right?"

"Of course," said Iris. "When a dragon dies, its body transforms into a single small stone."

"A dragon tear," he said, nodding. Then he shrugged. "It's all just make-believe, of course, but Mum always kept it with her. Said it reminded her there was still a bit of magic in the world if you take the time to look for it."

"But I don't have anything for you—" Iris started. Then on a whim, she stopped and reached into her handbag, extracting a small, thin book and holding it toward him. "Here. I want you to have this."

It was Jamie's turn to widen his eyes. "But it's your favorite one!"

"'The red dragon soared into the azure sky,'" she recited dramatically, "'its mighty wings pounding the rhythm of her heart.'"

Jamie laughed. "I should have guessed you'd have it memorized by now."

"I expect you'll return it to me in perfect condition," she said primly. "Just like I'll take care of this apparently worthless trinket for you."

"I said 'make-believe,'" he corrected her, grinning. "But definitely not worthless."

The blare of a car horn sounded behind them. Jamie pulled Iris out of the way as the car screeched to a stop nearby.

The door flew open, and Major Stevenson got out.

Iris immediately stepped into his path. "May I say goodbye to Galahad?" she begged. "Please? Where is he?"

The major stopped short of running her over, looking like he might change his mind and barrel through her anyway. "You *will* get out of my way!"

"But I—"

Jamie draped his arm across his sister's shoulder and steered her safely to one side. "Don't worry," he said to her as the major brushed past, "I'll check on Galahad when I get on board."

"But what if he's scared? Or lonely? Or—"

"Listen, he's in good hands. Trust me. I'll take care of him."

Iris collapsed against her brother's broad chest with her arms squeezed tight around him. She knew she needed to let him go, but she wanted to soak in how solid and real he felt a little longer. "Just come back to me. Both of you. Promise me."

He squeezed her back. "We will. I promise." He hefted his belongings and moved forward to climb the long plank up to the ship's deck.

Jamie turned when he reached the top and gave her a last smile and nod. Then he disappeared into the crowd of other soldiers aboard the ship. On the far horizon, the low rumbling continued, punctuated occasionally by bright flashes of light. Iris and her father stood beside the other families and watched until the ship departed, taking a piece of their hearts with them.

CHAPTER TWELVE
GENERAL WYVERN

French-Belgian border

General Wyvern, commander of the German military, stood on the terrace of the château with his hands clasped behind his back. His fingers were interlaced around a heavy black cane with a single bloodred stone fixed into its handle. The fact that he used the cane to help him walk did nothing to diminish the terror that his imposing, nearly seven-foot frame caused in all who stood in his presence.

"The Dragon." That's what many called him. Not to his face, of course. Though he rather liked the name.

The mountain retreat so conveniently abandoned by its wealthy owners sat perched on a cliff face. It was hundreds of feet above the valley floor, affording it a sweeping view of the French countryside. The emerald green Ardennes Forest spread as far as the eye could see, dotted here and there with tiny, picturesque villages. And somewhere beyond the pale blue horizon, the biggest prize of all—Paris. The German army had failed to capture the French capital in the last war two decades ago. But he would not fail this time. And after that—

"Herr General?" came a voice from behind him.

He spun on his heel. One of his officers stood stiffly in front of him, shrinking back slightly from the towering figure of the general. The newcomer quickly shot one arm straight out, fingers extended. "Heil Hitler!"

General Wyvern cursorily raised his own hand. "Heil Hitler!" He looked past the man and saw that the rest of his officers had gathered, standing at attention and awaiting his instructions. The general waved off the officer in front of him, and the man joined the rest of the small group.

Using his cane, Wyvern began to move slowly across the stone terrace. "Gentlemen," he said, "we stand today on the precipice of something marvelous. A new history is being written, and we are its authors." He paused in front of a large wine rack filled with dozens of dark bottles. After considering for a few seconds, he selected a bottle and slid it from its resting spot. Then he gently ran a hand along one side almost as if it were a sleeping infant.

"Our long period of false diplomacy," he continued, turning toward his officers, "empty claims and promises while we amassed our forces to strike, has lulled the French and British into a sense of complacency. In fact, they have even called this a 'Phony War.' As if they can simply open their eyes from a dream and it will all be gone."

He paused again, studying the men in front of him. "And so, this is the time we shall strike. Poland has fallen. Already, Belgium is on her knees." With one gloved hand, he began to squeeze the glass wine bottle. "And as our armies sweep to the north and south, we will trap the French and British armies unsuspecting in the middle." Tiny cracks started to form in the surface of the bottle. "Until at last, like a dragon's claw, we will close around and completely annihilate them."

The bottle finally exploded in his grasp, raining down broken glass and red liquid that pooled like blood at his feet.

CHAPTER THIRTEEN

IRIS

England

Iris watched the ship carrying Jamie and Galahad pull away from the shore and swing toward the open sea. The emptiness inside her felt as tall and wide as the cloudless blue sky. Out of the corner of her eye, she saw Maud approaching her. They nodded to each other, then stood side by side at the water's edge, staring after the ship even when it had disappeared into the gray mist rising from the ocean.

"They're gone," Iris said eventually.

"Somehow it doesn't seem real," Maud said. "I'm so sorry my grandfather wouldn't let you say goodbye to Galahad."

"I keep picturing him so scared and alone stuffed down in the hull of that ship," Iris said, swallowing a sob.

Maud's forehead creased in confusion. "Do you mean the one our brothers are on? Because I've been here since it arrived this morning, and there's been no sign of Galahad."

"Well, if he wasn't on the ship, then where is he?"

"I—" Maud said. "Hmm, I have no idea." She grabbed Iris by the elbow. "Come on. Let's go check his barn. Maybe he's still there?"

Iris's heart fluttered with a combination of excitement and worry. Where in the world was Galahad? She quickly let her father know she would meet him back at the house. Then the girls raced away from the harbor and across the village.

As they ran, Iris felt the knot in her stomach pinch tighter. Her mind tortured her with various scenarios: Galahad had been injured in some terrible accident. Or, even worse, the major had gone back on his word and—no, she wouldn't go there. She had to believe Galahad was still alive.

When they neared the barn, two soldiers stood outside its doors. She recognized the one named Harry, who moved forward to block their way.

"Sorry, girls, no visitors allowed," Harry said. "Major's orders. The dragon's to be kept strictly under lock and key."

"But why didn't he leave with the soldiers?" Iris asked, struggling to catch her breath.

"I can't discuss military matters with civilians," the soldier replied. "Even if one of them's the major's granddaughter."

"Oh, can't I at least see him?" Iris pleaded. She leaned around the soldier, trying to catch a glimpse of the dragon. "Not even for a minute?"

"My grandfather wouldn't mind," Maud added. "And I'd be sure to tell him what a terrific job you're doing."

Harry glanced over his shoulder at the barn. "Alright then, but just for a minute. And you'll have to say your hellos through the gaps in the walls. The major's made it very clear I'm not to open the doors for anyone without his—"

Iris rushed past the soldier before he'd even finished speaking.

"Galahad!" she called when she reached the barn. A muted bellow came from inside, making her heart leap. "Galahad, I'm here!" She frantically searched around the door and the front wall of the barn for any openings she might use to see the dragon.

"Over here," Maud said, and pointed to a small opening where a board appeared to have rotted away at about eye level.

Iris ran over and peered into the gray of the barn's interior. The smell of old hay and mildew wafted to her through the opening. Then a large golden eye appeared.

"Galahad!" She felt the knot in her stomach loosen a little at the sight of him. The gap was just big enough for her to shove her arm partway through. Her fingers found the scales of his snout and caressed him lovingly. "I was so worried about you. Why did the major leave you behind?"

"Hmm, maybe there's a way we can find out," Maud said.

"How?" Iris asked.

"Just come with me," Maud said, glancing at the soldier.

Iris said her goodbyes to Galahad and promised to return over the soldiers' protests that visitors were still not allowed. Then she followed Maud down a quiet lane on the outskirts of the village. As they walked, Iris quietly fretted over the new turn of events. If Galahad wasn't in France, then would Jamie be thrown into the thick of the fighting? The thought made her feel as if she might be sick.

The lane ended at a rambling, two-story Tudor mansion. With its severe gabled roofs and many darkened windows, it looked like somewhere a fairy-tale ogre might live. Iris knew it to be the home Maud shared with a very real-life ogre, namely Major Stevenson.

Maud jogged up the few steps to the front door and threw it open, calling into the empty space as she did. "Mother! It's me!"

"Margaret?" came a woman's voice from somewhere deeper in the house, using Maud's full name.

"Come on," Maud said to Iris and started down the long hall. "We'll just say hello quickly, then we'll see what we can find out about Galahad."

Iris found the inside of the house exceedingly dreary as they went down one dark hall, then another. The walls were all covered in almost-black wood paneling and a variety of dusty military artifacts. It was the perfect home for an army officer. But hardly so for a young girl. As they walked, the sound of a radio grew louder.

"Mother, this is Ir—" Maud said, turning into a room near the end of the hall.

"Come, come," interrupted a woman's voice. When Iris reached the doorway, she saw a pale-looking woman sitting propped up in bed. "There's a radio broadcast on just now with our new prime minister speaking," the woman continued, not bothering to acknowledge Iris. "Fellow named Churchill. Won't you turn up the volume a bit so I can hear?"

Maud crossed the room to a large freestanding radio and turned one of the knobs. A man's impassioned voice filled the room.

. . . *Centuries ago, words were written to be a call and a spur to the faithful servants of Truth and Justice: "Arm yourselves, and be ye men of valor, and be in readiness for the conflict; for it is better for us to perish in battle than to look upon the outrage of our nation—"*

"Turn it off! Turn it off!" Maud's mother said, waving her

hands in disgust. "Such useless drivel and glory mongering. Bah, he'll be just like the rest, then."

Despite the woman's opinion, Iris found herself deeply moved by their new leader's words. *Be ye men of valor.* Yes! Wasn't this precisely what she had argued with Maud about? That it was better to stand up and bravely face difficulties? To do *something* rather than nothing?

"Men of valor, indeed," the woman continued. She gestured toward the far wall, where a black-and-white photo of a man was displayed above an iron cross on a crimson ribbon. "Why, a lot of good that did your father, bless his soul. A Victoria Cross for valor in battle, and his remains lost in some godforsaken land." She turned toward Iris, giving the first indication that she'd actually noticed the girl. "And now Margaret's fool of a brother, gone and followed in his footsteps. It's enough to bring a wife and mother to an early grave."

"Mother, let me put another pillow behind your back," Maud said. She grabbed a fresh pillow from the divan and plumped it before helping her mother position it behind her back. "Is there anything I can get for you?"

"No, no, I think I'll just take some rest now. For all the good it will do me." She leaned back heavily against her headboard and closed her eyes.

Once Maud had softly pulled the door to the room closed, she turned to Iris with an embarrassed look. "Sorry about that. She's, well, easily excitable."

"Never mind that," Iris said, smiling. "You said there might be a way to find out about your grandfather's plans for Galahad?"

"That's right. Follow me." She led the way back toward the front of the house and stopped at a pair of large double doors. Testing both knobs and finding them locked, she lifted up on one of the knobs and jiggled it a little. There was a slight popping noise. When Maud pushed on the door, it swung open and she went inside.

Iris glanced quickly up and down the hall as if they were about to be caught doing something they shouldn't. Seeing no one, she crept after Maud. The room's walls were lined with maps, hunting trophies, and an assortment of guns, swords, and other weapons. "What is this place?"

"My grandfather's study," Maud responded from the other side of the room.

"And he lets you come in here?" Iris asked.

Maud stood beside a massive desk, searching for something in the filtered sunlight from the room's single window. "Not exactly. But what he doesn't know won't . . . Aha! Maybe this will help." She lifted a small packet of papers and began reading the top one before quickly flipping through the rest.

Iris crossed the room and looked over Maud's shoulder. "What are those?"

"They're telegrams between my grandfather and some captain whose name I don't recognize. This must be why he was in such a fluster when he arrived this morning. It says here that Galahad's transport has been delayed by more than a week due to storms."

Iris sank heavily into one of the chairs beside the desk and stared at the floor.

"What's wrong?" Maud asked. "You've been given all the extra time with Galahad. That's plenty of time to . . . I don't know, say, break him out?"

Iris startled. This had been the last thing she'd expected from Miss Do Nothing. Maybe there were even more layers to the girl than she realized. "What happened to 'That's the way the world works'?"

"Oh, you can't say you haven't thought of rescuing him." Maud dropped into her grandfather's leather swivel chair and spun around lazily. "Tell me something. I was watching you when Churchill was talking on the radio. You really believe that stuff, don't you?"

Iris nodded. "Does this mean you've changed your mind?"

"There's a part of me that wants to believe it too." Seeing a hint of a grin on Iris's face, Maud added, "A very . . . *small* . . . part of me."

Iris stood and began pacing from one end of the room to the other, processing the new information about Galahad. She had already laid the groundwork for the dragon's escape. And now that he could fly, Galahad could be safely among his former herd practically before a search party was formed.

She spun toward the major's massive desk and stared purposefully at Maud across the desktop. "Okay, I'll do it. I'm going to break him out."

CHAPTER FOURTEEN

MAX

French-Belgian border

Max stood frozen on the edge of the writhing mob of refugees. Through a narrow gap in the crowd, he saw his grandmother stumble to her knees. All the sound seemed to go out of the world—the angry cursing and yelling, the fighting, the screams of those trying to get clear. Then the gap closed, and she was gone.

"Stay, Plum!" Max called. Then he gulped and blindly leapt into the fray.

Almost immediately, someone slammed into him from the side, sending Max stumbling to his left. He regained his balance, only to trip over someone's leg and go down on all fours.

"Grandmother!" he called out.

A strong hand grabbed his shoulder and pulled him to his feet. Max whirled around, ready to kick and claw his way free from his attacker. But he froze when he saw his grandmother's smiling face. She had been the one to find *him*!

She grabbed his hand and peered around. "Come! We must get away from the crowd!"

Just then someone crashed into Max from behind. He spun around and looked up into a familiar angry face. It was the same man whose hat Max had accidentally shot with his arrow. Max backed up a step, his heart slamming against his ribs.

Suddenly, the crack of a rifle sounded over the clamor. Everyone stopped instantly and looked around for the source of the noise.

"My name is Captain John Clark of the British Expeditionary Force," called a commanding voice from nearby. Max swung his head in that direction. A tall, solidly built man in a brown uniform stood a few yards farther down the road from the refugees. He gripped a rifle in both hands.

"You will cease this bedlam immediately," the captain continued, "and carry on in an orderly fashion. Anyone who continues to cause trouble will be shot."

The officer stared around at the crowd, glaring at anyone who hadn't already turned their eyes to the ground. Apparently satisfied, he moved off to the side of the road to allow the refugees to continue west. Many in the crowd shook their heads as if waking from a dream, then gathered their belongings and quietly began shuffling forward again.

Max turned to his grandmother. "When I saw you fall, I"— his voice caught a little—"I thought for sure you'd be trampled."

"Your old grandmother isn't so helpless as you thought, eh?" She squeezed his hand. "Now, let us gather our belongings and hopefully put this episode behind us."

Max ran back and found Plum still guarding his things where he'd left them on the side of the road. "Good girl, Plum!" he praised her, and scooped her up along with the bow and remaining arrows, then rejoined his grandmother.

As they passed under the watchful eye of the captain, Max looked past the officer to stare at more British soldiers working in the field beyond. He'd been so busy trying to escape the fighting that he'd failed to notice the soldiers not far down the road. A small bubble of hope worked its way into his chest. Belgium's allies had come to their rescue after all!

But what were they doing? He'd expected stout fortifications of concrete and barbed wire. Instead, they seemed to be building a wall made merely of mud shoveled from the marshy ground to either side of the road. Was that really enough to stop the Germans?

Max saw one of the soldiers nearby pause and lean on his shovel while squinting into the east. Another soldier working beside him looked up, then over his shoulder to follow the first man's gaze. "Something wrong, mate?"

Max turned around curiously and walked backward while searching for what the men were looking at. It was impossible to see beyond a few hundred yards where the road disappeared around a bend into the trees. Soon his ears picked up a low whine that seemed to be steadily growing. Eventually, a motorbike and sidecar emerged from the trees, speeding toward them. Max shielded his eyes, trying to get a look at the rider. Was he French? British? No, there seemed to be a sharp point on the top of his helmet.

In the same moment that his brain processed *German*, a bright series of flashes erupted from the motorcycle's sidecar.

Gong!

Max whirled toward the sharp noise. One of the soldiers gaped at the splintered handle where the head of his shovel had been seconds ago. "Everyone down!" the soldier yelled.

Then the world burst into chaos.

Max reached for his grandmother's hand as a pair of German tanks rolled into view, but he was a second too late. Suddenly, people everywhere were running, pushing, and screaming. He was ripped away from her in the surge of confusion. How could this be happening again so soon?

"Max!" his grandmother's call came over the din.

"Grandmother!" he called as he jostled through the panicked mob. He pressed Plum closer to his chest.

Rat-tat-tat! came the sound of rifles nearby as the British unit returned fire.

"Max!" To his left, he thought. Only farther away now. But even as he started shoving his way in that direction, a terrible screeching noise filled the air. Confused, he stumbled and spun toward the sound. A large object plunged out of the pale blue sky, dropped from a German plane that buzzed low before arcing back toward the east.

Max stood transfixed as the bomb screamed downward like some sort of winged demon. It met the mud barrier he'd seen the soldiers building and exploded, sending two soldiers nearby spinning through the air.

Over all the noise, Max could barely hear the captain shouting "Fall back!"

Suddenly, more of the high-pitched whistling filled the air. One bomb. Two. Three. A chorus of death and destruction.

Max swung around, preparing to run, but found himself disoriented among the crazed mob. Explosions ripped through the air. Even from hundreds of feet away, the bursts of searing heat when the bombs met the ground prickled his bare arms. Their shock waves rippled through his body. Still in his grasp, Plum whimpered and wiggled agitatedly.

Max quickly looked left, then right, turning around in a full circle. Then his heart nearly stopped beating.

"Grandmother!" he cried out. This time there was no reply. Plum whined and stared up at him. "Grandmother!" he screamed again, frantically searching for her. But she was nowhere to be seen.

Someone crashed into Max from behind and knocked him to the ground. Blind panic had gripped the crowd. People were abandoning the road and throwing themselves into ditches, racing across grassy fields—anywhere to simply get away. Max scurried on hands and knees behind a tree to avoid being crushed in the stampede. Nearby, another plane buzzed low, tattooing the ground with its guns.

Tat-tat-tat-tat-tat!

More of the whistling screams. More explosions.

Max knew he had to move. To get away from this place if he wanted to live. He picked the last direction he'd seen his grandmother and ran. Plum's head bobbed in his arms as they raced through a meadow of yellow wildflowers now pocked with smoking black craters. Then over the ruins of a low wall that someone had once lovingly crafted from stacked river stones.

An old farmhouse sat solid and inviting in the distance. Maybe he could find shelter there. But in that instant the house's front wall vaporized with a mighty *ka-BOOM!* that sent dust and stone flying. Was there nowhere safe?

Another whistle shrieked through the sky, sounding like it

was right on top of him. Max instinctively threw his free hand over his head and tumbled to the ground. There was a sickening thud, and the ground beneath him seemed to quiver like jelly. He waited for the explosion, praying death wouldn't hurt. But after a few moments when nothing happened, he tentatively raised his head and saw he was face down in a patch of vegetables. A few feet away, an enormous bomb glistened in the sun like an overgrown turnip. A very deadly overgrown turnip.

A curious chicken wandered over and began pecking at the gleaming shell. Plum barked a warning at it, as if sensing the danger. Max blinked, returning from his thoughts and realizing his dog had the right idea. Something must have gone wrong with the bomb and it hadn't exploded. But their luck might not hold.

Max quickly pushed himself off the ground, and his eyes locked on the edge of a forest nearby. He ran for it.

CHAPTER FIFTEEN

IRIS

England

Iris paced the length of the major's study with growing excitement. She found herself unable to remain still as her brain spun into motion with the details of Galahad's escape. "I've already worked out some of the key pieces," she said, and explained to Maud how she had started a hole in the barn wall and learned of the dragon herd's new home.

Returning to the major's desk, where Maud sat listening intently, Iris noticed a chessboard sitting on a small side table. She picked it up and placed it on the desktop between herself and Maud. The knight pieces were shaped like knights in armor. And the queens were represented by dragons. She swept all the pieces off the board except for a dragon that she positioned in one corner.

"The only problem I haven't solved yet," Iris said, "is what to do about the guards." She placed two of the knights in the corner of the board, hemming in the dragon.

"Isn't Galahad a fire-breathing dragon?" Maud asked, and knocked down the knights. "Problem solved."

Iris stood them up again. "There must be some other way. Only, it seems impossible now that there are always two guards."

"Well . . . not always," Maud said. "Harry goes to visit his sick father in Exeter on Saturday nights." She removed one of the knights from the board. "That gives us about an hour or so with only one guard."

"Won't someone take over for him?"

"I doubt it. There aren't exactly a lot of someones left, with nearly the entire unit in France."

Iris sighed. "We can't possibly be ready by tonight. And I don't like the idea of waiting another full week, but that might be our best shot. Still, that leaves us with one guard."

The girls eyed the remaining knight for a few moments.

Then Iris noticed a flyer half-buried in the papers on the major's desk, and an idea sparked in her brain. "Unless we had a distraction," she said, and slid the sheet of paper out.

Both girls stared at it. It was an advertisement for the annual village boar hunt that was to be held that weekend. Every year, their village brought in a wild boar that was first hunted, then roasted and eaten in a lavish feast. Iris thought it was a truly appalling tradition.

"My grandfather was supposed to be the grand marshal," Maud said. "So I assume they'll have to cancel it now, even though the butcher's already taken delivery of the boar."

A smile slowly spread across Iris's face. "Maybe not."

"What do you mean?"

"Do you remember when I set the pigs free last year so they wouldn't be butchered?"

Maud laughed. "How could I forget? The village was in an uproar for days. My mother was even surprised by a pig hiding in our laundry!"

"So just imagine the commotion if a wild boar happened to escape."

"That is a truly diabolical idea," Maud said slowly, her eyes lighting up with mischief. "But what if it hurts someone?"

"With the war on, the village is practically deserted by nightfall. The only person out is likely to be the constable on his nightly patrol."

"And with a wild boar on the loose," Maud said, "he's likely to need plenty of backup."

"That's what I'm hoping," Iris said. She studied the flyer a moment longer, then stared up at Maud. "I think the boar hunt is back on."

The girls spent the next several days working out the remaining details of how they would rescue Galahad. Iris found it impossible to settle her anxious mind, between worrying that something would go wrong, like the dragon's ship arriving early, and waiting for letters from Jamie to assure her that he was okay. Her brother's absence was all the more painful at home, where even small things like the empty spot at the dinner table or the silent workbench in the barn where he frequently tinkered on new ideas would catch her unawares and take her breath away.

So she used whatever spare time she had to throw herself into volunteering at the local war office. There were instructional pamphlets to distribute on how to properly wear a gas mask in the event of a German raid. And things like butter and vegetables to collect to support England's rationing program.

Finally, Saturday arrived, the day they had planned to set Galahad free. Iris was just returning home from more volunteer work when she passed the village harbor. Her steps slowed, and her eyebrows furrowed together at the sight of all the activity happening in the normally sleepy port. It seemed that half the local population was there cleaning ships of all sizes and loading them with supplies. Iris stopped to ask an older fisherman what was happening but got only a muttered "dragon girl" in response. Maybe her father would know what all the fuss was about.

Arriving home a little later, she entered through the kitchen door to find the room in complete disarray.

"Dad?" she called. There was no response. She stared around at the cooking pans, utensils, and scraps of food scattered across the counter and table as if a band of hungry trolls had ransacked their kitchen.

What in the world?

She checked the parlor and the bedrooms. He wasn't in any of those places, but they again showed signs that someone had hastily rummaged through their things. She was starting to worry. Had something happened to her father?

"Dad?" Iris called again as she hurried outside and walked through the yard. As she passed the barn, she thought she heard voices. Was her father in the barn with someone? A loud clang echoed from inside. Her pulse racing, Iris slid aside the heavy door and rushed in.

The source of the voices was quickly revealed. An old radio sat in one corner tuned to a BBC news broadcast. An announcer was encouraging British women to join the Women's Land Army to help provide supplies for the troops abroad.

Iris scanned the barn for her father. He was nowhere to be found, but their old sailboat sat conspicuously out of place. The boat had been moldering in a dark corner, nearly forgotten, but someone had pulled it into the center of the barn. Even odder, their horse, Juniper, stood tied to the boat's small, wheeled tow cart.

The words from the radio caught her attention:

—evacuation of troops underway and is expected to continue for the next several days. The British Admiralty is requisitioning all seaworthy medium and small vessels available to assist in the effort.

A noise came from inside the sailboat. Iris climbed up onto the trailer to look over the edge. Inside, her father knelt on the deck with his back toward her, leaning over an open trunk.

"Dad?" she said.

Startling, he looked over his shoulder. "Iris!" His hands moved to carefully fold and restow a blue-and-white striped knit scarf in the trunk. Her mother's sailing scarf.

"I'm glad you're here," he said, blinking as his eyes darted around the boat. He seemed uncharacteristically flustered. "I could use your help with the preparations, love. There's so little time that I feel as if I'll run off and forget something important."

"Preparations? What's going on?"

"The British army has been ordered to evacuate France. The Germans have surprised everyone with the speed of their attack and have our boys trapped with nowhere to go except back across the Channel. Troops are already amassing at the French coast waiting to be ferried across." He pointed toward the ground, adding, "Hand me that sack there, will you?"

Iris gasped. "W-what about Jamie?"

"His unit is among those being evacuated. The sack, please?"

She knelt and peeked inside. It held enough food for a week—loaves of bread, half a dried ham, several apples, carrots, and various other items. That explained the state in which she'd found the kitchen. She hefted the sack up to her father waiting on the boat's deck.

"But where are you taking the sailboat? I mean, isn't the British navy handling all that?"

"They don't have enough ships," her father replied. "There are simply too many men to rescue and not enough time. Also, the French beaches where the troops are waiting are too shallow. They need smaller craft to ferry troops from the shore to the larger ships. So they've put out a call for all seaworthy vessels to join the effort. They're calling it Operation Dynamo. I've just been preparing to head down to the harbor."

Iris thought about all the boats that normally populated their village's small harbor. "And the navy has enough sailors to pilot all those ships?"

"Not nearly enough, no. They want the ships' owners to man their own craft."

"What?!" Iris exploded. "So you're simply going to head into war on a"—she waved her hands in disbelief at the little ship—"on a sailboat? The Germans have guns, and planes, and . . . and you've got nothing more dangerous than a fishing pole. Besides, we don't even know if the ship is fit enough to get you all the way across the Channel."

"I know the risks," he said gravely. "But if there's even the slimmest chance I can find your brother and get him back home safely, or help some of the other boys . . ." He trailed off, suddenly overcome with emotion. "Well, I have to take it."

Iris stared at him for a few seconds.

"Okay," she said finally. "Then I'm going with you."

"Absolutely not," her father said. He climbed down from the boat and strode away from her, signaling that that line of conversation was over.

"Why not?" she asked, trailing after him. "I already know how the boat works. You've said yourself—"

"Iris," he said, "we don't have time for this. And besides, I need you here, taking care of the farm."

Iris scowled. "But I'm so tired of taking care of the farm. I want to actually *do* something useful for once!"

"Now, I've already spoken with Widow Black on the next farm over," her father continued as if he hadn't heard her. "And she'll be available for whatever you need while I'm gone. I need to save every inch I can on the boat. I plan to bring back as many of those boys as I can."

"But, Dad—" Iris started.

"I can't," he said, his voice soft and thick with emotion as he stared at her imploringly. "I just can't have you putting yourself in danger too. Maybe I'll be able to find Jamie. Or maybe I won't. I don't know. I simply can't bear to risk losing you too. Do you understand?"

Iris let her gaze drop. "I understand."

"Thank you," he said, and pulled her into a hug. "Now, I

could use some help getting this old bucket into the water. What do you say?"

"Of course," she said, and climbed up onto the wagon's seat.

Her father coaxed Juniper out of the barn. The horse's tail twitched, and her head continuously swung around to eye the unfamiliar, noisy load.

Iris slid closer to her father, needing to feel his solid, reassuring presence to quell the despair growing in her chest. In her worst nightmares, she had never imagined losing him too. Would the war simply rip away everyone and everything she cared about?

As the harbor came into view, Iris let out a small cry of surprise. It had been busy earlier in the day. Now it was a scene of complete and utter chaos. Men, women, and children scrambled among boats of all types, from a large ferry to tiny fishing dinghies, all apparently preparing to head off to rescue the troops in France. Many of the boats looked barely seaworthy, much less capable of faring miles across the open water.

"The other way!" a woman yelled to a man on a small schooner, waving her hands toward the southeast. "France is the other way!" Two other boats rammed into each other in their haste to depart.

"Quite the rescue party, eh?" her father said with a laugh. "I think we'll ease into the water at the little inlet down shore a bit to avoid the mayhem in the harbor proper."

Iris knew his show of good spirits was just an act. He had to be terrified by the prospect of sailing toward a raging war. Toward a foreign shore about to be attacked by the German army.

The thought of her father alone in his little boat made her

heart squeeze. No, she couldn't do it—she couldn't let him go alone, no matter what she'd promised him.

They stopped at the place he'd indicated, and she helped him guide their little sailboat into the water.

When all was ready to go, her father turned back toward her. "Don't forget to close the barn for the night. And call Mrs. Black if you have any trouble at all. Also, make sure—*oof!*"

Iris threw her arms around his middle. "Just be careful and bring Jamie home, okay?"

Her father put his arms around her. "I will. With any luck, your brother will be back safe and sound by tomorrow night."

We need more than luck, Iris thought as a plan formed in her mind. She couldn't just wait here and hope her father and Jamie both returned safely.

As if reading her mind, her father tipped her chin up to look straight into his eyes. "Look, I know there's a strong rebellious streak in there. You came by it honestly from your mother." He smiled. "But I can't have you getting any ideas about, ah, borrowing another boat and doing anything reckless. Can you promise me that?"

"Yes, of course," Iris replied.

Satisfied, he turned his head toward the water. "Now, I'd better get going while the wind is good. The Channel has a reputation for being temperamental."

Iris reluctantly released her father. He climbed aboard the ship, then ducked low out of sight. When he stood again, he held out his hands to Iris.

"Here, I think she'd want you to have this," he said, handing a small blue-and-white striped bundle toward her.

Iris took it and stared down at her mother's favorite sailing scarf, her eyes growing wet with tears. "I love you, Dad."

"I love you too, my daughter." He cleared his throat and swiped a palm across his eyes before giving a sharp tug on the ship's rigging. The sail unfurled and the boat began to pivot toward the open water. "Wish me luck!"

"Good luck!" Iris called. As the sailboat shrank into no more than a speck on the ocean, anxiety encircled her like an iron fist closing around her chest. She didn't remember ever feeling so alone in her entire life.

Yes, she had promised her father that she wouldn't follow in another boat. That was fine. She wouldn't follow him in a boat. Because she had a much better idea.

CHAPTER SIXTEEN
MAX'S JOURNAL

France

Afternoon

I am alone. When the bombs and guns began, I ran and ran and ran and ran and ran until I could not hear them anymore. I was so afraid, I forgot about Grandmother. My hands shake so much I can barely write. How will she ever find me? How will Mother and Father find me? I do not even know where I am. I stare around at the tall trees that march as far as I can see in every direction like an endless leafy army. Only, they are just trees, and I am alone. I am here! Plum barks a greeting when she returns from exploring. Yes, Plum, you are here. I pull her into my lap, and she licks my chin. Together we wait in watchful silence as the daylight fades to orange, then gray, then black. As night comes, the trembling in my hands spreads until my entire body is shivering from the fear and cold. Is Grandmother also sheltering in a forest somewhere clutching her shawl around her shoulders against the chill? A scurry of tiny feet comes from nearby. Wind whispers in the leaves overhead. Forest noises are much more terrifying in the dark. Then a scream that sounds almost human echoes through the trees, startling a jolt of fear up my spine. I curl tighter around Plum and pray for it all to be over soon.

Morning

Sunlight streams through the leafy canopy above. We are alive! I flex my clenched fist and see the imprint of the six-pointed Star of David on my palm where I have clutched it all night. Was David always brave? Is it something you are born with, like the patterns of lines on your palms? I study the lines, wondering if the story of my life is written in them like a map, if only I knew how to read it. Then I remember: Yes! A map! I check the direction of the sun and aim the star toward the north, finding the point to the left of that just as Grandmother said. Come, Plum! We are going to Dunkirk!

Evening

Things I try to eat because I am so hungry my stomach growls like a wild animal:

1. *A few green berries: Very sour. Makes my stomach feel sour too.*

2. *A beetle: It squirms and wriggles going down my throat, and now I am wriggling as I imagine it in my stomach still squirming.*

3. *Tree bark: I have seen deer nibbling at it, otherwise I would not have thought to eat it. I test a bit on my tongue, but it is so bitter that I immediately spit it out.*

4. *River water: I drink enough that my stomach swells and I can forget that I am hungry. But only if I use my imagination very hard.*

I settle back from the river and wipe my mouth with my sleeve. Plum and I have found a bridge to shelter under for the night. Gunfire rattles in the distance and I automatically jerk my head toward it. Men shout far away. The bridge may hide me from men, but I cannot hide from fear. It follows me everywhere like a cold shadow. I am exhausted but unable to sleep. So I watch the river. It flows toward the east, maybe all the way to Germany where Mother and Father are. Maybe, even, they're miles and miles away beside the same river. I let my fingertips trail into the water and imagine they are doing the same and our fingertips touch. Goodnight, Mother. Goodnight, Father.

CHAPTER SEVENTEEN

IRIS

England

Iris turned and scanned the harbor. If she was going to do this, she would need help. And plenty of it. She spotted Maud helping with the loading of a schooner by the harbor's entrance and hurried in that direction.

"Maud!" Iris called as she neared.

Maud looked up. "Iris!" She handed an armful of oars to a waiting fisherman and then joined Iris at the foot of the pier. "Was that your father I saw leaving?"

"It was. He's hoping to find Jamie."

Maud bent over and started lifting more oars into her arms. "Can you believe all this? I think everyone has lost their minds if they think this is going to work."

Wait until you hear what I have planned, Iris thought. "I completely agree. I even thought for a minute that after I rescued Galahad, he and I would go look for Jamie ourselves. But I decided that probably wasn't the best idea after all."

"Right, well, aside from being incredibly dangerous and—"

"Because then I wondered: What if I didn't have just one dragon for the rescue, but a whole herd of them?"

Maud started and dropped the armload of oars, wincing as they all clattered back onto the pier. "Are you saying what I think you're saying?"

"If we had the rest of Galahad's herd, imagine all the soldiers we'd be able to rescue!"

"But how?" Maud asked. "You don't even know where the other dragons are exactly."

"That's true," Iris admitted. "But I think Galahad and I can find them together. And if we do, then I'm going to need some help. What do you think?"

"To be honest, I think you've gone completely insane."

"'Be ye men of valor,'" Iris said, quoting Churchill's speech. "'And be in readiness for the conflict; for it is better for us to perish in battle than to—'"

"Okay, okay," Maud said, putting up her hands in surrender. "I heard it all just as well as you did. But you know he didn't mean it's your responsibility to save the world, don't you?"

"I don't need to save the world," Iris said, shaking her head. "But if we can save even a few lives—including Jamie's and Jack's lives—don't you think we need to at least try?"

Maud stared at the ground as if deep in thought. "Well," she said finally, "if it means possibly rescuing Jack, then how can I say no?"

A shiver of excitement coursed through Iris's body. "And do you think you could maybe get a few more kids from the village to help too?"

"That shouldn't be a problem. Let me just finish up here quickly and I'll get started. Should we meet you somewhere?"

"At my house, later this afternoon?"

"I'll see you then. Where do we start?"

Iris leaned in closer to be sure she wasn't overheard. "We're going to break out Galahad as we planned. Tonight."

A few hours later, Iris led Juniper into their farmyard and untied the horse from the empty cart before leading her into the pasture to graze. There was still so much to do before she left. She thought through the broad strokes of her plan: First, rescue Galahad. Then they would fly north together to locate the rest of the dragon herd. And after that, they would fly to France to rescue as many soldiers as they could.

Making her way to the barn, she found the harness hanging where she had left it. She spread it on the ground and smiled at Jamie's cleverness. Leave it to her brother to make perhaps the world's first dragon harness. As she knelt there on the ground inspecting the careful weave of ropes, her thoughts were interrupted by the sound of voices outside the barn. Many voices. Her heart thudded against her ribs. What was going on?

Iris ran toward the open door, expecting the worst. However, when she rushed into the farmyard, she stopped dead in her tracks. A small army of kids waited there—some on bicycles, some on foot, some perched precariously on handlebars. They were all ages, from the youngest boy, who could have been no more than six, to a few kids who were older than her. They all stopped talking and turned toward her as she exited the barn.

"What in the world?" Iris asked, finding Maud's face among the crowd.

"You said you needed some help," Maud said, waving her hand at the other kids. "They want to help."

As Iris's brain struggled to process this unexpected scene, a boy stepped forward with a defiant look on his face. It was Tommy Wexford, the same boy who'd relentlessly teased her for years about Galahad. Iris braced for a snide remark from him. But then his expression suddenly crumbled, and the usually tough boy looked for a moment like he might be about to cry. He set his jaw again and said, "My dad's fighting in France. I want to do something."

Soon all the kids were talking over one another, telling of their fathers, brothers, uncles, and other family members who were all part of the British forces trying to evacuate France. Iris realized that they all felt as completely helpless and terrified as she did and were desperate to help.

As the commotion died down, one girl asked, "Maud says there are many more dragons? And you can get them to help us rescue our families?"

Iris shot a questioning glance at Maud before answering. "*Welllll* . . . I believe Galahad's herd migrated somewhere to the north. But I'm not exactly sure where, or even how many there are. Also, I'm not positive whether they'll agree to help us or not even if I *do* find them. All I can promise is I'll do my best."

Despite her cautioning words, the faces staring at her remained hopeful. She realized then it was all they had. *She* was all they had.

"Tell us how we can help," one of the older girls said.

Iris looked around as she thought about where to begin. If she found the other dragons, she would need at least a few of the braver kids to be dragon riders and help with the rescue in France. And there was her farm and its animals that needed tending while she was away.

After conferring with Maud, Iris split the kids into teams working on various tasks. Some assembled harnesses like the one Jamie had made for Galahad. Others carried buckets of water and feed to the farm animals. And still others kept an ear out in the village for any new developments in the evacuation efforts or news about Galahad.

At sunset, Iris called the kids together and thanked them for their efforts before sending everyone home for dinner lest any parents start to worry. It was time for her to begin preparing for Galahad's rescue, and she didn't want to reveal too many details in case anyone spilled the beans or reported her to the army.

As she watched the kids departing, Tommy came up to her. "Good luck," he said, surprising Iris with a brief smile before he turned to go.

"They all believe in you," Maud said, coming up behind her.

"I only hope I'm worthy of their trust."

"Well, you're off to a fine start as our fearless leader. After feeling helpless for so long, you gave those kids a purpose. A shot at doing something meaningful, even though they're 'only' kids."

"Were you able to check on our second guard, Harry?" Iris asked.

"I was, and he's still planning on taking the 8:10 train tonight to visit his sick father as usual."

Iris nodded. "And our distraction?"

"Tommy was happy to help with that. He says he'll even give the boar a solid whack on its rump right before he sets it free. That'll make sure it's good and mad when it gets loose."

"And what about you?" Iris asked. "Are you sure you want to help? I don't want to risk getting you in trouble with your grandfather."

"Let me worry about that," Maud said. "This is my brother's life we're talking about. I would do *anything* to bring him back safely."

"Then meet me by Galahad's barn tonight at eight."

CHAPTER EIGHTEEN

MAX

France

"What's wrong?" a voice shouted.

"I hit the trigger and nothing happened!" a second voice responded. "Must be a bad connection. Give me a minute."

"Can you fix it?" came the first voice again. "We need to blow this bridge now!"

The shouts seeped into Max's sleeping brain, growing in volume until he realized they weren't just another dream. He startled awake out of his deep sleep with one thought ringing in his head: *I've been found!*

"Okay!" the second voice said again. "Stand by for detonation."

Max rolled to his feet and staggered out of his hiding place under the bridge with Plum at his heels. His hands automatically went for his bow and arrow. His heart crashed against his ribs.

A soldier standing a safe distance away startled when he saw Max. The man started running toward the bridge and waving his arms. "Wait! Don't blow the bridge!" he shouted as the countdown started again.

"Three . . . two . . ."

Max dove for the ground and scooped Plum underneath him, bracing his body for the coming blast.

But instead of a huge explosion, he heard the second voice again. "Jamie? What's wrong? I was just about to—"

Max's eyes popped open. Two soldiers were jogging toward him holding their rifles!

He scrambled to his feet and raised his bow and arrow, swinging the tip of the arrow alternately at the two men.

"D-don't come any closer!" Max warned. He hoped it was too dark for the soldiers to notice the tip of his arrow wobbling.

Plum edged between his legs, barking fiercely.

The soldiers immediately slowed. The one in the lead shouldered his rifle and put up his hands in front of himself, palms out toward Max. "*Eaaaasy* there. We're not going to hurt you."

He was speaking English, Max realized. That was probably a good sign. Unless he was a German trying to fool Max into letting his guard down.

The first soldier looked over at his companion. "Give him a minute. I think he's just scared." Then, turning back to Max, he repeated, "We're not going to hurt you. We're part of the British army. My name's Jamie." He pointed toward the other soldier. "And this big oaf over here is Jack."

"Big oaf?" Jack repeated with a wry smile.

Max almost smiled himself. The tightness in his shoulders relaxed a tiny bit.

"Now you know our names," Jamie said. "Can you tell us your name?"

After a long moment, he managed, "M-Max."

"Okay, Max, it's a real pleasure to meet you," Jamie said. "Now, I know you must be really scared, but do you think you could lower your weapon so we can talk? And maybe call off your attack dog there?"

Max hesitated again. These men seemed friendly. And if they were Germans pretending to be British, then their accents were very good. "Plum," he said quietly, "it's okay." He lowered his bow and arrow but remained alert, just in case.

"Thank you, Max," Jamie said. "Can you tell me what you're doing out here? Where are your parents?"

"I was traveling with my grandmother," he explained, "and then . . ." His throat tightened involuntarily as he remembered the chaos. The bombs. The guns. People screaming and running everywhere. And his own screams for his grandmother going unanswered.

An older man strode toward them out of the night. "What's happening?" he barked. "We need to get this bridge down and move out. Now."

"Major Stevenson," Jack said. "We were just about to blow the bridge when Jamie noticed this particular bridge had its own fairy-tale troll." He shot a wink at Max.

The man eyed Max before turning back to his soldiers. "I don't care if it's got a troll or an entire troop of singing dwarves. If we don't bring that thing down in the next five minutes, we'll soon have a division of German Panzers blasting fireworks down our throats."

Max turned toward the far side of the river, where he half expected to see the entire German army crash out of the forest with guns blazing. The night was still and silent, but the air seemed alive with a feeling of lurking danger.

"We're on it, sir," Jack said.

The officer nodded. "We can't afford any delays. I'll get the rest of the unit started north. Join up with us as soon as you can." He strode away and Max could soon hear him calling commands to other soldiers who must have been hidden nearby.

"I'll get back to the charges," Jack said to Jamie. "What do we do with the kid?"

Jamie turned to Max. "Where were you headed when you were separated from your grandmother?"

"I promised to meet her at Dunkirk," Max replied. "Can you tell me if this road goes there?"

Jamie smiled. "You're in luck. Not only will this road take you there, but that's where we're headed too." He turned to Jack. "It looks like he's coming with us for now."

Max's heart leapt with relief at this bit of good luck. Now he wouldn't have to find his way to Dunkirk all on his own.

Jack's eyebrows rose slightly, but then he shrugged. "Give me twenty seconds," he called over his shoulder as he jogged away. "Then . . . *boom!*"

"Come on," Jamie said. "We'd better clear out before we become a permanent part of the landscape."

"Plum!" Max called, turning and searching the night. He heard a yip in reply and saw his dog trotting up from the river's edge with a wet snout. Max suddenly realized how parched his throat was and how good it would feel to have a long, cool drink of water. His stomach twisted painfully as if it wanted to remind him that he hadn't eaten for a long time either. But all that would have to wait. The Germans wouldn't care if he was hungry or thirsty.

Max waited for Plum to rejoin him, then together they raced away with Jamie into the trees. Moments later, he heard a loud *CRUMP!* Then another one. He peered out from behind the solid trunk of the oak where he was sheltering. A thick cloud of white smoke rose and dissipated into the night where the bridge had been moments ago, like a ghost that had been trapped in the structure for centuries.

"Wait for us here," Jamie told Max. "I'll go help Jack clear the rubble and make sure there's nothing left to help the Germans cross the river."

Max knelt and rubbed Plum's head as he watched Jamie disappear. Max was a little surprised to find that he had come to trust the soldier so easily. But there was something about Jamie. A look of kindness in his eyes, maybe. Whatever it was, Max felt that he could trust him. He was safe. That was something he hadn't felt since he'd left home.

Soon Jamie returned with Jack beside him. "Were those the last of the explosives?" Jamie asked.

Jack nodded sadly. "I suppose we'll have to bring the next bridge down with our bare hands."

The soldiers set off to find the rest of their unit, taking Max and Plum with them. Just as the sun was cresting the horizon to the east, they found their unit sheltering in a grove of blooming apple trees beside a squat stone farmhouse. The sun's first rays lit up the tree buds in glowing hues of gold, a moment of beauty that seemed impossible while the ugliness of war raged so close by.

Several men looked up as they entered the small camp. There were maybe a dozen of them in all, some leaning tiredly against trees, some sprawled out on the ground already snoring where they'd fallen, and others having a small breakfast, chewing slowly as if to make their rations last as long as possible. All their faces were streaked with grime and their eyes lined with dark circles from lack of sleep. The major that Max had met earlier turned away from a map he was studying and watched them for a moment. Max thought he read disapproval in the man's dark expression.

"Don't worry," Jack said, "the major has only eaten one or two children in his lifetime."

"Um, one or two?" Max said. "Have you known him a long time?"

"And lived to tell the tale. He's my grandfather."

"Oh," Max said.

"Don't listen to him," Jamie said. "Why don't you find somewhere to take a load off. I'll see if I can find us a bit of food."

Max nodded and not so much sat as let his legs collapse in the soft grass near the base of an apple tree. He leaned back gratefully against the tree's trunk as Plum climbed into his lap and briefly nuzzled his chin.

"Max? Hey, Max."

Max hadn't even realized he'd drifted off to sleep for a few moments before he opened his eyes. Jamie squatted in front of him, holding out part of a loaf of bread.

"I think the kid's tired," Jack said, lying on his back in the grass close by. His voice echoed inside the helmet he'd pulled over his face to shield his eyes from the rising sun.

"Guess we each have to decide what we need more," Jamie said. "Food or sleep."

"Why not both?" Jack asked. "I figure if I can walk in my sleep, then sleep eating should be easy. Fairly sure I even dreamed ol' Hitler was walking right along there with us the other night in a pink tutu."

Jamie laughed and bit into his bread. "Well, I prefer one at a time, if I can help it. Seems the guys lucked across a bit of bread left behind in the farmhouse cellar." The thick crust crunched softly as he chewed. "It's a little stale, but I'm not complaining."

Max tore off a bit of his bread and held it out for Plum, who gobbled it whole. Then Max bit into the remaining piece. If it was stale, he didn't notice. To his famished mouth, it tasted like the best bread he'd ever eaten in his life. He devoured it in seconds and then lifted his palm to tip the remaining crumbs into his mouth. When he looked over, he saw Jamie watching him.

"Sorry," Max said, reddening a little at his display of greediness.

"No need to apologize." Jamie laughed. "If there's one thing this war has taught me, it's don't wait for anything. You never know what the next day, or hour, or even minute might bring." He broke off another chunk of bread and held it out for Max.

Max hesitated only a second before his stomach overruled his instinct to politely refuse. He looked around at the rest of the small unit as he ate. "Is this all that's left of the British army?"

Jack snorted. "Don't take more'n a handful of Brits to handle the whole German army."

"At least, that's what a lot of us thought coming into this," Jamie said. "All bluster and bravado heading in, and now it feels like we're retreating with our tails between our legs. The rest of our unit hopefully is in Dunkirk already, or maybe even evacuated back home to Britain by now." He waved his hand toward the rest of the men. "We're the rear guard assigned to harass, mislead, and generally delay the German advance long enough for everyone else to make it off safely."

"And what happens when you get to Dunkirk?" Max asked.

"Don't know," Jamie replied, shaking his head. "I guess we're hoping for a miracle."

A miracle, Max thought to himself as he stared around at the small unit on which rested so much responsibility. From what he'd seen of the German army, a miracle was probably what it was going to take. Not just their lives, but the lives of his grandmother, his parents, and those of an entire continent would be either lost or forever changed by the relentless wave of German forces sweeping westward.

CHAPTER NINETEEN

IRIS

England

Iris dashed silently through the twilight heading toward the barn where Galahad was being held. Although the sun had barely slipped below the horizon, all the village shops and even the local pub were already shuttered. The war stalked the eerily quiet streets like a physical presence.

Thunder rumbled in the distance. Iris hoped it wasn't an omen of what was to come.

When she at last arrived at a small copse of trees overlooking the barn, she crouched in the shadows. A single guard leaned with his back against the door, his head lolling toward his chest. This much, at least, was going according to plan.

While Iris watched, suddenly a hand grasped her shoulder. A jolt of terror ran through her, and she whirled around. Fortunately, she had the presence of mind to throw her hands over her mouth to stifle her surprised scream.

"Sorry," Maud said, amused. "I didn't mean to startle you."

Iris lowered her hands to her thundering heart. "When does Tommy plan to free the boar?"

"Any time now," Maud said. "He said he'd wait for the train's whistle, then—"

The mournful call of a steam engine sounded from the far side of their village, signaling the train departing with the second guard on it. A minute later, an unearthly howl split the stillness of the night. It wasn't long before they heard the bangs of doors being thrown open, followed by the surprised cries of several men. The boar's howls continued, accompanied by loud crashes and the cracks of gunshots.

Below, Galahad's lone guard startled from sleep. His eyes wavered from the commotion in the village to the barn door and back again. Apparently deciding the dragon would be fine on his own, the soldier abandoned his post and dashed off toward the noise.

"Now's our chance," Iris said, breaking from the cover of the trees and sprinting toward the front of the barn.

Maud followed right on her heels. Overhead came another rumble of thunder. The first fat drops of rain started to fall.

When they reached the barn door, Maud tested the huge brass lock that fixed the top of the door to its frame. "Locked," she confirmed.

"That's okay," Iris said. "The hole I made in the back wall should be just big enough for us to slip inside."

Iris whispered into the dark crack between door and frame. "Galahad? Are you there? It's me." She was greeted by a familiar rumble of joy that tugged at her heart. "Hold on! We'll get you out in just a minute."

Iris dashed around the back and knelt by the loose boards.

However, when she shoved on the first one, it held tight. Confused, she tried the next one. It was also fixed solidly in place. She leaned her shoulder against it and pushed as hard as she could. It was no use. Her pulse raced as she turned toward Maud. "Someone must have—"

She froze in midsentence. There was no one there. A cold feeling settled into her stomach. What had happened to Maud?

Sprinting back the way she had come, she breathlessly turned the last corner and pulled up in surprise at what she saw. Maud stood innocently twirling the opened lock on her finger.

"I told you I could help," Maud said. She slid a small metal tool into her pocket before pulling the barn door open.

Inside, Galahad let out a soft roar. Iris ran to him and threw her arms around his neck in relief. Then she stood back, fingering the chain that trailed from his neck to where it was looped around one of the barn's supporting beams before looking back at Maud. "This is new."

"You think they suspected something?"

Iris lowered her small supply satchel onto the floor and threw the rope harness across Galahad's back. "Maybe. I don't suppose you have a hacksaw in your pocket too?"

Maud turned up her palms. "Sorry. But Galahad's strong, right? Do you think if he pulls hard enough, he can snap the chain?"

"That chain looks solid," Iris said dubiously. "It's worth a try though. What do you think, Galahad?"

The dragon rumbled a reply and started to slowly back away from the support beam. All the slack unraveled from the chain until it was a taut line from Galahad's neck to the beam. His muscles strained as he pulled on his leash. Finally, with a small bellow of frustration, he gave up and fell back, breathing hard.

"It's no use," Iris said. "It's too strong."

Maud leaned forward to inspect the stout wooden support beam. "Wait, he can breathe fire, right? Can't he simply burn right through this? Or at least weaken it enough that he can pull free?"

Outside, Iris heard the boar's squeals getting closer. And with them, the sound of men's shouts. Maud's eyes met hers. She'd heard it too.

"They're coming this way!" Iris said. Her eyes darted up the beam to the barn's rafters. "The fire might work, but he'll have to be careful not to—"

Galahad was already moving forward as she spoke, clearly agitated by the sounds from the boar. He spat a small fireball at the post. The stout wood smoldered for a few long seconds. They all watched anxiously to see what would happen. Then with a loud pop, a handful of orange sparks exploded from the post and a large flame sprang to life. A few of the sparks fell on the piles of loose straw on the floor. Wisps of smoke began to rise from the straw. The main flame worked up the barn's support beam slowly at first before gaining speed as it curled toward the roof. Nearby, two of the piles of straw flickered to life as flames quickly consumed the dry tinder.

Galahad roared and pulled on the chain in panic. Iris's mind raced as the fires rapidly spread. The dry, rotting barn was like kindling. It wouldn't be long until the whole structure was ablaze. The dragon continued to rear up with his eyes rolling wildly as he tugged on the chain. But it was no use.

Galahad was trapped.

CHAPTER TWENTY

MAX

France

The march northward continued as the hot sun climbed toward noon. Max studied the soldiers while he walked, marveling at the courage of the weary but determined band of men. They had put their lives on the line to stay behind and slow the German advance so that thousands of others could escape.

Eventually, Max's gaze returned to Jamie, whose thumb absently caressed the spine of a small book he kept in his front shirt pocket while he kept a wary eye on the surrounding countryside.

"My sister, Iris, gave it to me when I deployed for France," Jamie said when he noticed Max watching him.

"I'm sorry, I didn't mean to stare," Max said. "I was only curious."

"Not at all." Jamie slid the book from his shirt pocket and offered it to Max. "She's about your age, in fact."

"I never had a sister," Max said, taking the book. "Although my friend Peter says he'd be happy to give me his. Do you miss her?"

"We've had our share of sibling squabbles," Jamie said, laughing, "but I do miss her terribly. I've found it helps to read a little bit of her book every day." He patted the pocket over his chest.

"The rest of the time it stays here by my heart to remind me of her. Of home. In the darkest moments, it helps me remember why I'm here."

Max flipped open the book and read the first page. It was a story about dragons. It reminded him of one of the stories he was writing in his journal. Or, at least, trying to write. He couldn't quite work out the ending. He closed the book and handed it back to Jamie. "Is its cover made of metal?"

"It is." Jamie rapped twice on the cover with his knuckle, producing a solid thunk each time. "By about the third time she'd worn out the cover from reading the story so much, I decided to rebind it in tin. It's held up ever since. What about you? Do you like to read?"

Max reached around for the satchel where he kept his arrows and other meager supplies and produced the notebook he'd brought with him. He laughed when a few pages fell out as he held it up for Jamie's inspection. "I think mine might need a new binding too." Stooping down to retrieve the pages, he tucked them back inside. "This is more of a journal, though I do have a few stories I've written in it too. There's one about a heroic archer who battles an evil wizard. You're welcome to borrow it sometime . . ." He trailed off, suddenly feeling embarrassed. "That is, if you ever wanted to."

"Thanks, I'd like that." Jamie smiled, then tucked his book back into his breast pocket as up ahead the major called for a halt. The unit stopped, some of them keeling over gratefully right in the middle of the road where they stood.

Jamie nodded toward the bow on Max's other shoulder. "Speaking of heroic archers, feel like showing me your skills?"

Max self-consciously tried to tuck the bow out of sight. "Oh this, well, I'm actually not very good. It's more just a little kid's toy really."

"Nonsense," Jamie said. "I saw your form at close range last night. Your stance and the way you held your bow, well, I could tell you knew what you were doing."

Max felt a flush of pride in his chest. "My father made the bow and arrows himself," he said, now holding them up for inspection proudly. "And my mother knitted the quiver for me."

"They're obviously very talented," Jamie said, inspecting the craftsmanship before adding gently, "If you don't mind me asking, where are your parents now?"

It was a question Max asked himself every day. "I . . . don't really know. They left to help fight the Nazis, but I haven't heard from them in a long time." The bow's string seemed to make a mournful note when he plucked it. "I brought these along to help me remember them, even though I'm very out of practice."

"Would you like to practice a little now?" Jamie asked. "I could give you some pointers, if you'd like."

Max's legs felt numb from exhaustion, but then he pictured his grandmother and found strength in remembering his vow to protect her. "I'd like that. Thank you."

Jamie scanned both sides of the road, then led the way toward a wooden barrel that lay discarded in the grass nearby. "Here you go," he said, rolling the barrel onto its side so that one circular end faced Max. "Why don't you stand over there by that tree and see how close you can get to the center?"

Max walked over to stand by the tree Jamie had indicated and turned back toward the barrel. "Are you sure?" he asked dubiously, squinting at the barrel. "Maybe I should stand a little closer?"

"Give it a try," Jamie said. "You might surprise yourself."

"Here goes nothing," Max said under his breath. He nocked an arrow in the bow, pulled back on the string, and let the arrow fly. It sailed in a long arc before thudding into the soft mud about a foot in front of the barrel.

"Very good," Jamie said. He pulled the arrow out of the ground and jogged toward Max. "Let's make a few adjustments this time."

Max got the arrow set again and took aim at the barrel.

Standing behind him, Jamie patiently adjusted the boy's arm. "Raise your elbow just a touch. Good. And now we're going to turn slightly to adjust for the breeze. Perfect. Finally, hold your breath and let the arrow fly."

Max drew in a slow breath and held it. In the brief second of stillness, he felt as if the bow and arrow were an extension of his body. Then he released. The arrow twanged off the bow. A second later, it thunked into the lid of the barrel only a few inches off center.

"That was incredible!" Jamie said. "Think you can do it again? On your own this time?"

Max pulled another arrow out of his quiver and took aim, adjusting his elbow and stance as Jamie had shown him. Only, this time when he held his breath, in the brief second of silence before he let go, Plum let out a loud bark. Distracted, Max dropped his bow and looked up, shielding his eyes. A small speck appeared in the distant sky. Whatever it was, it was slowly growing as it headed their way. Soon he heard a buzzing noise that grew louder by the second, eventually becoming recognizable as the whine of an airplane's engines.

"If it's one of ours, it's way off course," Jamie said, now squinting in that direction too. "Everyone take cover!" he shouted. Instantly everyone was moving and pulling their gear out of sight under the nearest trees.

The plane slowly took shape until Max recognized the outline of a small fighter craft. But it was impossible to tell yet if it belonged to the German Luftwaffe or the British Royal Air Force.

"It can't have seen us yet," Jamie said, "but we'd better clear out too, just in case."

At that same moment, Plum erupted in a fierce fit of barking. Max tried to coax her back toward where the rest of the soldiers waited, but she wouldn't budge. Finally, he stooped to pick her up and carry her, but she dodged away from his hands. She tore off through the grass, then into the open road, still howling furiously.

"Plum, no!" Max shouted, and ran after her.

"Max!" he heard Jamie call behind him.

"I have to get her!" he called over his shoulder.

Max chased Plum onto the empty road as the sound of the approaching plane grew louder. The dog's tiny legs churned surprisingly quickly. Max soon found himself gasping for breath as he gave chase. Ahead, the whine of the plane's engines changed, and Max looked up. One wing dipped toward the ground as the fighter changed its path to angle directly toward them. It was close enough now that Max could just make out Germany's iron cross painted on one side. His hammering heart skipped a beat in his chest.

"Plum!" he cried, and dove for the dog. His hands closed

around her. He rolled and tucked her close to his chest as she squirmed to get away. The roar of the plane was so loud it seemed almost to be inside his head. Max darted his eyes toward the sky. The plane loomed impossibly close. His heart shot into his throat. The fighter had swooped low to the ground, heading right for him! His vision seemed to narrow so that all he could see was the glare of its metal in the sun like a ball of fire. And he was frozen there in the middle of the wide-open road, unable to move.

Suddenly, a tall figure stepped into the path between the fighter and Max. Startled, Max looked up and saw Jamie standing there with his rifle leveled, calmly taking aim. The plane's twin machine guns started to spit fire, and seconds later Max heard the steady crack of asphalt as bits of the road exploded a hundred feet in front of them.

Chug chug chug came the steady roar of the plane's cannons.

Closer. Closer.

What happened next seemed to flash by in a staccato of sounds and scenes barely occupying the space of a few seconds. Over the noise, a single, sharp crack of Jamie's rifle. In almost the same moment, Jamie's body lifting off the ground and jerking backward as if he'd been no more than a rag doll. Then the sound of the plane's engines changing. Max watching it wobble in the sky before dipping to one side. Its wings catching the tops of some trees along the road. In the next moment, the entire aircraft exploding in a huge inferno.

Max felt his body violently spun around and thrown backward by the concussion.

Then . . . nothing.

CHAPTER TWENTY-ONE

IRIS

England

"We have to get out of here!" Maud shouted.

The flames were all around them now. Iris reached for Galahad's chain, then yelped and yanked her hands back from the scalding-hot metal. "I'm not leaving Galahad!"

"But he's a dragon! Fire won't hurt him, right?"

"Yes, but the roof collapsing on him will!" The rafters above them groaned. Streaks of orange raced across the beams—the entire roof was on fire. Iris spotted a shovel propped against one wall. She ran toward it and brought it back toward Galahad, where she swung the metal end against the chain again and again. Beads of sweat dotted her forehead in the heat by the time she stopped to catch her breath.

"It's no use!" Maud said. "The whole barn will come down before you're through."

Iris spun around, looking for anything else they might use to free Galahad. Over the dragon's terrified bellows, she could hear men shouting outside.

The guard appeared in the open doorway, shielding his face with one arm as he peered into the barn. "Is someone in there?"

"Help!" Maud cried. "The dragon is trapped!"

The man started to edge toward them. But the burning timber over the doorway collapsed right in front of him, blocking the way in. Iris's breath caught in her throat. They were trapped now too!

"Hold on!" the man yelled. "I'll go get help!"

Iris instinctively threw herself onto Galahad when an ear-splitting screech of rending wood filled the barn, followed by a terrible cracking noise. Bits of wood and other debris rained down all around. She covered her head, expecting the entire structure to come crashing down. But when nothing else happened for several seconds, she tentatively lifted her head and looked around.

The beam that Galahad was leashed to had cracked and was now resting precariously on what seemed to be barely more than a splinter of wood. Above them, rain pelted in from a large hole in the roof. Unfortunately, it wasn't enough to quench the fire, which raged on stronger than ever.

"Galahad!" Iris cried over the noise of the fire and rain. "If you can fly, I think you might be able to pull your chain free where the wood is weaker there."

Iris grabbed the harness to help herself scramble onto Galahad's back, then held out her hand to Maud. "Come on!"

"I don't know," Maud said nervously.

"I thought you said you weren't afraid of dragons?"

Maud looked around, evidently trying to come up with another plan. "I'm not. It's the falling-off part that scares me."

"It's the only way!" Iris said. "But we don't have long."

Another large, burning beam thudded to the ground nearby,

sending sparks flying. Maud dashed toward Galahad. She grabbed Iris's hand and catapulted herself onto his back behind Iris.

"Hold on!" Iris said.

Maud wrapped her arms tightly around the girl's waist.

"Now, Galahad!" Iris shouted.

With a sickening lurch, Galahad used his powerful hind legs to launch them off the ground. They wobbled in midair as he unfurled his wings to their full length and beat them uncertainly at first, then more confidently. The chain slowly slipped up the beam toward the weakened section as Galahad rose higher and higher.

"You're doing it!" Iris encouraged him.

The entire barn groaned in protest as Galahad pulled against the weakened beam. Below, the fire churned hotter, fanned into a fury by the beating of the dragon's wings. Iris could barely stand the heat of its flames on her face as Galahad struggled to free himself. It was going to be a near thing, she knew. Then finally, with a terrible cracking noise, they lurched backward. The chain had come loose at last!

"Fly!" she screamed, and buried her face against Galahad's scaly neck. Seconds later, the dragon and girls exploded through the destroyed roof in a shower of orange sparks. A clamor of groans and screeches came from below as the barn finally succumbed to the flames. Iris felt the welcome patter of cool rain on her skin and raised her head. Far below, dark figures pointed up at them from the edges of the burning structure. The last standing wall of the barn leaned inward, then fell.

It was over. Galahad was free.

CHAPTER TWENTY-TWO

MAX

France

The first thing Max's brain registered was darkness. Then a dull ache in his head that seemed to radiate out from the base of his skull. It was almost enough to make him want to retreat back into unconsciousness.

Jamie! Plum!

The names floated up from the recesses of his mind. With enormous effort, Max shoved aside the pain and wrestled through the cobwebs clinging to his brain.

He jerked awake with a gasp and found himself lying flat on his back, staring up at the underside of a canopy of trees. His head throbbed painfully. The green leaves overhead bobbed and moved rhythmically. Or maybe he was moving. He couldn't tell. He tried to sit up but found himself tied down. The first thought that rang through his head was *I've been captured by Germans!*

"Well, look who's awake," came Jack's voice. He spoke in a low voice, for which Max was thankful due to his splitting headache.

Max tilted his chin up and back. There was Jack, grinning down at him and carrying whatever Max was lying on.

"Sorry to have to restrain you, mate," Jack said. "Couldn't

133

have you rolling off and into the trees on your own during our march. You know, if you'd needed a nap, all you had to do was say so."

"Where's Jamie?" Max croaked.

"Right here, Max," came Jamie's voice from nearby.

Still feeling groggy, Max let his head loll to one side and saw Jamie being transported on a makeshift stretcher.

Jamie tried to smile, but it ended up looking more like a grimace. On the ground between them, Plum pranced and yipped excitedly at seeing Max awake.

Max attempted to lift his arm to wave at her before remembering he was tethered in place. The gentle swaying motion from their march was making him queasy. He squeezed his eyes tightly shut and groaned.

"You'll be wanting to lie still for a bit, I expect," Jack said, as if reading his mind. "Nasty business that, with the Me-109. But you came out on top with nothing worse than a whopper of a bruise on your head."

"What happened? All I remember is the plane and then . . . nothing."

"Let's put it this way," Jack said. "The stretcher you're strapped to was once the wing of a German Messerschmitt. It's not exactly going to be needing it anymore."

Max's eyes went wide. "You mean, Jamie hit it?"

"In one shot," Jack said, and whistled appreciatively. "Not a bad bit of shooting there, though I wouldn't recommend making a habit of it. He'd have punched his ticket into the great beyond if not for a little luck of the literary persuasion."

Max wasn't sure what Jack meant by that. He studied Jamie. The soldier's shirt was torn back, and white bandages were wrapped tightly around his torso. A large, angry-looking bruise was visible around the edges of the bandages. Despite the obvious injury to Jamie's body, he realized something was missing. "Why isn't there any blood?"

"Because that bruise you see isn't the only souvenir Jamie got from your little skirmish," Jack replied. "Want to show him, Jamie?"

With a grunt, Jamie felt around on his right side and held up a small object. It took Max a few seconds to register what he was looking at. It was the book Jamie's sister had given him, only now it had a jagged shard of metal embedded in its cover. "Is that a . . . ?" His voice trailed off, not quite believing what he was seeing.

"Fragment of a machine gun shell?" Jack finished for him. "Best we can figure, it shattered on the road in front of him and caught him in the chest on the rebound. Still had enough force to punch him backward several feet. Hit him right over the heart. If it hadn't been for that book, well . . ."

Max gulped, his head feeling suddenly woozy again at the realization of how narrowly they both had escaped death.

"Iris is going to kill me when she sees what I did to her book," Jamie said.

Jack raised one eyebrow. "Somehow I think she'll get over it."

"And, Max," Jamie said, searching the boy's face, "you're . . . okay?"

Max closed his eyes to assess how he was feeling. "I think so, other than my head pounding and feeling sore all over." He opened his eyes and searched for his dog again. "What about Plum?"

Hearing her name, the dog yipped happily and tried to hop up next to Max to lick his face.

Jack laughed. "Fit as a fiddle, I'd say."

"Well, as soon as I'm feeling better," Max said, "she and I will have a long talk about never doing anything like that ever again."

"Don't be too hard on her," Jamie said. "If it wasn't for her sharp hearing, the rest of our unit might have been spotted. We've managed to elude the Germans so far, but they can't be very far behind."

A muffled command to halt came from somewhere ahead and they stopped moving.

"Oi!" Jack said to the soldier carrying the front of Max's makeshift stretcher. "Let's set him down here."

The men gently set their patient on the ground beside a large oak tree. Jack then started working on the ropes that had been used to keep Max's body in place. "Think you can sit up?" he asked Max. "You'll probably be wanting a little water by now."

Max nodded. His throat felt like he'd swallowed a handful of sand. As the tethers came loose around him, he edged up onto his elbows. Why did his entire body ache so badly? He waited for a wave of dizziness to pass before sitting up all the way and taking a long drink from the canteen offered to him. Plum immediately crawled into his lap and squirmed happily while he hugged her tight with his free arm.

"Need a little help?" Jack asked.

Max lowered the canteen and looked across at Jamie struggling to sit up.

"I think so," Jamie replied, pressing his hand against his chest. "Maybe . . . give me a minute though."

When Jamie indicated he was ready, Jack gently slid his arms under Jamie's shoulders and helped haul him into a sitting position. Max could tell the pain must be excruciating, but Jamie closed his eyes and focused on taking in long, slow breaths.

Not trusting himself to walk yet, Max crawled through the leaves on the forest floor toward Jamie with his forehead creased in concern. "Here, you can have some of mine," Max offered, holding out the canteen to Jamie.

Jamie nodded and took it gratefully. He tipped his head back, poured the cool water carefully into his mouth, and took a tentative swallow. Then he coughed, spitting most of the mouthful onto the ground. "It even hurts to drink," he said, and chuckled, only to wince again. "And laugh."

"My grandmother says that pain is your body's way of telling you it's healing," Max said. "So I guess it's sort of a good thing, in a way." The boy's eyes fell when he mentioned his grandmother.

"I can tell you really miss her," Jamie said.

Max nodded, then bit his lip and blinked fiercely.

"Well, she sounds like a very wise lady," Jamie said. Just then his stomach emitted a loud growl. "And what do you think she would say about grumbling stomachs?"

"Probably that it's your body's way of telling you it's time to eat," Jack replied. "Unfortunately, we ran out of rations yesterday morning. We've been surviving on what we've been able to forage from the forest, which isn't much."

"When did we leave the main road?" Jamie asked.

"Early last night," Jack replied. "Narrowly missed being spotted by a German convoy. They've got us fairly surrounded now. Fortunately, we found this road—if you can call it that—heading generally in the direction of the coast."

Max heard a crunch of leaves off to his right. Major Stevenson emerged through the trees, striding purposefully back toward them.

"You're both awake," he said to Jamie and Max. "That's excellent news." He turned and addressed the unit. "We'll stop here for a brief rest before we press on. I'm afraid we have to keep moving to keep ahead of the Germans."

When Stevenson had left, Jack turned back to Jamie. "Anything we can get for you? More water? Some beef Wellington with red wine sauce?"

Jamie humphed softly at this and winced, clutching his chest again. "Actually, I was hoping Max might be able to read a little of his story to us." He held up his own book with the metal shard embedded in its cover. "I don't think mine's in any shape to read anymore."

Max looked up, surprised. "Um . . . I, are you sure? It's just, it's not all that good."

"Come on, Max, let's have it," Jack urged. "I'd wager you're a far better writer than you let on." He retrieved Max's journal for him and handed him a small flashlight. "Here you are, mate. Just keep the light hooded in case there are any German scouts nearby."

Max nodded and directed the flashlight down at his lap, where it cast a yellow circle on the open page. Another young soldier joined them. His name was Boone, but he'd quickly earned the nickname "Boo" because he had a tendency to jump at the slightest provocation. Boo drew his legs close to his body and lowered his chin to his knees expectantly.

Max flipped to the first page, then glanced up at his audience, feeling his neck flush with embarrassment. Jamie smiled encouragingly, and Max took a deep breath as he lowered his eyes to the page: "Once upon a time, there lived a man named Sebastian who had a gift possessed by no other man. For Sebastian could speak to dragons."

Soon, Max was once again lost in the story, his mind carried away on dragon's wings into the quest to defeat the evil wizard. From time to time, his peripheral vision registered a form moving out of the deepening night to join their small group and listen. By the time he stopped reading and finally looked up, he was startled by what he saw.

Nine men . . . ten . . . no, the entire unit sat quietly in a semicircle in front of him, their tired but attentive faces waiting expectantly for what came next. All the crushing tension of their forced march—the constant fear of Germans, the sore and blistered feet, the lack of sleep and food—seemed to be forgotten under the trance of the story.

His story.

Max could hardly believe it. If there was any magic still left in the world, he reflected, then surely this was it.

Jack's voice came out of the dark, breaking the spell. "Well, you can't jolly well stop there. Does our chap Sebastian escape or not?"

Max laughed. "I haven't quite figured out how the story ends yet, but there's a little more." He had just opened his mouth to continue reading when a bloodcurdling scream knifed out of the dark.

CHAPTER TWENTY-THREE

IRIS

———

England

Sitting astride Galahad, Iris watched the rush of activity around the inferno below. Despite the steady rain, the remains of the barn continued to burn. The dragon slowly circled the pillar of smoke that rose into the night.

"Now what?" Maud asked behind her, clinging tightly to Iris's waist.

"Now we take you home before Galahad and I go look for the dragons."

"No way," Maud protested. "I promised to help. And I'm going to. Anyway, they'll have alerted half the village by now. Anywhere you try to land, they might have someone waiting to capture or even shoot Galahad."

Maud was right. After all they'd gone through to free the dragon, Iris couldn't risk him being recaptured now. "But my supplies. I lost them in the fire. We don't even have anything to eat."

"We'll figure something out," Maud said. "Just promise not to drop me."

Iris smiled at the girl's indomitable spirit. "Okay then. Let's go find some dragons."

Galahad beat his wings, propelling them forward, and their journey into the north began. Iris wasn't exactly sure how fast the dragon could fly, but her father had said the journey north was a few days on foot. She judged that might be only some hours' time by air. Then the real search would begin. She felt her heart thump a double beat. Even if they found the dragons, would they be in time to save their brothers?

"We're . . . flying," Maud half whispered behind her after a time.

Iris glanced over her shoulder. On the heels of their narrow escape from the fire, she hadn't allowed herself the time to enjoy the sense of awe her friend was feeling. The wind whipping through their hair. The sense of complete freedom. "Amazing, isn't it?"

Iris stared into the impenetrable blackness of the night sky ahead, wondering what lay waiting there for them. Far below, the occasional light shone from a lonely farmhouse as the hours slid by. Maybe inside each of those homes, someone was staring up at the sky, worrying about a brother or a son away in the war. The war had torn so many families apart. But at the same time, it had brought together many unrelated people into a sort of makeshift family united by their common fears and worries.

Suddenly, Galahad shuddered and seemed to falter. "I-is he okay?" Maud asked as her arms tightened around Iris's middle.

"I'm . . . not sure," Iris said. She leaned forward so he could hear her. "Galahad, is something wrong?"

A series of rumbles came from his throat in reply.

"He says he's feeling a little tired," she translated for Maud's benefit. Iris rubbed his neck encouragingly. "We'll get you some rest soon."

By the time the first traces of dawn lit the sky, Galahad's head visibly drooped as he flew, and his breathing grew increasingly labored. She knew he couldn't go on much longer.

"There's the ocean!" Maud said, pointing up ahead to where the first rays of the sun glinted on a golden strip of water.

As they arced over the shore, Iris studied the lonely coastline, thinking it was the perfect sanctuary for a herd of dragons. Galahad shuddered beneath her again, and she stroked his neck soothingly. For now, their search would have to wait.

"Let's land there," she called to Galahad, and pointed to an open stretch of sand.

Once Galahad had thumped down onto the beach, Iris quickly scrambled off and came around to his head. The dragon's golden eyes seemed dimmer somehow. Her heart squeezed in her chest, seeing him like this. She examined the shoreline and spotted a sheltered bower big enough for a dragon to curl up and rest. After helping Maud down, she led Galahad there. He crumpled to the ground and immediately closed his eyes. Iris sat by his side and stroked his neck until his labored breathing settled into the even patterns of sleep.

"Do you think he's sick?" Maud asked quietly, coming up to kneel beside Iris. "Maybe it's the emotional trauma of being kept in captivity for so long?"

"Maybe . . ." Iris said uncertainly. Whatever it was, she hoped some rest would do him good.

It was Galahad who woke her sometime later. Iris sat up quickly, initially disoriented. She brushed sand from her cheek from where she'd fallen asleep and looked around, remembering their mission. The sky was slate gray. The best she could tell, it was already late afternoon. She was surprised they had all slept so long.

The dragon nuzzled playfully into her neck.

"You seem to be feeling better!" Iris said, and laughed with relief.

Galahad rumbled a reply from deep in his throat.

Maud pushed herself up on one arm where she'd been lying nearby. "What's he saying?"

"That he's starving!" Iris said. Overhead, a distant peal of thunder drew her gaze back to the sky. Dark clouds scudded slowly in from the north.

Addressing the dragon, Iris said, "I know, and I'm so sorry. Only, I'm anxious to use whatever daylight we have left to start our search. And at the very least, we might find somewhere to shelter from this storm. Do you feel up to flying?"

Galahad stood and stretched his wings in response. Iris and Maud climbed onto his back, and moments later they were soaring along the coast, studying the barren beaches for any signs of dragons. It was easy for Iris to imagine that no living thing had ever set foot on this fog-shrouded shore.

Iris had no idea how long they'd been searching when she felt a wet drop plop onto her forehead and slide down to the tip of her nose. More joined that one, and soon the rain picked up to a drizzle. The girls clung to Galahad as the wind steadily increased, buffeting them and swirling their hair around their faces. Overhead, thunder cracked again. The sky grew darker as night set in, making their search more difficult. Eventually, the light rain progressed into a heavy downpour that soon soaked them through to the skin. Up ahead, a bolt of lightning arced out of the sky, followed by a closer boom of thunder.

"Should we try to find shelter?" Maud called over the wind.

"Just a little farther," Iris said, trying to think of some way—any way—they could keep up their search despite the storm. With each passing minute, she felt with increasing dread that time was running out. Too much was riding on the success of their mission. Just then, another white-hot bolt stabbed toward the earth so close that she could feel its heat on her face. Galahad swung hard to the right in surprise.

"Iris!" Maud screamed.

Her stomach twisting in fear, Iris spun around in time to see Maud tumbling backward. The girl's fingertips scrabbled frantically at the dragon's back but couldn't find a grip on the rain-slicked scales. At last, one hand managed to grasp the fringe of the rope harness with a white-knuckled grip as she toppled off the dragon's back and hung dangling in midair. Galahad bellowed in fear.

"Grab my hand!" Iris cried, throwing out her arm toward Maud.

Maud's free hand shot toward hers. But the movement caused the rope to snap under her weight. Iris's fingers closed on empty air.

With a cry of terror, Maud plummeted out of sight.

"Galahad!" Iris yelped, but the dragon was already banking around and down, evidently having felt the sudden lessening of weight. Iris squeezed her knees tighter around the dragon's back and clung to the harness to avoid falling off too. She squinted through the nearly blinding rain, looking for any sign of her friend. Between the storm and the dark, it was impossible to see beyond a few feet in front of her. She hoped Galahad could spot Maud with his better night vision.

Then another bolt of lightning crashed down from the sky. Not far below and just a bit to their right, Iris spotted a dark figure flailing in the sky.

"There!" she shouted to Galahad.

Her heart thudded harder at the rocky coastline racing up toward them, which was also illuminated in the brief flash of light. All went black as the lightning faded, leaving Iris blind again.

The dragon dove toward Maud. Did they have enough room, or would they be smashed to bits on the jagged rocks? The wind screamed in Iris's ears. Or was it Maud's screaming? She couldn't tell.

Suddenly, Maud's body appeared out of the darkness, her arms windmilling frantically. Iris stretched and grabbed for her with one hand. Her fingertips found the billowing edge of Maud's sleeve. Iris snapped her fist closed around the fabric and yanked with all her strength, pulling Maud into a tight hug. And none too soon. The sound of crashing waves exploded in Iris's ears as Galahad quickly pulled out of his dive. Iris felt her stomach drop sickeningly as the dragon clawed back toward the sky.

Iris clung to Maud, who continued to tremble either from fear or the cold, or probably both. Whatever the case may be, she knew they had traveled far enough for the night.

"Let's get you somewhere out of the rain," Iris said.

"Y-yes, p-please," Maud said shakily.

Iris gazed through the storm, trying to orient herself. The lightning flashed again. She saw a sheer cliff rising above a row of sharp, pointed rocks, and partway up what looked like a dark opening in the rock. An odd feeling of déjà vu gripped her.

She rubbed Galahad's neck and pointed. "Can you take us there? We might be able to find shelter from the storm."

The dragon angled toward the opening. The rain stopped pelting them as soon as they crossed the threshold into the cool dryness of a cave. They were enveloped in total blackness. Judging from the sound of the echoes of the rain on the cavern's walls, it was a fairly large space. Iris helped Maud down from Galahad's back. She looked toward the entrance, where the rain continued to sluice down from the sky.

"Th-thanks." Maud's shivering voice came out of the dark.

"I'm sorry I pushed us to go farther tonight. I shouldn't have put us all in danger like that." Iris cautiously ventured farther into the cave, twisting her hair together and squeezing the water out of it. Her foot kicked something on the ground that shifted when she nudged it. She knelt to feel what it was. "I think I found a bit of driftwood over here," she called back to Maud. "Maybe Galahad could make a fire for us."

She found a few more pieces of wood, enough to make a small pile. Soon they had a cozy blaze going. Galahad curled around the fire, and both girls settled in against his warm bulk, staring around at the cave. Orange and yellow light cast dancing shadows across stalactites hanging far over their heads.

"Is something wrong?" Maud asked beside her.

Iris glanced in her direction. She was encouraged to hear Maud's voice had already regained some of its usual self-assuredness.

"It's only"—Iris got up and wandered in a slow circle around the fire, studying their surroundings—"when I first spotted this cave, I had the strangest feeling I'd been here before."

"Have you?"

"I'm fairly certain I haven't. But still . . ." She studied the shape of the cave's opening, and suddenly a lightbulb went on in her brain. She spun toward Maud. "Of course! The rocks shaped like dragons' teeth. The slash in the cliff face. They were both in a drawing my mum made. My dad said it was the place the dragons went after they left our village!"

Maud looked around uncertainly, noticeably less excited than Iris had expected by her discovery.

"What is it?" Iris asked. "You don't look so certain."

"Only . . . if this is where the dragons went . . ." Maud said slowly. She cupped her hands around her mouth and shouted "Hello!" into the emptiness all around them. The only sound that came back was the echo of her voice. *Hello . . . lo . . . lo . . .* She turned toward Iris. "Then where did they all go?"

Feeling her spirits deflate a little, Iris stared around the cave again. There didn't seem to be the least trace of the dragon herd. She had never considered that the dragons might have moved on from this place. Which meant now they could be virtually anywhere.

"Well," Iris said eventually, "I suppose we can't go back out in the storm, so we might as well wait it out here where it's dry. Maybe we can search again in the morning." She tried to sound optimistic, though inside she felt as hollow as the cave they stood in.

"Sorry," Maud said softly.

Iris sank back against Galahad's side again. Outside, she heard the wind continue to pound the surf against the jagged rocks below, as if the storm was trying to dash to pieces her grand plan for finding the dragons and rescuing her brother.

CHAPTER TWENTY-FOUR
MAX'S JOURNAL

France

Night

I have eaten so many marshmallows that I think I might burst. And to think, we may never have found them, if not for the peacock. Maybe I should explain. We heard a shriek from the forest, but it was too dark to see what made the noise. Boo thought it was an evil spirit. To me, it sounded more like a woman's scream. When we investigated, we found it was just a silly peacock. Boo was so angry that he chased the peacock through the forest, crashing into trees and bushes and using English words I've never heard before. The chase led us to an old building with wooden crates sitting around inside. Guess what was in the crates? Marshmallows! So many marshmallows that we are eating, and laughing, and even throwing them at one another. One soldier pretends to clutch his stomach and fall when a marshmallow hits him. Only he doesn't seem to be—

CHAPTER TWENTY-FIVE

IRIS

England

When Iris woke sometime later, the cave was quiet. Their fire must have died out at some point as she'd slept. All that remained of the storm was a soft *drip drip* somewhere near the mouth of the cave. Galahad's side swelled gently in and out where she lay curled against him. It seemed that whatever had been ailing him earlier had passed.

She was just about to sit up and stoke the fire back to life when she sensed something nearby. Something large moving silently in the gray murk. Then a huge, dark head slid into view directly in front of her. A pair of golden eyes stared into her own—eyes that did not belong to Galahad.

"Iris!" Maud hissed.

"I see it," she said softly. Her heart thumped loudly against her ribs.

Slowly, Iris lifted one hand, moving it toward the dragon's snout, which was long and rounded at the end like Galahad's. The mouth parted slightly to reveal a row of gleaming, sharp teeth. But Iris didn't pull back. The dragon's eyes followed her hand until, a few inches away from making contact, it flinched away from her touch. A soft mewling noise rumbled from its throat as the dragon shifted farther back into the shadows.

"It's okay," she soothed, rising carefully to a sitting position. "We're friends." She fumbled around until she found their small pile of loose driftwood and slid a piece onto the glowing remains of their fire. With a small pop, the flame sparked back to life and filled the cavern with a low amber glow.

Beside her, Maud let out a small gasp. "Oh my goodness."

The soft yellow light revealed a dragon slightly larger than Galahad. However, instead of Galahad's muddy brown, this one's scales were a rich, shimmering blue. They caught the fire's glow and cast it back as rainbows on the walls of the cave. The dragon's head swung from the girls to Galahad, who was now awake too. He shrank back under the newcomer's scrutiny. The two dragons studied each other for a few seconds, their heads bobbing and turning inquisitively in a slow dance.

Suddenly, the blue dragon's head shot out and thumped against Galahad's long neck. Surprised, Galahad yelped and tumbled over onto his side.

Maud put a hand on Iris's arm. "What's happening?"

The new dragon emitted a soft, tentative rumble and Galahad lifted his head curiously.

"I think"—Iris said, grinning—"I think she wants to play."

In the next moment, the blue dragon pounced at Galahad, nipping at his flank. Galahad yelped again and bounded away. He studied the other dragon for a heartbeat. Then he sprang toward her, narrowly missing as the larger dragon deftly dodged his attack. Soon both dragons were bounding about the cave, their playful growls and shrieks echoing in the large space as they took turns going on the offensive and retreating.

"I think Galahad's made a new friend," Iris said, laughing.

Maud's eyes lit up. "We should name her! Maybe something from the King Arthur legends to match Galahad. There's Guinevere, of course. Or maybe Morgan, but"—she studied the blue dragon—"she doesn't strike me as an evil enchantress."

"What about Malory?" Iris asked.

"Malory? I don't remember her."

"I mean from Sir Thomas Malory, the author who originally compiled the Arthurian legends."

Maud considered. "I think I like it. And I've always thought there's a bit of sorcery in how writers create their stories, so it's got that magical element to it. Okay, Malory it is." She nodded toward the dragon. "Speaking of, I think Malory is trying to tell us something."

The dragons had stopped leaping around the room and now stood close together, exchanging a series of low guttural noises. Then Malory backed up toward the rear of the cave a few steps and bleated softly, first toward Galahad and then the two girls.

"I think she wants us to follow her," Iris said.

Iris and Maud walked slowly toward the blue dragon. Malory watched them approach for a few moments before turning and shuffling farther into the cave. They followed her, leaving behind the comforting glow of the fire.

Iris peered into the yawning blackness, her heartbeat picking up as she imagined what might lie ahead. "Hold on. I'll be right back," she said to Maud, and hurried back toward the fire.

She found a thick piece of driftwood on the cave floor and dipped one end into the flames. Within a few seconds it smoked and caught. When she returned to Maud's side, the makeshift torch illuminated a small halo of light around them before it was swallowed in the dark of the cave.

"Good thinking," Maud said.

Malory led them onward. As they traveled farther, the chill in the cave deepened despite the warmth of the flame. Occasionally, Malory's golden eyes glowed at them when she peered back to confirm they were still following.

Galahad had chosen to walk alongside his new friend. Iris could just make out their low rumblings of conversation. Iris's heart swelled knowing how much it meant for Galahad to finally interact with one of his own kind.

"What do you think people taste like?" Maud asked, breaking the silence.

Iris stutter-stepped before catching herself. "That's kind of a morbid question. You're not changing your mind about being scared of dragons, are you?"

"Of course not. But I'd feel better knowing a dragon wouldn't eat me unless it absolutely had to."

Iris wasn't sure how to respond. Fortunately, a sparkle of light at the end of the tunnel offered a distraction. "Wait, does it look to you as if the cave gets lighter up ahead? Or am I just seeing things?"

Maud squinted into the distance. "I think you're right!"

The girls hurried toward the light. Soon the tunnel grew noticeably brighter. Iris could make out the shapes of rock formations around them. Occasionally, she also thought she saw large shapes moving in the half-light, but when she turned toward them with her heart thumping in her chest, they were gone.

Suddenly, they stepped out into a massive cavern that opened up before them, lit with the golden glow of sunlight. On the far side, a waterfall thundered down toward the cavern's floor far below. The girls stopped at the edge of a stone ledge and stared around in wonder.

"Did you see where Malory and Galahad went?" Iris asked.

Maud gasped beside her. "There!"

Iris followed her gaze up toward where a shaft of bright sunlight pierced down through an opening far above. But the sun's brilliance was easily outdone by what else she saw.

Dragons.

They were everywhere. And in nearly every color imaginable—blue, red, green, and many more. Their scales seemed to sparkle and shift as if infused with magic while they soared through the vastness of the open space or crouched on rocky perches along the cliff walls.

"They're . . . beautiful," Iris breathed. In her wildest dreams, she had never imagined there were so many dragons. She spotted Galahad circling and diving among them. Her eyes grew misty at seeing him so happy among his long-lost family at last.

"With this many dragons," Maud said excitedly, "we can rescue everyone's family from the war!"

Tears began to slip down Iris's cheeks as an immense wave of relief and joy washed over her. She pictured Jamie, Jack, and all the other village children's brothers, uncles, and fathers soaring home to safety on a fleet of dragons. "Yes!" she cried, laughing through her tears. "I think we could evacuate perhaps the entire British army!"

Maud snapped to attention, saluting. "Royal Air Force, Dragon Fleet at your service!"

The girls giggled and threw their arms around each other. But even in the midst of Iris's jubilation, a tiny sliver of doubt wormed its way into her thoughts. She had no idea how she was going to get the dragons to join them in their rescue mission. Would they come willingly?

Iris felt a rush of wind beating downward on her. When she looked up, she saw an enormous dragon descending toward them. Iris stepped back from the ledge, her pulse thumping loudly along with the sounds of the huge, leathery wings. She instinctively raised one arm over her head against the whirl of debris as the dragon came to rest on a rocky outcropping about a hundred feet away.

Iris studied the dragon as it folded its wings against its body and silently met her gaze. Scales of a deep golden color tarnished dull with age covered the massive head, which was easily as large as her tractor at home. A row of sharp horns traced back along the top of its snout toward a pair of amber eyes, where they diverged into two larger ivory horns that swept back from its head like a crown toward a body bigger than her family's barn.

Galahad and the blue dragon Malory descended from the sky and landed by Iris's side. A hush fell over the cavern, filled only by the rushing of the waterfall in the distance.

At last, when the huge dragon spoke, the slow, deep voice came without the beast making any movement: *Greetings, human children. How have you come to this place?*

She glanced across at Maud, who seemed as confused as her.

Then Iris startled, realizing the dragon's voice must have somehow been inside her head. She wasn't sure if she should reply in kind and instead said out loud, "M-my n-name is Iris." She paused to take in a deep, calming breath before continuing more confidently, "And this is Maud, and Galahad. We have come from the south seeking your herd. May I ask your name?"

"What's happening?" Maud asked under her breath.

"I think he can project his voice directly into our heads," Iris replied.

As if confirming, the voice came again. *Well met, Iris and Maud. Dragons do not follow such conventions as human names, but at one time humans spoke of me as Belrath.* His eyes swung like huge lanterns to look past her shoulder. *And what of this youngling you call Galahad?*

Iris flicked her eyes toward Galahad, who was cowering back from the huge dragon. "Galahad is the name I gave him, after a brave knight. I believe he was once a part of your herd. I found him alone in the forest years ago, and we have grown up together. He's my best friend."

A human and a dragon . . . friends? Belrath said. *That is a curious notion. My memory reaches far, and I can recall few instances of true friendship with humans. Indeed, the very reason we have retreated to this lonely refuge is to escape them and the harm they have done to our kind.*

Iris's heart sank. This conversation wasn't going the right way at all if she was going to ask him for their help. "I'm truly sorry for the way humans have treated dragons in the past."

The dragon studied her for a long moment. *You have returned the one you call Galahad safely to our herd, and you have my deepest thanks for that. But I sense that you have come with still another purpose.*

Iris's mind went blank. All the words seemed to have fled from her brain.

"You can do this," Maud said softly, reaching out and squeezing Iris's hand.

Nodding, Iris continued. "That's right. There's another reason we came here. You see, a war is going on in France. Our friends, brothers, and fathers are trapped there by the German army and need help escaping." She paused. "They need dragons to carry them home."

Several agonizing moments passed before Belrath's voice echoed in her head again. *I know of this place across the waters called France. But what have dragons to do with human affairs? Humans have fought and killed one another for millennia and will continue to do so for many millennia hence. We do not involve ourselves in such matters.*

"Only—"

As I have said, the dragon cut her off, *I am grateful that you have returned our young one to his herd. But that alone does not erase years of hostility between humans and dragons. I invite you now to take your leave and return whence you came.*

"But, please, you don't—"

I bid you farewell, Belrath said with finality. His great wings unfolded and swept downward once—*thwump*—then again—*thwump.*

"No, wait!" Iris cried, and ran toward the cliff's edge. But her words were swept away. The dragon rose slowly from his perch, the gale from his wings buffeting the small outcropping where they stood.

Unprepared for the force of the wind, Iris stumbled backward and fell. Her teeth clacked together painfully as she sat down hard on the stone floor. A jolt of pain and disappointment seared through her body. All her hopes for rescuing her brother dashed in a single moment. Hot tears sprang to her eyes as she leaned forward, covering her face with her hands. How had she come this close only to fail? This had been their one hope. Their last desperate gamble to save their families. She feared that she would never see Jamie's smile again. Never hear his laughter echo through their home.

Eventually, Iris became aware that everything had grown still around her. Through her tear-filled eyes, she saw that the enormous golden dragon had returned to his perch. What was he doing? He seemed to be staring at her intently. No, not her exactly, but—

She tilted her head downward, following the dragon's gaze.

On her chest, her mother's dragon tear—the one Jamie had given her before he had shipped off to war—dangled in midair. The blast from the dragon's wings and her fall must have jerked it free from beneath her blouse. And now the blue stone caught the sunlight, where it hung and blazed with light.

How do you come by such an item as this? Belrath's question carried a tone of interest but also a hint of danger.

Iris clutched the necklace and held the stone toward Belrath in her open palm. "It belonged to my mother. My brother gave it to me before he left for the war. Do you . . . know something about it?"

And your mother . . . she is the one called Charlotte?

Iris's heart thumped harder. It had been years since she'd heard her mother's name. "Yes, her name is Charlotte. Or rather was, that is. She died years ago when I was little."

I am truly sorry to hear of her passing. When I spoke earlier of the few humans that dragonkind have been able to call friends, I counted your mother as one of those friends.

Iris's chest ached with an intense feeling of loss and love for her mother. "She wore it wherever she went, but I always assumed the stone was nothing more than a pretty piece of jewelry."

Then you have never heard of a dragon tear?

Iris's breath caught. Was it possible that the story her mother had told them all those years ago was true? "She said that when a dragon dies, its spirit transforms into a beautiful stone, like this. It's the most wonderful story, but that's all I assumed it ever was—a story."

Years ago, Belrath said, *relations between humans and dragons had grown intolerable. It soon became clear that we must depart their company. Your mother was a great friend to my own mother, who was our leader at that time. It was your mother who helped us find this haven, where we have lived in peace for many years. My mother was already very old then. When she died not long after, we gifted Charlotte with this dragon tear—my mother's spirit—as thanks for her invaluable aid.*

Iris's mouth fell open in astonishment. "Does this mean you'll help us?"

Belrath stared at her for a long time. Suddenly, a deep, throaty rumbling filled her head. The dragon was growling. She had pushed too far.

But as she listened, she realized it wasn't a growl at all. Belrath was laughing!

I can see your mother's spirit lives on in you, the dragon said. *She was never one to give up without a fight. And for that, we owe her a deep debt of gratitude.*

As Belrath spoke, Iris felt her spirits, so recently crushed, find new wings.

However, he continued, *I fear dragons do not make decisions quickly. Perhaps this is why humans are ceaselessly at war. Instead, dragons take our time to consider all paths before choosing one.*

"How long do you need?" Iris asked, her hope fading again.

That is difficult to say. Time is not the same for dragons as it is to humans. But in your terms, perhaps some weeks or even months.

"Months!" Iris exclaimed. "But we only have days. Maybe not even that before my brother"—she swept her hand toward Maud—"and many others . . . They could all be captured or even killed!"

I am sorry, the dragon said, *but this is our way.*

Iris nodded slowly. "I understand. And I am grateful for your consideration. But I hope that you will understand that we can't wait for your decision. Lives are at stake, and we need to act as quickly as possible." She looked toward Galahad, an unspoken exchange passing between them. "I know that we have only just reunited Galahad with your herd, but we hope you will allow him to accompany us on our mission."

If that is his choice, said Belrath, *then I will not stand in his way.*

For the first time, the blue dragon Malory shifted forward and stood before the leader of her herd. A series of low rumbles came from her throat.

Soon Iris heard Belrath's voice in her head again. *It would seem that my daughter wishes to accompany you as well. I feel that her decision is ill considered, but she is old enough to choose her own path.*

His daughter? Iris thought. She spun toward Maud, her spirits rebounding a little despite Maud's sour face.

"Two girls and a pair of dragons . . . against the German army?" Maud asked.

Iris shook her head. "Not just girls, remember? Women of valor."

CHAPTER TWENTY-SIX

IRIS

England

Iris swept the tendrils of hair out of her face and peered down from atop Galahad as they flew toward the south. She could see for miles and miles, but the distance to Jamie in France seemed endless.

To Iris's left, Maud's arms clung tightly around Malory's neck. She seemed determined to prove she'd overcome her fear of flying by flatly refusing to use the rope harness. Malory had flown for a long time without a harness, Maud had argued, and was unlikely to take well to it anyway.

Iris marveled at her friend's bravery.

Friends.

Was that what they were? Yes, Iris reflected. She supposed that after all this, they had become friends. It had been a long time since she'd had a true friend. Or, at least, a friend that wasn't a dragon.

"The kids back home will be waiting for word from us," Maud called over the sound of the rushing wind. "Should we let them know what happened?"

"We haven't got any time," Iris said, staring ahead at the

darkening horizon. "It's a more direct route across the Channel this way, and we've already wasted too much time finding the dragons." She silently prayed it wasn't already too late.

"Our efforts weren't completely wasted," Maud reminded her. "Because we've got Malory to help us now."

"And I'm very glad for that," Iris said, glancing over at the blue dragon, whose scales lit up like fire in the last light of the dying day. But two dragons were a far cry from the whole army of dragons she'd been hoping for.

"How much longer can the dragons go before they need a rest?" Maud asked.

"What do you think, Galahad?" Iris asked, rubbing his neck. Beneath her, the dragon gave a low rumble. "He says he can keep going." She looked over at Maud's dragon, who had probably been flying for many more years than Galahad. "And Malory doesn't look tired at all."

The blue dragon shrieked her assent.

"If the evacuation is still happening, there should be a trail of ships to guide the way to France," Maud said.

It was a big if among many unknowns that lay ahead. The girls fell silent as night stole over them. Iris watched below for any landmarks they might use to help guide their way. Before long, the lighted homes dotting the dark countryside increased in number until they seemed to merge into one large glowing jewel that sprawled as far as the eye could see.

"I think that's London!" she called over to Maud. She had never imagined that her first visit to the huge metropolis would be from the air.

Soon the lights lessened again, then went out altogether. The temperature rapidly fell, and she spotted the sparkle of a tossed wave in the moonlight. They had arrived over the English Channel. However, other than the occasional glow from the cabin of a lonely ship, she was disappointed to see few vessels to guide their way to France. She realized most of them would probably run with their lights off at night to avoid attracting attention from Germans.

This might be even harder than she'd thought. But there was nothing she could do about it now. She felt a deep weariness settle over her, all the way to her bones. Not just from physical exhaustion but from the mental strain of worry, and fear, and everything else that had plagued her brain seemingly every waking moment since Jamie had left. Sometimes it even chased her into her dreams too.

There was seemingly no safe refuge. She resolutely stared into the night for so many hours that she lost all track of time. The next thing she knew, she was blinking her bleary eyes at a pink glare that rimmed the sky. She yawned and shook her head to clear the cobwebs from her brain. Finally, morning had arrived.

"Alright, Galahad?"

The dragon's reply had an edge of such weariness to it that it made Iris's heart ache. Whatever had been bothering him the previous day had seemed to go away, but Iris feared pushing him too hard.

Far below, she spotted what looked like a navy destroyer flying the British flag. Maybe they weren't off course after all.

"Is that land?" Maud's voice called from her right. Her eyes were rimmed red as if she hadn't slept at all either.

Iris followed her gaze toward a long bank of patchy fog that coiled across the water ahead of them. The wind shifted, temporarily opening a view of what appeared to be a long, dark coastline. A thrill shot up her spine. It must be France!

As they flew nearer, a beach materialized out of the fog. But it was unlike any beach she had ever seen. Extending from the sand out into the water for hundreds of feet was a large, dark mass that shifted with the tide as if it were alive.

"What in the world is that?" Iris asked.

"I have no idea," Maud replied.

They swooped downward beneath the thickest fog for a better look. "It's . . . people!"

The dark, undulating shape on closer inspection resolved into long lines of soldiers snaking out into the ocean from the sand. Hundreds—no, thousands of them stood in water up to chest deep, like an enormous octopus with its tentacles reaching out into the waves. They were probably waiting for ships to carry them back to England. The sheer magnitude of the rescue operation took Iris's breath away. She couldn't imagine there were enough boats, destroyers, trawlers, and dinghies in all of England to carry so many men.

Directly below, she spotted a medium-sized fishing scow whose deck was completely packed with bodies like sardines. It crawled slowly toward the open sea under its heavy load. Closer to shore, more soldiers clambered out of the water onto a ship that was barely bigger than a raft. It quickly swamped under their weight and capsized, leaving the men sputtering in the water. Still another group of men were trying to board a sailboat while an older man already on board waved a pistol at them, probably fearing his ship would have the same fate as the raft. A desperate few had even apparently built their own makeshift vessels out of discarded items like old tires, crates, or buoys and were attempting the roughly sixty miles to England with nothing but their bare hands to use as paddles.

Everywhere she looked was complete chaos.

"How are we ever going to find Jack and Jamie in all this?" Maud asked.

"I have no idea," Iris replied wearily. "I suppose we'll simply have to start asking."

The dragons dropped lower, and the girls scanned the crowds of soldiers waiting in the water and along the beach. Faces tilted upward in their wake and followed their flight. Iris could hear murmurs of mixed surprise, curiosity, and even fear. Probably very few of them even knew that dragons still existed. What would they make of a pair of dragons being ridden by girls?

"There!" Iris pointed at a thin concrete pier that stretched out into the ocean. A larger ship was berthed there, taking on soldiers under the direction of a man who moved with the air of command. Galahad made a wobbly landing on the end of the pier and sighed loudly when they came to rest. He was even more exhausted than Iris had realized.

The soldier closest to them quickly paled at the sight of the dragon and made the sign of the cross on his chest. Another nearly fell off the pier entirely but managed to catch himself at the last second.

Malory glided down beside them, and Maud slid off the dragon's back to the pier.

"You there! Halt!"

Iris spun around, her heart leaping into her throat. The officer they'd seen earlier stood ten feet away with a dark scowl on his face. Behind him, three soldiers had their rifles trained on the girls and their dragons. And beyond them, a few hundred more soldiers stared at the newcomers, having temporarily forgotten about boarding their ship.

The officer leveled a finger at the dragons. "You have ten seconds to explain your business with these beasts before I order my men to open fire."

Galahad rumbled angrily, and Iris reached out her hand to soothe him. After his last encounter with soldiers, the dragon was understandably on edge with more rifles pointed at not just him but Iris as well.

"We're on your side," Iris said, raising her hands. The sight of the guns pointed in their direction brought her back to the terrifying moment when she'd thrown herself between the major's rifle and Galahad. "We heard about the evacuation effort and are here to help. My name is Iris, and this is my friend Maud. These dragons are from a herd that once lived by our village." She slowly lowered her hands. "They won't hurt anyone."

The officer continued to glare at them. "Does it look like on top of everything else I need to add babysitting children to my list of concerns?"

"Respectfully, sir," Iris said, emboldened by a small spark of anger at being dismissed as a child, "from the look of things, it seems that you could use all the help you can get."

"You've got a lot of cheek speaking to me like that," the man shot back. "My orders are to get more than fifteen thousand men onto ships and safely home in only two days. You'll excuse me if I fail to see what a pair of girls and their dragons can do to help our situation."

"It's true we only have a couple of dragons," Iris said. "But we can help transport soldiers to waiting ships."

"Maud!" someone shouted. A commotion arose in the crowd of waiting soldiers, and an older man with unkempt salt-and-pepper hair pushed through the crowd. The decorations on his uniform indicated he was also an officer.

"Maud! What on earth are you . . . ?" The new officer's voice trailed off as he took in the two dragons, then Iris. His face hardened. "And what is she doing here?"

"Captain Wexford," the first officer said impatiently, "do you know these girls?"

Wexford? Iris thought, and suddenly realized the man was Tommy's father from their village back home. His time in Dunkirk seemed to have aged him enough that, combined with his unexpected appearance, she'd failed to recognize him at first. Would he help them? Or—

"Do your parents know you're off playing with dragons?" Captain Wexford scolded. He moved forward, as if he planned to march them straight back home to England himself.

"We're only looking for our brothers!"

"They aren't even here," Captain Wexford said with a heavy sigh.

"What do you mean they're not here?" Iris asked, panic growing in her chest. "They've already been evacuated back to England, then?"

"No, I mean they haven't even arrived at Dunkirk yet," he said. "They both volunteered for the rear guard."

"What does that mean?" Maud asked, frowning.

Captain Wexford swept his arm, taking in the coastline where thousands of men awaited transport. "It means they're doing their best to stall the Germans so others can escape with their lives."

Iris felt a swell of pride. That sort of selflessness sounded just like her brother. She planned to give him a solid whump over the head with a broom as soon as she found him, but she knew he'd do it again just the same.

"All these men you see here," the captain continued, "these are just the last of the tens of thousands that have already been evacuated. Talk is, we'll be pulling up stakes by tomorrow morning. Maybe sooner if we can ever get enough blasted ships. If your brothers know what's best for them, they'll come running. Otherwise, they could show up to an empty beach with no ride home. Or else a German welcome party if Hitler's army arrives before they do."

"How do we find them?" Iris asked, hearing the rising panic in her voice.

Captain Wexford turned and looked back toward land, pointing. "That'll be where the fighting is. They're bound to be there. That is, if they're still . . ." He trailed off.

Iris heard her heart thumping loudly in her ears as she watched an ominous cloud of thick black smoke curling into the sky in the direction the captain had indicated. *If they're still alive*, the man had meant.

"Of course, I can't allow the two of you to go there," Wexford continued. "You're heading straight back home to your parents in England." He grabbed Iris and Maud by the wrists and began dragging them toward a makeshift gangway connecting the pier to the waiting ship.

Iris heard Galahad rumble nearby, while Malory crouched low, hissing ominously. Several soldiers leveled their rifles at the dragons. Beyond them, the crowd of waiting men began shouting angrily and shoving forward, desperate to board the ship before the German army arrived.

Over it all, a low droning noise filled Iris's ears. She thought maybe it was the sound of blood rushing through her head as she panicked. "No!" she protested. "We have to save them!" She tried to yank her arm away from the man's iron grasp, but it was no use. He was much too strong.

The captain jerked her forward again, and Iris found herself standing at the base of the flimsy bridge leading onto the ship. The bridge bobbed and weaved with the vessel's motion on the water. She looked down to where the ocean dozens of feet below churned and slapped against the steel hull in the narrow gap between the pier and the ship.

The tide momentarily shoved the ship against the pier. Iris flinched at the terrible screeching noise of steel on concrete. Her stomach turned over. If the walkway collapsed while she was on it, she'd fall and be crushed to death.

Had she come this far only to be either killed or packed off for home again? She had to think of something—anything to get away and find out what had become of her brother. On top of everything else, the strange droning noise was growing louder and louder until it seemed to fill her head.

Then a loud cry pierced the air:

"Luftwaffe!"

Iris spun around as a pair of German planes swept down out of the low fog cover. Her entire body went rigid. On the pier, hemmed in by a steep drop to the ocean on three sides and a mob of panicking soldiers on the other, she realized with terror that she had nowhere to run. And the German fighters were headed right for her.

CHAPTER TWENTY-SEVEN

MAX

France

Blood.

Max couldn't move.

Bullets whizzed and pinged around him, but he couldn't tear his eyes away from the wet stain rapidly soaking the British soldier's side right in front of him. Yes, he had already experienced far more bombs, and cannons, and gunfire than he thought he'd ever witness in his lifetime. But the stark reality of the blood was what finally drove into his brain the realization that he could die at any moment.

One second here. The next . . .

"Fall back!" someone screamed nearby. "Take cover in the trees!"

Max felt a hand tugging on his arm. Then Jamie's voice, as if Max was hearing him from underwater. "Max! We have to go!"

Finally shaking off his stupor, Max blundered after the fleeing soldiers. Tree trunks seemed to explode all around him with the impact of bullets. The acrid stench of gunpowder burned his nostrils. Jamie raced along beside him, keeping one arm protectively across Max's shoulders as they ducked low and sprinted away.

By the time Max's lungs burned and his feet throbbed so

badly that he thought he couldn't run another step, they finally collapsed in a thicket beside the rest of the soldiers from their unit. In the gray light of dawn, Max thought they all looked like a band of reanimated corpses with their torn clothing and mud-stained faces. A few yards away, the injured soldier grimaced as another soldier ripped his bloody shirt away and pressed the fabric against the wound to slow the bleeding.

Max looked away, suddenly feeling ill.

"Are we safe?" Jamie asked the major.

"I think we are, for now," the officer said. "It must have been a couple scouts who stumbled across us, instead of an entire division. Otherwise, we wouldn't have made it out alive."

"Still," Jack said, "now the Germans know we're still out here. I expect they'll be wanting to repay the favor of us harassing their movements all the way north."

Major Stevenson nodded gravely. "There's a village just up ahead. We'll take cover there for now. It appears to have been abandoned and mostly destroyed by German shelling, but it might still have supplies that we can use."

A few hours later, Max stood in a bell tower in the small French village the major had mentioned. He gazed toward where the pale blue of the sky met a thin line of darker blue that he guessed had to be the ocean.

"Is that . . . Dunkirk?" he asked, his breath catching in his throat at the thought that after this terrible, exhausting journey, he was finally nearing his destination. Still, he knew that even when he arrived there, his journey wouldn't quite be over. Not until he'd found his grandmother. He didn't imagine that would be easy in an entire city.

"I think so," Jamie replied. "Only . . ." He stared hard into his binoculars with a frown. At last, he shook his head and lowered his hands without finishing the thought. The quick movement caused him to flinch and emit a low groan.

Max could tell the soldier was still in pain from being struck in the chest by the fragment of an artillery shell so recently. But somehow he never complained. Max wondered if not complaining was part of being brave. Not two months ago, Max had accidentally stubbed his toe, and his grandmother had finally shooed him out of the house to escape his endless moaning.

Max moved around to the other side of the bell tower and looked down. Ten feet below was the slate-tiled roof of the small schoolhouse that had miraculously escaped the devastation done to the rest of the village. He watched as other soldiers from their small unit picked through the rubble that was once a village square, looking for food or anything else they could use.

"Be careful to keep a low profile," Jamie said, motioning for Max to lower his body. "You never want to make yourself a target for a sniper."

Max quickly dropped down low enough so that he could just see over the edge of the enclosure. His gaze darted around the surrounding countryside, which seemed to bristle with imaginary sniper rifles.

"What do you make of it?" Jack's voice echoed up from below, where he held a rickety wooden ladder in place.

Jamie shook his head. "I'm not sure. There seems to be a lot of aerial activity over the coast. With any luck, it's the RAF helping with the evacuation. Otherwise, maybe it's already too late and the Germans have beat us there. Funny thing is, I could have sworn one of them was a dragon."

"That's the sleep deprivation for you," Jack said. "Maybe just keep the safety on your rifle in case you mistake me for an ogre."

Max smiled a little at that. Jack's sense of humor reminded him of his mother. Even in the darkest moments, she'd always think of something funny to pick up Max's spirits.

It was quiet for a few minutes, then Max heard Jamie's voice next to him. "What have you got there? It looks important."

Max followed Jamie's gaze to his hand, which—seemingly of its own accord—had extracted the golden star from his pocket.

"It was my mother's," Max said. "It *is* my mother's," he corrected himself, trying but failing to keep the tremor out of his voice. Had he already given up on ever seeing his parents again?

Jamie put his hand on Max's shoulder comfortingly. "It's okay to be scared."

Max didn't answer right away. Then he said in a small voice, "When they left, they asked me to be brave for them. But no matter how I try, I . . . I just can't."

"From what I've seen," Jamie said, "you're much braver than you think. I mean, look at how you led an entire unit of grown men who were afraid of a little peacock."

Max laughed a little at that.

"Sometimes bravery is as simple as putting one foot in front of the other," Jamie continued. "Then doing it again. And again. No matter what happens. Just look at how far you've come already—crossing almost an entire country to find your grandmother."

Max nodded, considering his words as he absently traced a fingertip through the mortar in between two of the stones that formed the bell tower. "I promised I'd find her in Dunkirk. When I first lost her, that seemed so impossible. But I know she would do anything for me. Maybe it seems like a small or insignificant thing, but I want to show her how much I love her. That I would do anything for her too. No matter how hard it is."

"That's not insignificant at all," Jamie said. "That's called having a mission. Something that helps you be brave by keeping you going day after day. Even during a war."

Max stared down at the small star in his hand, considering the soldier's words, which so closely echoed his own thoughts from just days ago. "Do you have a mission?" he asked.

"I suppose you could call it that. Or her, that is." He stared away toward the north. "I mentioned my sister, Iris. Every day, I remind myself that everything I'm doing here to delay the German advance—all the sleepless nights and endless miles of marching—is another day she's safe at home."

"How do you know you'll succeed?" Max asked.

Jamie shook his head and shrugged. "I don't. But I do know that I can't stop trying. Not while there's still hope." He looked over at Max. "And I can tell you won't either. Not while there's hope for your parents and grandmother. If there's anything I can do to help, all you have to do is ask."

"Thanks," Max said, and looked down at his feet. "But I already feel like I've been a burden on you and your whole unit. Maybe my mission is getting in the way of yours."

"Never," Jamie said, and squeezed Max's shoulder. "How about we help each other accomplish our missions together?"

"I'd like that," Max said. He tucked the star back into the safety of his pocket. The pair stayed there in silence for a while.

Then from below came Jack's bellow: "You two fall off up there or what? Also, I don't like the way your dog is eyeing me, Max. If we don't find her some food soon, I think she might start gnawing on my leg."

Max laughed again and leaned forward to look down.

Jack was sitting cross-legged with the dog in his lap. "Don't you do it, Plum," he warned.

But at hearing her name, the dog began leaping up and down while licking at his face with her tongue. "See?" Jack asked, laughing and twisting his face away from the slobbery assault. "She's out for blood! It's been nice knowing you, gents!"

Jamie shook his head. "Sounds like we'd better rescue Jack before it's too late."

Max climbed down the ladder and scooped up Plum in his arms.

Jamie came down stiffly after him. "Have you looked in these old boxes?" he asked Jack. "Maybe we'll get lucky and find something edible in them."

The base of the bell tower doubled as a storage room for the schoolhouse, and two stacks of boxes sat in one corner. Jack moved across and yanked open one of the top boxes. A cloud of yellow dust ballooned out of it. The big man gave a mighty sneeze.

"That'll be chalk in that one," he said, and sneezed again. "S'pose that was my fault. Always thinking first with my stomach, my mum always used to say."

He moved the box to the floor and began more carefully opening the others. While the men were doing that, Max wandered back into the main room with Plum at his heels. "If I were going to keep food in a school, where would it be?" Max mumbled to himself while roaming the room with his eyes.

Plum darted from side to side with her nose down, excitedly exploring the unfamiliar scents in the room. She stopped suddenly in front of a large bureau set between two windows on the north-facing wall, then turned back toward Max and whined.

"Find something, girl?" he asked. He crossed the room toward her and pulled the door open excitedly. However, the cabinet's contents were disappointing. Inside were only a pair of mud-splattered galoshes and a raincoat that hung patiently as if still waiting for a schoolteacher who might never return.

Max was about to close the door and keep searching when Plum put her paws up on the door frame and whined again. He reached inside and slid aside the raincoat. Then his eyes lit up.

In an alcove behind the coat was a stack of cans labeled FOIE GRAS. He wasn't sure what that was, but it looked like it might be food. However, he did recognize the neatly wrapped parcels beside them. Chocolate! It was even the fancy Belgian brand that his grandmother bought only on special occasions.

Max felt a sudden wave of homesickness overcome him, but it was quickly dispelled by a sharp pain in his stomach. He was starving! But when he reached for the treasures, his hand froze in midair. He felt a little guilty taking the food, as if the teacher might return at any second and rap his knuckles.

He heard footsteps behind him, then Jack's voice: "Oh ho, Max! What have you found there?" The man leaned over Max's shoulder and plucked a few cans from the secret stash. "Fwaa graa, ooh la la!" he said in a droll French accent, reading the label on one of the cans.

Jamie grinned. "Nice work! This should make for quite a feast!"

Max stooped and scratched Plum behind the ears. "It was Plum who sniffed them out." The fact that they'd helped find food for the soldiers made a warm glow spread in his chest. Maybe he wasn't entirely a burden after all.

He helped move the food to a large desk at the front of the room next to one of the dusty boxes he recognized from the storage room.

"What's in the box?" Max asked, peering into the top curiously.

"Bunch of pencils," Jack said over his shoulder as he moved toward the front door of the schoolhouse. "Jamie says he's got an idea of how to use them. Excuse me a minute while I let the lads know dinner is served." He leaned out the door and gave a low whistle.

"It's just an idea I had," Jamie said, motioning to the box of pencils. "But that can wait until after we eat."

He took one of the cans of foie gras and stabbed into it with his knife before prying the lid open. A pungent smell filled the air.

"It smells like Plum after she's been rolling in the mud," Max said, and wrinkled his nose.

Jamie laughed. "It does sort of have an odor of wet dog. Let's hope it tastes better than it smells."

"After weeks of near starvation, I'm not feeling choosy," Jack said, rejoining them and grabbing one of the cans. He tipped it upside down and let the pinkish-grayish lump slide out with a wet sucking noise and fall into his mouth. He swallowed it in one gulp, then shrugged. "I don't think I'll make a habit of it, but it ain't bad either."

The remaining soldiers from their unit began to file through the front door of the schoolhouse. Max waved, spotting Boo among them. He was glad to see the soldier on his feet, even though he looked a little pale. Perhaps it was because they were the two youngest among the group, but Max felt a sense of kinship with him.

One of the soldiers paused and sniffed the air. "What's that smell?"

Boo froze and stared at Jack's sleeve. Then he tore his gear bag open and yanked out his gas mask, quickly sliding it over his face. The soldier next to him gasped and fumbled for his mask too.

"What is it?" Jamie asked, rising to his feet. "What's wrong?"

Boo pointed a shaky finger at them. "Mustard gas!"

CHAPTER TWENTY-EIGHT

IRIS

France

Iris watched in horror as the machine guns blazed to life on the pair of planes. Their bullets raked the nearby beach, where soldiers helplessly scrambled for cover that was nowhere to be found. The aircraft rocketed over the pier. Several dark objects dropped from their wings and screamed downward through the air.

"Get down!" Captain Wexford shouted, and yanked the girls behind him just before a horrendous concussion shook the air.

A painful ringing noise echoed in Iris's ears. The blast left her disoriented for a few seconds. She looked up again in time to see geysers of flame erupting from several points on the deck of the boat they'd just been about to board. With a sickening moan, the entire ship leaned away from the pier. The gangway collapsed like it was made of matchsticks and disappeared into the churning surf below. Soldiers who had already boarded were running and throwing themselves into the water to get clear of the sinking vessel. Then with a mighty splash, the ship collapsed onto its side with enough force to send a tidal wave that threatened to capsize several nearby waiting boats.

As the ringing in her ears subsided, Iris heard the droning of aircraft engines growing louder again. She whirled around. The two German planes had swung around for a second pass.

"There are more of them!" Maud shouted.

Looking where her friend was pointing, she saw a half dozen new enemy fighters roaring down to join the attack. More bombs. More strafing machine-gun fire. Three more British rescue ships and a destroyer caught flame and slowly succumbed to the waves. A few soldiers tried firing at the invaders with their rifles, but they had no effect. The Germans continued to terrorize the British and French forces unchecked.

"Surely the British army has some way of fighting back?" Iris asked the captain.

He shook his head helplessly. "We were ordered to destroy our antiaircraft guns to avoid them falling into German hands."

"What?!" Maud said, her eyes wide in disbelief.

"But what about the Royal Air Force?" Iris asked. "Can't they help?"

"They're running patrols periodically," he replied. "But there's only so much they can do. I'm afraid in the meantime we're simply sitting ducks out here with no choice but to throw our arms over our heads and pray. Now come with me. I need to get you girls off this pier before those fighters come this way again. There's nothing anyone can do until they're gone."

Maud watched the destruction, her eyes blazing. Suddenly, she tore away from the captain's grasp and ran toward the dragons still perched on the end of the pier.

"Maud!" Iris called after her. "Where are you going?"

"Come back here, young lady!" Captain Wexford shouted.

Distracted, he loosened his grip on Iris's arm. She took the opportunity to yank herself away and run after Maud. "You'll get yourselves killed!" he yelled at their backs.

Iris caught up to her friend as she was climbing onto Malory's back. "What in the world are you doing?"

"Didn't you hear the man?" Maud asked. "They need an air force!"

Iris stared at her, then up at the fighter planes tearing through the sky. "Are you quite mad?"

"Maybe!" Maud yelled as she and the blue dragon launched off the pier. "But I can't just sit here and watch."

Iris paused for a heartbeat before she slid onto Galahad's back. Her hands shook as she clutched the harness and wrapped its coils around her wrists three times as an extra precaution. She was exhausted and in no condition for a swim in the Channel.

"Galahad," she said, "if we ever make it out of this alive, remind me to make better choices about my friends." She tugged on the harness and the dragon shrieked a battle cry before leaping into the air after Maud and Malory.

Iris scanned the sky, her brain working frantically to come up with a plan. How were they going to take on the German planes with their machine guns and bombs? Far ahead, Maud clung low on the blue dragon's back as the pair streaked through the air behind an unsuspecting Luftwaffe aircraft. As Malory closed the distance, Iris realized they did have at least one advantage: The dragons were faster than the enemy planes.

Iris waited to see what her friends would do. Would they use Malory's red-hot breath to catch the plane on fire? Or maybe try to use her claws to pierce holes in the craft's fuselage? She watched the dragon glide into place directly over the cockpit, pacing the German fighter. Noticing the shadow that had fallen over him, the pilot slowly tilted his head up toward the underbelly of blue scales and wings directly above. Maud leaned out past Malory's back and waved.

Then with a swipe of her razor-sharp claws, Malory sheared the plane's wings clean off with a terrible screech of rending metal. Iris felt her jaw drop with amazement. The dragon had instantly transformed the airplane into a torpedo. The craft's nose dipped downward, and it screamed toward the ocean. Seconds later, the pilot ejected from the cockpit and watched the remains of his aircraft plow into the water with an enormous splash as he floated downward under his parachute. A cheer went up from the British and French soldiers watching the whole thing.

Iris couldn't help but laugh. "She is definitely, one hundred percent, certifiably mad."

In the next moment, she heard the rattle of machine-gun fire from behind her. Galahad quickly dove and spun away. Iris felt the heat of the shells as they whined through the air, narrowly missing her and Galahad. She swung her head around to look over her shoulder. While she'd been watching Maud, she hadn't been paying attention to the other planes. Now a German was right on their tail.

Iris ducked low, wrapping her arms around Galahad's neck. The dragon roared and dropped suddenly toward the water. Iris felt her stomach lurch into her throat and her feet momentarily lift into the air as they plummeted. The plane buzzed harmlessly overhead, not able to copy the dragon's maneuver. But before she could breathe a sigh of relief, the *splat splat splat* of machine-gun fire hitting the water erupted to their right. Her head jerked in that direction. Another fighter was almost on top of them.

"Galahad!" she cried. "Look out!"

Startled, Galahad dodged directly toward the oncoming plane and blasted it with a column of fire. For one terrifying heartbeat, Iris's gaze met the pilot's. Behind his goggles, his eyes widened in surprise while the front of his plane melted as if it were hot butter. It fell out of the sky like a rock and catapulted over the slate-gray waves before crashing to a stop with a geyser of water and steam.

She stared downward anxiously, searching the ocean. Finally, the pilot's head bobbed above the surface, and he started to swim toward shore. Iris's heart slammed once extra-hard against her chest as it started beating again. That had been too close.

She scanned the sky, looking for Maud and Malory, only to find them dodging and weaving away from two more planes chasing them. "Quick! We need to help them!" she shouted to Galahad.

Galahad arced through the air toward the blue dragon. Seeing Galahad coming straight at them, the German planes quickly scattered out of his path. But in almost the next second, Iris heard more machine-gun fire and Galahad banked hard right to avoid being hit by another spray of bullets. She searched the sky as the dragon dodged and weaved. Even more German planes had joined the fight. There were just too many of them. But she couldn't simply run away and leave the men on the ground defenseless.

Iris cast her gaze around desperately, trying to find some solution. Then a little farther down the coast, her eyes settled on a row of gigantic circular structures. One of them had already been hit in the firefight. The thin trail of black smoke that poured out of it over the British and French soldiers reminded her of the oil fires that frequently plagued the tractor on their farm back home. It must be an oil refinery.

"Galahad!" she shouted. "Can you get us over to Maud and Malory?"

The dragon soared toward their friends, pulling up alongside the blue dragon.

"I'm beginning to think this wasn't my best idea," Maud shouted to Iris, struggling to make herself heard over the din.

"Don't worry!" Iris called back. "I think I may have a better one. Follow us!"

Galahad banked downward and swooped toward the domed oil tanks. When they drew close enough, he unleashed a steady stream of fire from his mouth. Malory did the same on another row of them. Iris spun around to look over her shoulder. The oil in the tanks was ablaze. She flinched as one exploded and coughed thick black smoke that was carried downwind over the soldiers on the ground.

"One more time!" Iris shouted to Maud, and swung around and hit the oil tanks with another fiery blast. There were more explosions, and soon a thick blanket of smoke obscured the beach. She gagged, tasting the acrid smoke in her mouth.

"It smells horrible," said Maud as the blue dragon flew up next to them, "but I think it did the trick. Look!"

No longer able to spot their targets below the covering of smoke, the German planes peeled away one by one and headed back toward the east.

"We did it!" Iris grinned.

"Thanks to your idea," Maud said. "What do you think we should do now?"

Iris stared off toward the south, where more black smoke continued to crawl skyward. "Well, we have at least some idea of where our brothers might be. I hate to leave the soldiers behind here, but I'm afraid our brothers' situation is even more desperate. Also, Galahad and Malory must be dreadfully exhausted. So I'd suggest we head south and find some shelter where they can get some sleep. We don't know when we'll be able to rest again."

As they banked away from the coast and flew south, Iris felt a rising feeling of dread. The French countryside looked like it had been ravaged by a terrible fire. Everywhere she looked, trees lay toppled over, buildings crumbled, and abandoned military vehicles were overturned. Much of the landscape was charred black and smoking.

Eventually, they spotted a large structure sufficiently away from the main road to possibly offer some protection. The dragons set down in a small clearing behind the building—a solid-looking white barn that had been spared from destruction. After checking for any German soldiers, the girls and dragons crawled into the barn's hayloft and gratefully collapsed into the warm hay, where they all instantly fell asleep.

CHAPTER TWENTY-NINE
GENERAL WYVERN

German Front, France

It was barely dawn, and General Wyvern was already in a foul mood. His officers gathered in his command tent for their new orders, looking still half-asleep at that early hour. In the flicker of the tent's lone gas lamp, these leaders of hundreds and thousands of fighting men saw something terrifying in the general's eyes. One by one, they cowered away toward the far side of the tent, where they huddled together in nervous silence.

For weeks, Wyvern had relentlessly pounded on the British and French forces with the full might of the German war machine. Yes, *he* had driven them back, beaten and bloodied, toward the coast. And yes, even now *he* had given them no choice but to flee for their lives back to England.

It was in these terms that he thought, giving himself the sole credit for Germany's victories. Because he knew that his superior mental prowess, his unbending discipline, and his very will to destroy his enemies were the reason that the Third Reich continued to march mercilessly westward.

However, despite everything he had done, somehow the spirit of the Allied forces still flickered with life. Somehow, the British and French continued to stand up and fight. And in particular, one meager unit had proven to be a thorn in his side. They had continually dogged and harassed his lines and slowed their advance toward the coast. And now, he had missed his chance to deliver the final, crushing blow.

But he had his orders. Orders directly from Hitler himself. And they were to turn immediately south toward Paris. Very well. He would let the last of the British and French stragglers escape to England for now. There would be another opportunity later.

When everyone had arrived, Wyvern began. "Gentlemen, I have gathered you this morning to detail new orders from the Führer." He limped with his cane toward a large map of France that hung on one wall and was just about to speak again when there was a commotion outside his tent. Behind him came the sound of running feet, then: "Herr General, a word."

The general did not immediately turn around, but instead closed his eyes, fighting to control the flame of anger that erupted in his chest at the interruption. If it had been any other man but his second-in-command, the unlucky soul might have found himself already unconscious or worse, struck down by a blow from the huge general's walking stick.

"What. Is. It?" the general asked at last, biting off the end of every word.

"F-forgive me, s-sir," the man said. "I thought you would want to know right away." He shifted closer to his commanding officer and lowered his voice. "Dragons."

At this word, Wyvern's head jerked around. "What did you say?"

Glancing at the other men still standing nearby, the lieutenant lowered his voice further and continued, "There are reports of dragons helping the British at Dunkirk, sir. The way it was told to me, a half dozen gigantic winged beasts gobbled up most of our planes and chased off the rest by turning the sky black as night with their fiery breath. It sounded half fanciful to me. Especially the last detail . . ." He looked down at the ground as if unsure whether to continue.

The general waited impatiently for him to finish. "Well?" he said through clenched teeth.

The man flinched visibly. "Sir, they say the dragons were ridden by . . . well, by little girls."

Wyvern blinked, this last bit of information taking even him by surprise. And it took a lot to surprise the battle-hardened general. Dragons helping the British? And ridden by girls? He stared down at the glinting red orb on the handle of his cane. If there was any truth to the report, he knew what he had to do. Somehow, he would capture these dragons and turn them to his own purposes. Hitler would forgive him disobeying orders. After all, even Hitler himself would kneel when Wyvern, with a dragon army at his command, brought not just Paris to its knees but the entire world.

"Gentlemen," he said to his gathered officers, "we will proceed to Dunkirk. And let no one who gets in our way remain alive."

CHAPTER THIRTY

MAX

France

Boo backed toward the door of the schoolhouse holding his gas mask firmly in place.

"Hold on," Jamie said, and put his hands out with palms turned toward the terrified soldiers. "I know we're all on edge, but let's not panic here."

Boo pointed at Jamie's sleeve. "Look! It's yellow!" To Max, the soldier's voice sounded strange and distorted behind his thick rubber mask. "The Germans must have gassed the village and some of it was trapped in this building!"

Max's heart hammered against his ribs. He'd heard talk among the soldiers in Belgium of mustard gas and the terrible things it did to people. Had he been breathing it this whole time? He looked at the cuffs around Jamie's and Jack's arms. They must be some sort of early warning sleeves that changed color when toxic gas was present. And both were yellow.

Jack looked down at his arm with a spark of fear in his eyes. "What color's it supposed to be?"

"I . . . I can't remember." Jamie shot a glance at the sleeves of the men who had just entered the room, but theirs were caked with mud.

Max sprang to his feet in panic. The room swam in front of his eyes. Did he suddenly feel dizzy, or was he only imagining it?

The commotion in the room rose. The soldiers in front turned and collided with those still coming in through the door, unaware of the situation inside.

"What's happening?" a voice barked above the clamor.

Major Stevenson shoved through the crowd, then stopped when he arrived at the front. Some of his men wore gas masks on one side of the room, while Jamie, Jack, and Max stood frozen on the other, unsure what to do. Then the major strode across the wooden floorboards and wiped his hand across Jamie's sleeve. The yellow brushed off easily, and he held up his hand. "Chalk dust." He sniffed the air. "And, if I'm not mistaken, goose liver."

There was a moment of stunned silence. Then Jack began to laugh. At first it was a low chuckle, but it grew into a full-on belly shaker. Soon Max felt a little laugh escape his mouth as the contagious sound worked its way around the room until eventually everyone was howling with laughter and slapping one another's backs.

"Look at us," Jack gasped, "a bunch of boorish Brits almost done in by French cuisine."

Once the merriment began to die down, Major Stevenson raised his hands in a gesture for quiet. "We all got a good laugh out of this little incident, but I think it was a useful exercise to illustrate the importance of keeping a level head. If we're going to survive out there, we're going to need everyone to think and work as a unit. One man panics, and we could all end up dead." He paused and turned his head, meeting each of their gazes. "The soldier standing next to you is not just a man. He's your brother. And we're all getting through this together or not at all. Are we all in agreement?"

Each man shouted an emphatic "Yes, sir!" before Stevenson continued. "Good. Now, we've managed to get this far. The coast is in sight, but there's no telling when we'll run into the Germans again. There isn't much cover from here on out, but we've scouted ahead and found an abandoned vineyard a bit up the road. That should provide us a good spot to hole up for the rest of the day. Then we leave at dusk. And if luck is on our side, by dawn we'll be on ships heading home."

"Amen to that," Jack said, and clapped his hands. "The moment I set foot back in ol' Blighty, I'll be on my knees kissin' the ground."

"And I'll be right there next to you," Jamie said. He broke off a piece of chocolate and handed it to Max with a grin. "I guess we should have started with the chocolate, and we could have avoided this whole mess." He walked over to talk with Major Stevenson as the other two finished eating.

"My grandmother always says, 'Why save dessert for last?'" Max said. He bit into the candy and let the smooth sweetness roll around on his tongue, then quietly prayed that his grandmother was safe somewhere and they would be reunited soon.

The rest of the unit finished their quick meal and started exiting the schoolhouse through a blown-out window in the rear. Max watched them climb out one by one and melt into the trees bordering the small village.

When Jamie returned, he hefted the box of pencils off the desk. "Think I could get a little help with a small project? I told the major that we'd meet up with the rest of the unit at the vineyard when we're done."

Max jumped to his feet. "Sure! Let me know what I can do." Plum barked beside him. "And Plum says she'll help too."

"Does this mean we're going to finally hear about this mysterious plan of yours?" Jack asked.

"It does," Jamie said. "Could you grab a few of those unused charges we saw and meet us on the road leading north out of the village?"

"Aye, sir." Jack saluted and lumbered out of the room.

Jamie looked at Max. "And meanwhile, the two of us can get started. Ready?"

He helped Max climb through the back window, and they followed a well-trodden footpath through the woods. Max might have imagined they were taking a pleasant afternoon stroll if not for the backdrop of the destroyed village and lingering smell of ash. Plum sniffed the ground, looking for squirrels or other wildlife, but they seemed to have abandoned the area just like the human residents.

The path soon met up with and followed alongside a canal that sparkled gaily in the sunlight. As they had moved farther north into the lowlands nearer the French coast, Max had seen more of these man-made canals crisscrossing the landscape. Fortunately, they hadn't needed to go through any yet. Max didn't know how to swim.

While they walked, he slid his bow off his shoulder and nocked his last arrow. He closed one eye and moved the tip of the arrow around the landscape in search of a target. An old, gnarled stump appeared on a small rise about thirty feet ahead. Max took aim and let his arrow fly. A second later, he heard a satisfying hollow thunk of the arrow hitting home. He stopped and gaped. It was about a foot off center, but still he'd managed to hit the stump.

Ahead of him, Jamie rested the box he was carrying on top of the stump and yanked the arrow out. "You've been practicing!" he said, and smiled.

Max was thankful that the dappled shade hid his blush. "A little."

"Well, better be careful, or the major will try to recruit you!" Jamie handed the arrow back to Max. "Hmm," he said, turning and looking downhill to where the forest gave way to green fields and pastures pocked here and there by black craters. "I think that may be the spot I've been looking for."

He started down the hill. Max and Plum bounded after him, crunching through the leaves. First checking that the road was clear in both directions, Jamie upturned the box of pencils and dumped them into a patch of mud along the roadside.

"What are you doing?" Max asked. Plum trotted up to the pile of ruined pencils and sniffed at them, then looked up at Jamie as if questioning the human's strange behavior as well.

"Call it an early warning system," Jamie said. "In case the Germans arrive before we've cleared out. I could use some help if you want to copy what I do."

Max watched the soldier kneel beside the pencils and scoop

a handful of them out of the mud. Then Jamie started sticking them point downward into the crevices where the road's surface had cracked or been reduced to dust.

Max followed Jamie's lead, and soon they had a tiny forest of muddy shafts bristling from the road.

"I hope your plan isn't to sprout those pencils back into trees," Jack said, coming up behind them, "or I'm afraid you'll be sorely disappointed."

Jamie inspected the box in Jack's hands. "Those should work perfectly. And no, this is a trick I've heard the Germans use. They stick pencils upright into the road like this because—"

"Ahh," Jack said. "Because they look just like detonators. So refugees think the road's mined and impassable. Kind of a twisted mind game, ain't it?"

"No argument there," Jamie said.

Jack rubbed his chin thoughtfully. "I like the idea of turning the tables on the Germans by using their own trick against them."

"Exactly. Or at least, that's how I hope it works."

"Oh, it'll work alright," Jack said. "But I'd better get started in case they decide to join the party early." He set down his box and, after disguising the detonators with mud, he placed them at random intervals among the pencils already stuck in the road. When he was done, Max couldn't tell which was which. A shudder ran through him as he imagined stumbling across their trap.

Jamie hid the empty boxes in the brush, then rejoined Jack and Max. "Now let's get some shut-eye if we can," he said. "Something tells me we'll have a long night ahead of us."

A little farther down the road, they came to a vineyard lined with grape trellises. Back among a copse of trees sat a sprawling French château.

"This must be the place," Jamie said.

As they started down the path leading to the house, Max noticed that his feet were soon squishing with every step. When he looked down, he saw honey-colored liquid pooling around his shoes.

Noticing his confusion, Jack said, "From the smell of it, I'm guessing it's some sort of alcohol. Brandy, most likely. The vineyard owners probably opened their vats and let it flood out into the grounds to keep the Germans from getting it. No sense sharing your best vintage with the blokes who're invading your country." He pointed. "Though you might want to keep little Plum from tasting too much herself."

Max quickly stooped to pick up the dog, whose little tongue was already lapping at the amber liquid.

Jamie gave a low whistle as they approached the house. It was answered by a similar whistle from inside. They jogged the rest of the way to the door. He waved his hand, motioning Max, Plum, and Jack to follow him inside. Max paused at the top step and scanned the countryside for any sign of Germans. Had he looked up, he might have been just in time to see a pair of dark, winged shadows flit across the sun a second before he closed the door.

CHAPTER THIRTY-ONE

IRIS

France

The dragons swept low over the treetops, heading south. Iris's gaze had barely left the thin line of smoke that still spiraled into the sky ahead since they had taken to the sky to continue their rescue mission. It was now a faint, wispy beacon compared to the thick black column it had been the day before. She just prayed it didn't mean they were already too late.

"Shouldn't we wait until dark?" Maud asked. She squeezed her knees around Malory's neck expertly, as if she'd been riding dragons for years. "What if we're spotted?"

"We'll just have to take that risk," Iris replied from Galahad's back. "It's driving me half-mad not knowing if they're okay."

As they drew nearer, she turned to study their surroundings, half expecting to come upon an entire German battalion at any moment. Their path took them over a sprawling estate crisscrossed with grapevines, but oddly its grounds glistened as if they had recently been flooded.

"Let's land there," Iris said, pointing to a small clearing in the trees up ahead. "That will give us a chance to check it out first and see if it's safe or not."

"Good idea," Maud said. "I keep getting this creeping feeling like Germans are lurking somewhere nearby."

The dragons glided down among the trees, and the girls slid off and quickly scouted their immediate surroundings. What had initially looked like a natural clearing in the woods was in reality a very unnatural gap blasted by a stray bomb or mortar round. Once-majestic, old-growth trees now lay broken and uprooted as if a giant had used them for toothpicks. As Iris turned toward the village, she noticed that the tops of some trees had been sheared clean off.

"I don't know about you," Maud said, "but I'm sure glad we weren't here whenever all this happened."

"I know what you mean," Iris said. "And I fear it's likely even worse in the village."

Galahad made a sad bleating noise.

Maud sighed. "But I suppose we'll probably have our best chance of finding our brothers there."

They quietly picked their way through the woods until they came to the edge of the village. Iris crouched in the shade of an elm and surveyed the village for several minutes. Nothing moved or made a noise, only the occasional stir of wind that carried the pungent scent of ash on it, along with another odor that she didn't want to guess at.

"Do you see anything?" Maud whispered next to her.

Iris shook her head. "Nothing. It looks like it's safe."

Satisfied, they moved into the village and walked slowly down its empty streets. On every side were the stark mementos of war. A cottage with its empty front door frame still intact like a surprised mouth gaping inward at four walls that had been reduced to rubble. The twisted metal of a bedframe where not long ago someone had slept and perhaps dreamed of happy things. The body of a dog half buried under the ruins of a fireplace where it had likely sought shelter from the chaos of noise and light when the attack had begun. Everywhere death and destruction.

So much death and destruction.

Only a small schoolhouse near the village's edge seemed to have escaped intact. For a few seconds, Iris stared up at the bell hanging silently in its adjoining tower, then turned back toward the village. She felt compelled to say something. Anything to eulogize the horror that she saw all around her. Her stomach hurt, but the hurt in her heart was so much worse. These were people's homes. Their memories. Their lives. All erased as if they didn't matter at all. She roamed slowly through the village's remains in a daze.

Which is why when danger arrived, she didn't realize it until it was too late. The only warning was the noise of a brick clattering into the ruins to one side of them. Her brain had already dismissed it as a natural shifting of the destroyed structure when the air suddenly erupted with shouting voices.

"Halt!"

"Achtung!"

Iris whirled around, only to find herself roughly tackled to the ground, where she was pinned with a knee against her spine. Somewhere nearby she heard Galahad's terrified shriek. She jerked her head in that direction. A half dozen gray-uniformed soldiers dragged him to the ground under heavy steel chains.

"Galahad, no!" Iris cried, thrusting one hand in his direction. But another hand grabbed her elbow and wrenched it behind her back. She felt the burn of rope as her wrists and ankles were tied together. Her heart thumped in her ears. *No! This can't be happening!*

All she could do was watch helplessly as Maud and Malory were similarly subdued. Iris jerked and bucked against her restraints, but it was no use. Iris squeezed her eyes shut against the tears of fear and frustration that threatened to pour from them. How had they come all this way only to be captured? She was Jamie's only hope, and now . . .

A dark shadow moved past her like an eclipse. Iris's eyes blinked open. An enormous man in the uniform of a German officer limped slowly by, leaning heavily on a black cane. He stared intently at Galahad and Malory and made a deliberate circuit of the dragons without speaking.

When at last he stopped and carefully knelt by Galahad's head, the excitement in his voice was unmistakable. "How exquisite," he said in a hushed tone. "So the reports were indeed true. And now after searching for so long, I have finally found you." He paused before whispering, "Dragons."

Galahad cowered back from the man's gaze. The dragon's large golden eyes rolled wildly toward Iris, but she was powerless to give him any measure of comfort.

Eventually, the German turned to the girls. "And I suppose these are the fierce Valkyries who wreaked so much havoc on my forces. Mere children!"

Iris felt a flame of anger course through her body. "Let us go!" she demanded. "We've done nothing to you."

"I am afraid that will not be possible, my little Valkyrie. But you have my word that no harm will come to you." He looked back toward the dragons. "Unless, of course, it becomes necessary as a source of motivation for your little pets here."

Cold fear crept down Iris's spine. "W-what do you want with them?"

Before he could answer, another soldier jogged up and held out his arm in salute. The officer waved away the gesture impatiently. "What is it?"

"General Wyvern, our scouts have spotted what appears to be a small unit of British soldiers in hiding not far from here. What would you like us to do?"

"That must be them," Wyvern said, tightening his fist around the top of his cane. "Very good. Prepare a greeting party, and we will be off to deal with them at once." He turned back to Iris. "You see, my dear, there are times when the fates clearly reveal their favor with gifts to those who are destined for greatness. You asked what my plans are for your dragons. Perhaps a demonstration will prove more eloquent than mere words."

Iris felt her chest tighten. Who were the British soldiers they had mentioned? And what did the general plan to do with Galahad and Malory?

"Bring them," the general commanded.

Iris felt herself being yanked to her feet and shoved from behind. She staggered forward a few steps, then regained her balance. Thick steel chains were wrapped around the dragons' snouts like muzzles. Malory shrieked and bucked against her restraints, while Galahad resisted more halfheartedly, as if he had already become more accustomed to yielding to human will.

They were marched to the rear of a line of German soldiers who led the way out of the village and onto a paved road heading north. At the front were a pair of motorcycles with sidecars outfitted with large machine guns, followed by several armored cars carrying more heavy artillery, then the soldiers on foot leading Iris, Maud, and the dragons.

Iris frantically scanned their surroundings, looking for any opportunity to escape. But there were simply too many soldiers and nowhere to run. Flying was out of the question because the dragons' wings had been secured back flat against their bodies. Plus, the general himself had opted to bring up the rear in his sleek, shiny motorcar to personally ensure all went according to his plan.

As they approached a bend in the road, their steady march came to a halt. Iris heard a shout from up ahead. The general impatiently mashed his horn and drove to the front of the motorcade as the soldiers parted to let him through. Iris stood on her tiptoes to see what was happening.

"Why have we stopped?" General Wyvern demanded as he reached the front and stepped out of his car.

"Sir," one of the motorcycle riders said, "the way ahead appears to be mined. We can't get through."

The general limped forward and bent at the waist inspecting the road's surface. Iris wasn't quite close enough to see for sure what the strange sticks were that bristled from the cracks going all the way across the asphalt. She squinted harder, not quite believing what she was seeing. Were those . . .

"Pencils!" Wyvern exclaimed. "Our own forces have set this

ruse. They merely appear as detonators to slow the movement of the enemy. You will simply ignore them, and we will continue on."

The soldier stared down dubiously at the road. "Sir?"

"Ach!" the general cried. "What has become of the fearless German soldier?" He leaned down, yanked one of the pencils from the road, and thrust it toward the soldier, who flinched away. "There is your detonator, dummkopf!" Then he snapped it in two and tossed the broken pieces into the brush at the side of the road. "Now go before I let one of my new dragon friends devour you!"

The man saluted and quickly climbed back onto his motor-cycle. Iris watched the general return to his motorcar. He had just swung the door shut when the motorcycle started forward. The second motorcycle followed, then the armored vehicles.

Crunch snap crunch went the pencils as the German military vehicles started to drive over them.

Then suddenly: *BOOOOM!*

The explosion carried enough force for Iris to feel its pressure and heat ripple through her body all the way at the back of the column. She stumbled backward in surprise as another *KABOOM!* ripped through the air.

Iris reacted on instinct, grabbing Maud's hand and pulling her down. They huddled together with their hands over their heads in the middle of the road. Her heart rattled crazily in her chest. The blasts felt as if they had been right next to her.

BOOOOOM! A third explosion shook the ground.

Suddenly, everything was happening all at once. Men run-ning and shouting. The dragons shrieking and pulling on their restraints. And above it all the general screaming things in German.

Iris couldn't understand what he was saying, but his voice was thick with rage.

After what seemed like an eternity, the chaos began to die down. Iris untucked her arms and ventured to raise her head and look around. Up ahead, the pair of motorcycles that had been in the lead lay overturned on the side of the road, blackened and smoking. One of the armored cars had been flipped completely upside down and rested on its roof with two of its tires blown completely off. She couldn't see what had become of the soldiers who had been driving them.

The general stalked among the wreckage with his chest heaving. His fingers clenched and unclenched on the head of his cane. "The Tommies think they are so clever," he seethed, and struck at the few remaining pencils still in the road. They snapped and scattered into the brush at the roadside. "Turning our own ruse against us. We shall see who is the cleverest." He spun on one heel and motioned to his remaining convoy. "Come! It is time to put an end to these meddlers once and for all."

Iris felt herself being jerked back to her feet and forced to march forward at double time. Her brain spun as she processed what the general had just said. *Tommies.* She knew that was the Germans' name for British soldiers. So he thought British soldiers were responsible for setting this trap? As she passed the site of the explosions, something about the cleverness of the trick reminded her of . . . But no, could her brother actually be close by?

"What's wrong?" Maud muttered under her breath.

"It's Jamie," Iris whispered. "I think it's possible he helped make this trap. He's always had a brain for this sort of thing."

"And maybe Jack too," Maud said. "He was the sapper for his unit. They're the ones who know how to blow things up. So maybe they worked together on this?" She paused before adding. "If it *is* them, then we have to warn them somehow."

Iris looked around at the grim faces of the German soldiers and shook her head. "I think all we can do now is pray they heard the explosions and are already far away from here."

A cry went up from the front of the column to halt. The unit stomped to a stop at the foot of a long drive leading from the road to a French château set a few hundred yards back in a grove of trees. The shadows of the trees in the late afternoon stretched across the long rows of grapevines that striped the fields.

"Herr General," said a soldier, walking forward and addressing the commanding officer, "we have spotted movement inside. We believe the British are still here."

General Wyvern climbed out of his motorcar and strode forward to take in the scene. With his stiff movements and tight expression, the man looked like a bomb set to explode at any moment.

The towering officer stopped pacing and sniffed curiously. Iris noticed a strong, sour odor that was somehow familiar, but she couldn't quite place it. No wait, she knew what it reminded her of. It was the odor that frequently wafted out of the tavern in her village back home. But what could be causing it here?

Kneeling, the general swiped a bare finger along the ground and brought it to his nose. A grim smile spread across his face as he turned toward the girls. "Why, it seems our vineyard owners have spilled all their brandy. Such a pity. However, it seems that fate has smiled on me once again. Because, you see, I believe I may have an even better use for their fine vintage than drinking it. Perhaps I might even leave the owners a small note of thanks." Rising to his feet, he motioned to the men restraining the dragons. "Bring them." Galahad and Malory bucked and struggled as they were dragged forward and their muzzles removed.

Suddenly, Iris had a glimmer of what the general had planned. Her stomach turned over so violently, she thought she might be sick. Forcing the wave of nausea down, she struggled forward against her bindings. "Stop!" she gasped. "You . . . you can't!"

"Oh, but I can," the general purred. "Or rather, it is your dragons who will do the job for me. They can understand what I am saying, yes?"

When Iris didn't respond, Wyvern nodded to her captor and one of Iris's arms was wrenched painfully behind her back. She gritted her teeth, not wanting to give the German the satisfaction of hearing her cry out. Finally, when she could barely stand the pain anymore, she made a quick, single nod.

The general smiled and turned toward the dragons. "Excellent. Therefore, my friends, your task is simple: You will ignite the field with your fiery breath. And our British friends will no longer be a problem."

Through tear-filled eyes, Iris saw Galahad stare mournfully back, seeking her face. When their gazes met, she felt as if someone had punched her in the gut. *No,* she mouthed. *You don't have to do this.* But she found herself powerless to move. To strike out. To do anything to stop the inevitability of what was rushing toward them. She wasn't sure how, but she knew that her brother was trapped inside the house just a few hundred yards away. And the Germans were going to use her sweet, kind Galahad to murder him.

When the dragons didn't move, General Wyvern nodded again to the men holding Iris and Maud. A white-hot pain lanced through Iris's shoulder as her arm was twisted even further. She yelped out loud, not able to hold it in this time.

Galahad was trembling all over. He bleated at Iris with such sadness that she felt as if her heart was breaking.

"You will do as I say," the general said, his voice lowering menacingly, "or your dear girls will suffer my wrath."

Finally, with a mighty bellow, Galahad swung around and leveled a stream of fire on the open field. A second later, Malory joined him.

General Wyvern stared on with an unearthly orange flicker lighting up his eyes.

CHAPTER THIRTY-TWO

MAX

France

Max jerked his head toward the sound of the explosion. The muffled boom had come from a distance. But it had still been uncomfortably close to the house where Max and Jamie had taken shelter with the rest of the unit.

Then there was another. And another.

Max rose cautiously from where he'd been playing with Plum in a back room and crept toward the front of the house, careful to keep below the line of sight from the windows as Jamie had taught him.

"What is it?" Max asked Jamie, who was already on the alert and peering outside.

"It sounds like someone found our trap," Jamie replied without looking away from the window.

"Do you think it was the Germans? What do we do?"

"Be on the alert," Major Stevenson said, coming up to join them. "But hold our position. Sunset will be here soon, and that's our best bet to slip away unnoticed."

The rest of the unit gathered in the deepening shadows of the front room. "See anything?" one of the soldiers asked Jamie.

Jamie shook his head. "Not yet."

Max pulled out his star and began rubbing it nervously between his thumb and forefinger. Why wouldn't the sun hurry up and set already so they could leave?

"Here they come," Jamie breathed.

Max looked up quickly and spotted a column of gray-uniformed soldiers marching rapidly up the same road that he, Jamie, and Jack had traveled a few hours earlier.

Jack leaned closer to the window. "And if I'm not mistaken, that big fella there leading the way in his fancy car looks to be scrapping for a fight. Hope we didn't kick the ol' hornet's nest with our little trick."

"No quick movements now," the major said. "Let's hope they pass by without spotting us."

But not much sooner had he said this than the German column abruptly stopped at the bottom of the drive leading up to their hiding place.

"Too late for that," Jack said. The big man slowly lifted his rifle and rested its barrel on the ledge of the window in front of him. Max's knees started shaking. He doubted their small force would be able to hold off so many Germans for long.

"Galahad . . . how?" Jamie said with bewilderment.

"What is it?" Max asked, trying to get a closer look.

"I think . . . if I'm not seeing things, that's . . ."

Then Max spotted it too. The Germans were leading a pair of large creatures to the front of their lines. The last golden rays of sunlight danced across the lead creature's body and wings. As if these were mystical beasts born from the pages of a fairy tale.

"Dragons!" Max gasped with wonder.

Jamie's eyes frantically darted around the enemy formation. "And if Galahad is here, then that means . . ." Then his fingers tightened on the edge of the windowsill. "No!"

A shrill scream rang through the air. Max spotted two young girls struggling to free themselves from the Nazi soldiers who held them. What was going on? "Do you know that girl?"

Without taking his eyes off the scene, Jamie replied in a stunned voice, "One of them is my sister."

"And the other'll be mine," Jack growled. He started to rise. "I don't know how she got mixed up in all this, but—"

"Maud?!" Major Stevenson exclaimed, lurching forward so violently, he almost lost his balance. It was the first time Max had seen the stoic officer lose his composure. "I don't care how many Germans are out there, I'll—"

He never got to finish his sentence. In the next second, the dragons let loose twin blasts of searing flames. The streaks of angry orange and yellow lent an ominous glow to the falling twilight as they raced across the lawn with such speed that they seemed to spread and consume everything in their path within seconds.

"The brandy!" Jamie said, leaping to his feet.

"Looks like the Germans brought the matches," Jack said grimly, "and we're in the middle of a lake of liquid fuel. I figure we've got about two minutes to get out of here before we're cooked like a Christmas pudding."

"Head for the canal!" Major Stevenson ordered. "It's our best shot. Quickly now, everyone run like the wind and there's a chance we'll make it."

The soldiers needed no other encouragement. Everyone darted for the back door in a hasty retreat.

"Plum!" Max called. "Plum! Where are you?" A responding bark came from the back of the house and Plum came bounding toward him. Max breathed a sigh of relief. He scooped up the dog in his arms and raced after the other soldiers with his bow and quiver bouncing against his back.

Bursting out the back door into the gathering dusk, Max stumbled on the concrete stairs leading down into the yard and fell to his knees in the grass. Ahead, the dark silhouettes of British soldiers raced away from him across the open field.

Don't leave me!

But in the next moment, Jamie was beside him. "Alright, Max?" he asked, and helped him back to his feet.

Max nodded and took off again after the other men already disappearing in the dark. Something flickered in his peripheral vision. When Max spun his head toward it, his legs turned to jelly. The fire! It had already overtaken the house and now raced across the field directly toward them. He shot a glance in the other direction. Another arc of flame was sweeping toward them from that side too. The two flames must have encircled the property and were closing on them like a trap from both sides. How long did they have until they were cut off completely? Minutes? Seconds?

"Just keep going, Max!" Jamie urged. "We're going to make it!"

But Max was no longer sure. He was panting now. And the muscles in his legs were starting to ache. He didn't know how much longer he could keep up their breakneck pace. Then the sound of a splash from up ahead reached his ears. The canal! It was too dark to see it, but it couldn't be far now.

Finding a second wind, he bolted for the water. He didn't dare look to see how close the fire was now, worried that his legs might simply quit on him. The heat of the flames singed the bare skin of his arms and face. His eyes stung from the smoke. That was enough to know it was too close. It would be such a relief to feel the canal's cool water—

Oh no!

In his blind panic, Max had forgotten one critical thing: He didn't know how to swim!

Tongues of fire licked toward him from both sides. He had no time to think. Only act.

"Hold on, Plum!" he shouted. Then he sucked in a huge breath.

Closed his eyes.

And jumped.

CHAPTER THIRTY-THREE

IRIS

France

The Germans took Iris, Maud, and the dragons back to the ruined village serving as their base of operations. The general ordered the girls confined to a tent under guard while the dragons were led off farther into the camp.

"Where are you taking them?" Iris cried.

The general ignored her. One of the soldiers held the tent's flap open while another roughly shoved her inside. She stumbled and fell onto the hard ground. Pain lanced up her leg from where her knee connected with the packed earth. A moment later Maud was pushed into the tent as well, and the flap fell closed again, leaving them in the dark.

Iris thought she heard Maud say something to her, but the voice seemed to be coming from the end of a long tunnel. All her senses seemed to have gone dull since the horrible moment she saw the flames racing toward the house where she suspected Jamie was hiding. He had to have escaped. He *had* to. If her attempt at a rescue operation had led to his death, there was no way she could keep on living. Her grief would consume her with the same fury as the fire that had swallowed up the house.

215

"Iris!" Maud said urgently, shaking her this time. "Come on, snap out of it!"

Iris wrestled with the fog that seemed to fill her head. "I can't. It doesn't matter anymore anyway." She paused, struggling to speak past the lump in her throat. "You were right. If I hadn't tried so hard, if I'd just left it alone like you said, none of this would have ever happened."

Maud sank to her knees, her shoulders shaking with quiet sobs. "I d-don't want to be r-right," she gasped. "Don't you get it? I *need* you to be right. All that stuff I said about the way the world works? I wanted you to prove I was wrong. That it really, truly matters if we try." She sucked in a long, shuddering breath. "Otherwise, it means my father, and now maybe my brother . . . they both threw away their lives for nothing."

Iris was so stunned by this revelation that she was momentarily speechless. That behind Maud's facade of grim self-assurance was an injured heart still reeling from the loss of her father. A heart that needed her now.

"'Centuries ago, words were written.'" The words came slow and soft from Iris's mouth almost before she knew she was saying them. Her voice trembled with the soul-crushing pain she was feeling, but as she spoke, she felt her spirit spark with life as if compelled to speak. "'To be a call and a spur to the faithful servants of Truth and Justice.'"

Maud's eyes rose to meet hers as she spoke, before they finished together, "'Arm yourselves, and be ye men of valor.'"

They held eye contact for a long, silent moment where an

understanding passed between them. Then the silence was abruptly broken by the tent flap snapping open to reveal the German general peering in at them.

"If you would be so good as to join me," he said, "I find I am in need of your assistance."

Iris shot a glance at Maud. The last thing she wanted to do was help this cruel man. But if it reunited them with the dragons and—just maybe—provided an opportunity for them all to escape, then she would take it. They had come so far. She wouldn't quit now, no matter how bleak things looked.

"Women of valor?" Iris whispered as the general turned away.

Maud nodded. "Women of valor."

Iris rose to her full height as she exited the tent and paused to look around. The camp was a beehive of activity, with soldiers rushing around in every direction. Up ahead, a long line of canvas-topped transport trucks was being loaded with weapons and supplies. The general led the way toward those same trucks, walking unevenly through the rubble of the village with the aid of his stout black cane.

"We plan to rendezvous with our other divisions within the hour," the general told them. "And, by a week from now, Paris will be ours. Now that we have successfully captured your dragons, there will be no further need for delay."

"If you think we'll help you use Galahad and Malory to fight your battles, then you're wrong," Iris said defiantly. "Dragons are peaceful creatures, not meant to be used as weapons of war."

"Oh, your pets have names, do they?" General Wyvern replied.

"How very touching. But as our amusing bit of entertainment at the vineyard demonstrated earlier this evening, your dragons will in fact make excellent weapons."

Iris's stomach churned at the suggestion that murdering a group of soldiers was this man's idea of entertainment. "Then you'll no doubt be highly amused when an entire herd of fire-breathing dragons descends on your army to rescue their friends," she fired back.

The tall general froze, and Iris instantly realized her mistake. He turned toward her with a strange gleam in his eyes. "So there are . . . more of them?"

Iris didn't respond. She didn't need to. The general clearly read the answer on her face. Her blunder may have just endangered the entire herd of dragons.

"What do you plan to do with them, then?" she asked. "And what do you need us for?"

For a moment, she wasn't sure if the general had heard her. He appeared lost in thought, staring at the red stone embedded in his cane's handle.

"Come," he said at last, turning to lead them on. "You will find out soon enough, my little Valkyrie."

As she followed behind him, Iris tried to get a closer look at the red stone, wondering about the general's fascination with it. What was it? Then it caught the beam of a headlight as they walked past and sparkled almost like it was alive.

Iris gasped.

She was surprised she hadn't seen the resemblance until now. Her hand went automatically to the blue stone hanging around her neck. The red stone in the general's cane was a different color, but otherwise it was exactly the same size and shape as hers.

They were both dragon tears.

A cold hand of fear gripped Iris's chest. She could barely breathe. Where had he gotten the dragon tear? Were there even *more* dragons somewhere beyond the herd that she knew of? Clearly, if there were, the general's reaction to her earlier revelation showed that he didn't know the answer to that question either.

"Ah, here we are," the general said. They had arrived at the back of one of the transport trucks. A small contingent of soldiers ringed the vehicle but stood several yards away, as if keeping a safe distance. An angry bellow echoed from the truck's cargo area, and she immediately understood why. Clearly, the dragons were inside. And they were not happy.

"Which brings us to how you may be of assistance," General Wyvern continued. "As you can hear, your friends are rather inconsolable. You will be kind enough to placate them until we arrive." He yanked aside the canvas flap on the back of the truck.

Iris stared into the dark interior, unable to see more than something large shifting in the gloom at the back of the cargo hold.

The general held out a hand to assist them into the truck. "There our handlers will take over and prepare them to aid with the next phase of our plan: the utter destruction of Paris."

Over my dead body, Iris thought.

She ignored the general's offered hand and climbed into the truck's cargo area. Once inside, she rushed forward and found Galahad curled in one corner. Thick chains lashed him down to metal hoops fixed into the bed of the truck. A large steel clamp had been used as a makeshift muzzle, probably to prevent him from scorching any unwary Germans.

His pitiful bleat instantly brought tears to her eyes. She fell to her knees and cradled his head in her arms, furious that anyone would try to hurt him. He shuddered under her touch, and the dull, feverish look was back in his eyes. Fear stabbed through her heart. Whatever had been ailing him a couple of days ago seemed to have not only returned but gotten worse.

"What have they done to you?" she whispered. It had been her job to protect him, and she had failed. But she wouldn't fail again.

"Sorry to interrupt your reunion," Maud said beside her, "but we sort of need to figure out how we're going to escape. And fast."

Iris turned away from Galahad. Maud knelt nearby, caressing Malory's lithe neck. Unlike Galahad, the blue dragon didn't seem completely crushed by the recent events. Instead, a small spark glowed in her eyes. She was ready to fight. Good.

"I know," Iris said. "But we still have a little time to come up with something."

"Less time than you think."

"Why do you say that?" Iris asked.

"Because once their handlers take over with the dragons"— Maud paused and pointed at Iris and then back at herself—"then they no longer need us."

Iris gasped. "And he said they plan to meet up with them within the hour."

"Meaning, if we don't get away first, this could be our last hour alive."

CHAPTER THIRTY-FOUR

MAX

France

Max plunged into the icy water of the canal and sank like a rock. *I'm going to drown! I'm going to drown!* his brain screamed over and over again. He instinctively hugged Plum tighter. But his arms closed around empty water. Where was she? Fighting back his panic, he forced himself to open his eyes.

And immediately felt another surge of panic.

Which way was up? His heart hammered as the disoriented feeling threatened to overwhelm him. An orange glow filtered through the murky water. That had to be the fire, which meant the surface must be that way too.

But when would it be safe to come up for air? He couldn't hold his breath for very long. Already his lungs were tightening with the automatic need to inhale more oxygen. Which was worse: drowning or being burned alive?

Max felt the current carrying his body downstream. Was he imagining it, or was the orange glow above fading the farther he went? He waited as long as he could, and when his lungs were practically on fire and dots of light prickled the edges of his vision, he kicked out his legs to push off the bottom of the canal. Seconds later, his head shot out into the cool night.

Wheeeze!

He sucked in a huge lungful of air.

If the air was cool, that meant the current must have carried him clear of the fire. Unfortunately, he didn't have long to celebrate the fact before he started sinking again. He thrashed his arms against the water in a futile effort to swim.

"Plum! Where—" His shout was choked off by water flooding into his mouth as his head went under again. Equal parts water and air filled his lungs. He felt his foot touch something solid. He shoved against it with all his might in a desperate attempt to reach the surface. Seconds later he bobbed up into the night again, choking and sputtering.

A yip came from nearby. "Plum?!"

"Max!" someone shouted.

Several strong hands grabbed him and hauled him onto the grass along the water's edge. Max crouched on all fours, shivering, while his lungs coughed up what seemed like enough water to fill an ocean. A tiny rough tongue found his ear. When his coughing fit finally subsided, he collapsed on his back on the grass with a wet, squelching noise and pulled his dog into a tight hug.

"Plum, you're okay!" he sighed with relief. The dog licked the end of his nose while her body wiggled with delight.

"That was quite a scare you just had. Are you okay?"

Max looked up to see Jack and Jamie squatting beside him with their eyebrows pressed together in looks of concern. The rest of the soldiers from their unit were a little farther away, wringing out their clothes. It was completely dark now, and the night quiet enough that he could hear the sucking noise of one soldier peeling off his wet boot and the water running out when he turned the boot upside down. Max turned his head back upstream. An orange glow from the fire still burned in the distance. They were safe. For now.

"I'm fine——" he started to say before being overcome by another fit of coughing. He turned onto his side until it passed.

"Might have mentioned you needed a little help in the water back there," Jack said, grinning. "The second I saw you plunge in on your ear, I said to myself, 'That boy don't know how to swim.'"

Max smiled. "I sort of forgot about that, with the fire and the——" He sat up quickly, his face growing more serious. "Were those really dragons back there? And your sisters . . . what did they have to do with any of it?"

Jamie turned his head back toward the burning vineyard. "That's what we intend to find out."

"Right," Jack said darkly, "as soon as we figure out how to take on an entire battalion of Nazis with no weapons but our bare hands." He tilted the muzzle of his rifle at the ground and a stream of water poured out. "Lot of good these'll do us now."

"At least we have one advantage," Max said.

Jamie cocked his head. "What's that?"

"Well, they probably think we're all dead, right?"

"You're likely right there," Jack said. "Probably thinking their fire show finished us off for good."

Jamie was nodding slowly. "Which means they won't be expecting a couple spies doing a little nighttime reconnaissance on their camp. They couldn't have gone far, but we have to move quickly. What do you think? Are you up for it?"

"When do we leave?" Jack said, already rising to his feet.

"Let me talk to the major, then the two of us—" Jamie started.

"You mean four of us, right?" Max interrupted. "Plum and I are going with you."

"Make that five," said another voice. Max looked over and saw Boo stand to join them. "Sorry, couldn't help overhearing your conversation. If your sisters are in trouble, then you've got my help."

"Call it six," another soldier said.

"Seven."

Soon the entire unit had gathered around their small group, pledging their support. Everyone except the major, who now approached with a grim expression on his face.

Major Stevenson stopped and folded his hands behind his back as he surveyed the men. "Is this a mutiny I'm hearing? Our express orders are to make for the coast and evacuate to England." He paused and cleared his throat. "There are times to follow orders. And there are times when circumstances require you to make your own. And I believe this is one of those times."

"But, sir," Jamie said, "we can't allow everyone to put their lives at risk. Not when we're this close to the coast and escaping the Germans. Even in the best-case scenario, if we managed to rescue the girls and get to Dunkirk, it may be too late to find any ships left to get us home."

"I said it before," the major replied. "We're not just a unit any-more. We're a family. And when one of our family is in trouble, we're all in trouble. We're not going to leave your sister and my granddaughter behind."

A murmur of approval came from the exhausted, bedraggled group of men. Max felt a lightness in his heart he hadn't felt for many weeks. He'd lost his entire family, but he'd become part of a new one.

"And I'd wager," the major continued, "that more than a few men here might be interested in a bit of payback to the Germans for nearly roasting us alive."

At this, the soldiers clapped and cheered.

"So what now?" Jamie asked, finally finding his voice.

"For one thing," Jack replied, "I suggest we stop standing here jawing about it and go do something while we've still got the cover of night in our favor."

After the major outlined a quick set of plans, the men grabbed what gear they had left and set off at a jog back in the direction they'd come from. They guessed the Germans had most likely set up camp in the nearby village for the night rather than marching onward to the south.

Max trailed behind Jamie with Plum at his side. They were careful to keep to the shadows and tall grass along the road to avoid detection by any enemy scouts who might still be lurking in the area. Overhead, a sliver of moon provided enough light to guide their way without risking revealing their location. When they passed the vineyard, pockets of fire still raged where anything remained to burn. The black, smoking husk of the house where they had been hiding earlier that evening still pulsed with an eerie orange light through its vacant windows, as if the building's heartbeat was slowly fading into the stillness of death. Max shivered at the thought that they had all barely escaped the inferno alive.

Eventually, they reached the tree line near the village and found the same trail they had traveled earlier that day. At that point, the men split up into smaller groups to scope out the best approach to the enemy camp.

"Do you think the Germans are even still here?" Max whispered to Jamie.

"I can only hope so," Jamie replied. "Otherwise, we may never find Iris and Maud."

But as they approached the village, this worry was quickly put to rest when voices speaking German carried to them on the night breeze.

Jamie raised a cautioning hand. They silently crept forward and hunkered down in the shadows on a wooded knoll overlooking the village. Despite the late hour, the German camp was bustling with activity. Men moved hurriedly through the rubble-filled lanes of the destroyed village, hastily pulling down tents and moving supplies into waiting trucks.

"Well, at least we know they stopped here," Jack said under his breath. "But maybe not for long. Does anyone see where they might be keeping the girls?"

"My guess would be there," Jamie said, pointing toward a large truck near the village square. "There seem to be an awful lot of guards for one truck, don't you think? As if they're keeping something important inside."

"Like a pair of dragons?" Max asked.

Just then a mournful, inhuman bellow came from inside the truck. One of the guards stepped around to the back impatiently and barked, "Keep them quiet!"

"That must be them!" Max said excitedly.

"If so, then they're practically at the dead center of the camp," Jack said. "It'll be nigh impossible to get to them, especially without any weapons."

Max scanned the scene. Everywhere he looked, there seemed to be German soldiers. The only place where there wasn't a man in a gray uniform was the area around the schoolhouse they had explored earlier on the edge of the village.

"It's too bad we don't have any more of that goose liver," Max whispered. "That stuff probably smells bad enough to clear the whole camp."

"Max, I think you may be a genius." Jamie shifted his gaze to the schoolhouse that lay dark and silent below them. "Jack, do you think we can get in there undetected?"

Jack followed his stare and shrugged. "Don't see why not. Why? What are you gonna do?"

Jamie grinned at him. "The impossible."

CHAPTER THIRTY-FIVE

IRIS

France

Iris had just begun forming an escape plan when the night erupted around them. Soldiers yelling. Feet racing. Bursts of gunfire. From inside the enclosed bed of the truck, it was impossible to tell what was happening.

"Is someone attacking the camp?" Maud shouted. "We have to get ourselves and the dragons to safety!"

Iris moved at a crouch toward the back of the truck, half expecting a mortar round to explode nearby at any moment. "Let me take a look outside."

She had just reached to pull open the canvas flap when a huge man burst through the opening, nearly colliding with her. Iris fell backward to the floor in surprise and sat there staring up at the man with her heart thudding in her chest. In the dark, she couldn't tell the color of his uniform. Was he friend or foe?

"Jack?!" Maud exclaimed behind her. Then, "Ugh, what's that smell?"

"Nice to see you too, sis," the soldier said with a smile.

Iris found her heart was pounding for an entirely different reason. Because if Maud's brother was alive, then—

The flap parted again.

"Are they in here?" another voice asked.

"Jamie!" Iris shouted. She threw her arms around her brother's neck and clung to him fiercely. For what seemed like an eternity, she found herself unable to speak as sobs racked her entire body. In her mind, two words kept repeating over and over. *He's alive!*

Finally, with tears streaming down her cheeks, she pulled away to look at him. He appeared solid and unharmed after the fire. "H-how?" she managed to choke out.

Jamie cleared his throat with difficulty, clearly struggling with emotion himself. Then he looked past her to Maud and the two dragons in the back of the truck. "We'll have more time to talk later. Because believe me, I've got questions for you too. But there's no time for that now. We don't have long to get you out of here before the Nazis figure out our little ruse. Can the dragons fly?"

"Not with necklaces like these," Jack said, tugging on one of the heavy chains. "It'll take me some tools and a little time to get them free."

Jamie frowned. "I guess there's nothing for it then. We'll just have to take the whole truck. Let me see if I can get this bucket of bolts started."

"Okay," Jack said, "whatever you do, make it quick. The clock is ticking."

"Jamie, wait—" Iris started to say, but the canvas flap was already falling closed behind him. She'd only just found him again and wasn't ready to let him out of her sight.

"Don't worry," Maud said, scrambling for the rear of the truck. "I'll keep an eye on him. I might even have some skills that'll come in handy. Anyway, I think Galahad needs you more right now. So you stay here and help Jack with the dragons while I see if Jamie needs a hand. Okay?"

Without waiting for an answer, Maud stuck her head out of the truck, glanced around quickly, then slipped out after Jamie.

Meanwhile, the commotion outside continued unabated as if a full-scale battle was raging through the Nazi camp. Iris turned back toward the dragons with her head spinning. This was all happening so fast. And at the same time, maybe not fast enough. Her leg bobbed up and down, and she felt like she might burst with nervous energy.

"You remind me of a top that's wound too tight," Jack said, and glanced across at Galahad, who was making low moaning noises while he pulled against his chains. "I think you're making your dragon friends more nervous."

"Sorry," Iris said, and stopped to lay a calming hand on Galahad's forehead. His scales felt hot with fever. She watched Jack attempt to pry apart the metal clamp over Malory's mouth with his bare hands. "I guess I'm not very good at doing nothing."

Jack grunted. "Then I can see why you and Maud get on so well. If you want to do something, you might look around this truck bed and see if there's a stash of tools somewhere. It'll probably be under one of these benches if it's anywhere." He flexed his fingers and gestured to the dragons' restraints. "Because it's looking like it'll take more than a little elbow grease to get through these."

"I can do that!" she said. She moved toward a bench on one side. When she pulled on it, it hinged open, revealing a compartment underneath full of tools of all kinds. "What do you need? Monkey wrench? Sledgehammer? Hacksaw?"

"Oh ho, a lady who knows her tools!" Jack said, impressed. "Unless there's a set of lockpicks in there, better hand me the sledge. We don't have time for a finesse job."

She handed him the hammer. He positioned one of the locks that held the chains in place flat on the floor, then swung the sledge with both hands.

BANG!

The lock rattled but held. However, it now had a sizable dent in it.

Jack waited for another explosion outside to mask the sound of his blow, then swung again.

BANG!

Iris cringed, wondering if someone would hear and come investigate. While Jack was working, she grabbed a pair of pliers to attempt to pry open the muzzle on Malory's mouth. *Creeeeaaaaak.* The metal of the muzzle separated agonizingly slowly. The muscles in her arms began to tremble from the effort. But just as she was about to give up, the device broke open with a loud *POP!* that sent Iris tumbling backward.

The blue dragon roared and shook her head.

Jack eyed Malory warily but continued working. "Maybe you can ask your friend there not to sink her teeth into my backside."

"I think she's more interested in German cuisine at the moment." Iris leaned forward to run a soothing hand over where the muzzle had rubbed against the dragon's scales. Then she moved over to free Galahad's snout as well.

A low rumble vibrated through the truck, and in the next

moment a small partition between the cab and the cargo portion shot open. Maud grinned back at them, kneeling next to Jamie, who sat in the driver's seat, studying the truck's dashboard.

"So you know how to hot-wire German trucks now?" Iris asked.

Maud pointed to where a set of keys dangled from the ignition. "No need. I guess even Nazis keep a spare set under their floormats."

"Jamie, I'm so sorry"—Iris grunted as she tugged on the pliers—"about all this." Galahad's muzzle popped free and clanged to the floor. The dragon immediately leaned in to nuzzle her neck. "Galahad and I were supposed to be the ones rescuing you."

"Don't worry, you may still get your chance," Jamie said. "We're not in the clear yet. Now hold on to something. This could get a little bumpy."

He shifted gears and eased down on the gas pedal. The truck lurched into motion, and he guided it in a wide arc heading back toward the north. Iris nearly toppled over when the truck wobbled over a pile of rubble, but she shot out her hand and grabbed one of the metal ribs that supported the canvas top. When the tires were clear of the obstruction, the truck picked up speed.

Iris looked out the windshield as they wound their way out of the village. Some sort of haze seemed to hang in the air, making it difficult to see. Whatever it was, it smelled terrible. She coughed as some of the stuff filtered in through the open windows of the truck. "What in the world is that?"

"Only a little mustard gas," Jack said beside her. He swung the hammer again and the lock finally shattered into pieces.

"Wait . . . what?" both girls cried at the same time, clapping their hands over their mouths and noses.

"Relax," Jamie said. "It's only a little concoction we made to fool the Germans and give us an opening to pull off our rescue. We were counting on them not knowing what the real stuff looked and smelled like, and I guess we were right. But I'd like to be well clear of here when they figure out those homemade bombs were filled with nothing more deadly than chalk dust and goose liver."

"Did you know your brother's a genius?" Jack asked Iris. He tugged on one of the chains and it rattled loose, freeing Malory's legs. "A little cracked in the head now and then, but a genius nonetheless."

"I can't take all the credit for this one," Jamie said. "Max was the one who provided the inspiration."

"Who's Max?" Maud asked. "Is he another soldier in your unit?"

"You'll meet him soon enough," Jamie replied. "We're supposed to meet up with him and the others along the road just north of here."

While everyone else was talking, Iris moved toward the back of the truck to see what was happening behind them. It was hard to see clearly with the night and lingering haze of chalk dust in the air, but no one seemed to be pursuing them. At least, not yet.

A ball of worry sat in the pit of Iris's stomach as she thought of General Wyvern. Something told her he wouldn't remain fooled for long.

A pair of headlights swung into view behind them. Iris's heart leapt into her throat. It had to be the general's roadster. She spun around and shouted, "They're following us!"

Jamie's eyes flicked toward the rearview mirror. "Guess it's time to find out what this old girl can do." The truck's rear tires spun, throwing loose gravel as he shifted gears and floored the accelerator. "Maud, see if you can find the headlights. Our secret's blown anyway, and I'm not sure I can make it out of here blind."

"On it!" Maud said, and leaned forward, studying the dashboard. She yanked a knob and a thick cloud of smoke belched from the back of the truck. "Sorry!" She tried another and the night in front of them filled with a yellow glow.

Iris held tight with both hands as they swerved and dodged through the last remains of the village. The truck jolted along, causing the dragons to roar in fear each time a particularly sharp turn sent the vehicle yawing far to one side on the edge of overturning. By the time they rocketed onto the main road heading north, many more headlights had joined the chase. Leaves and dust swirled in the wake of the fleeing truck, making it look like a hurricane was chasing them, carrying with it the entire German army.

"Why aren't they shooting at us?" Maud shouted over the whine of the truck's engine.

"Probably don't want to risk hitting the dragons," Iris said. She watched as their pursuers continued to gain on them. "But there's no way we'll be able to outrun them."

"Doesn't mean we can't fire back," Jamie said.

"With what?" Jack asked, looking around and then holding up his hammer dubiously. "You're forgetting maybe that all our rifles are waterlogged?"

"No, I mean literally fire back," Jamie said. "You've got the dragons' mouths free, right?"

"Aha," Jack said, "the Germans used dragon fire on us. It's time we return the favor."

"Exactly. Only, I'm thinking that concentrating their fire directly at the German vehicles will only temporarily keep them at a safe distance. Eventually, we'll run out of gas, or the dragons will get tired, and we'll be caught. We need something that will get them off our tail long enough to let us escape."

With a screech of tires, they came around a bend and entered a section of the road with thick forest on both sides. Iris nervously watched the dark forms of the trees leaning over the truck as if they were reaching out to grab her and her friends. Suddenly, an idea came to her. She whirled back toward Jamie.

"The trees!" she shouted. "If we can start a forest fire behind us, the flames may block the Germans from chasing us."

Jamie leaned forward and studied the trees in the truck's headlights. "It's worth a try. Jack, can you give the dragons an opening to do their work?"

"Already on it," Jack said, and grunted as he tore at the canvas top. With a loud ripping noise, part of it came free directly over the dragons.

"Concentrate their fire on the trees beside and behind us," Jamie said. "We don't want to get burned by our own trap."

Iris shot a nervous glance back at the gaining headlights, then turned to Galahad and Malory. "Do you understand?"

Both dragons rumbled their agreement. Then, raising their heads through the opening in the roof, they opened their mouths and sprayed streams of fire into the trees on both sides of the truck. The wood instantly exploded into flames from their superheated breath.

Galahad collapsed with a loud thump into the truck bed, looking completely spent. Iris knelt by him and stroked his scales. "Just a little longer, and hopefully this will all be over."

"It's working!" Maud called.

Iris looked up in time to see tongues of orange and yellow arc upward through the branches overhead and down to the underbrush below. As the inferno quickly spread in all directions, the roadway behind them lit up under a tunnel of fire. It might have even been beautiful to watch, Iris reflected, if not for the fact that it illuminated the swarm of Nazi vehicles still gaining on them.

As the fire continued to expand, the trees began to groan ominously. Their burning limbs creaked and swayed under the strain of the blaze weakening their attachment to the old, gnarled trunks. Suddenly, a flaming branch fell out of the canopy and directly into an open German jeep. The surprised driver swerved and collided with the armored car next to him before both screeched to a stop. Flames licked across the hood of the jeep, and the soldiers abandoned their vehicles.

Another branch fell. Followed by another. Then with a mighty moan, an entire tree collapsed and fell across the road onto their pursuers. It sent up a shower of sparks as it collided with a truck and blocked the road and part of the German convoy behind it. But that still left plenty of soldiers chasing them. Including the general, who deftly dodged and weaved his car among the falling bits of tree limbs and burning embers.

"Guys, I think we may have a problem," Jamie shouted from the front of the truck.

Iris whirled around. The raging fire had somehow outpaced

them and was quickly transforming the road ahead into another tunnel of flame.

"These old woods must be drier than we thought," Jack said. "And now we're about to be broiled alive for a second time in one night."

"Hold on," Jamie said, squinting into the night. "There might be hope for us yet. I think I can see a break in the fire up ahead where the forest ends."

"I see it too!" Maud shouted. "We can make it!"

Two huge trees on either side of the road in front of them began to lean inward as they succumbed to the fire. A terrible groaning noise filled the air from the collapsing trees. Their trunks made sizzling and popping noises while flames wreathed circles around them, spreading higher into their topmost branches.

"I can't look!" Iris cried. She buried her face in her hands, peeking out between her fingers.

"Come on," Jamie urged the truck faster. "Come on."

Iris watched as the path ahead slowly narrowed between twin pillars of fire falling toward each other. The heat was already so intense that her bare skin tingled as if it might combust at any moment. A single bead of sweat ran down her cheek and traced her jawline. In just seconds, the opening would close. And they would be trapped. Burned alive.

CHAPTER THIRTY-SIX

MAX

France

It's definitely been too long, Max thought. Something must have gone wrong. He felt like he had been waiting for days for any sign of Jamie and Jack. All he could do was squirm restlessly. And wait some more.

A shadow passed over the grassy spot to the north of the forest where they had all planned to meet. Max looked up and saw that a cloud had slipped in front of the moon. The night was so black, he could only hear Plum's snuffling as she explored the ground nearby but could no longer see even the faint outline of the dog's shape.

Would they all even be able to find one another? He shivered, his clothes still damp from their escape through the canal.

Earlier, two soldiers from their unit had returned. Then another three. Everyone had been assigned to launch their fake mustard gas bombs into the German camp from different sides so as to create the most possible confusion for the rescue mission. Soon everyone was accounted for. Everyone except Jamie and Jack.

"They'll make it, Max," Major Stevenson said, noticing the

boy's discomfort. "Those two are survivors. They always find a way."

Max suddenly noticed he could see Plum again, even in the dark. He stared up at the sky, but the moon was still hidden behind a bank of clouds. And there wasn't the least hint of a sunrise on the horizon. Looking around, he noticed a faint orange glow coming from the nearby forest. It grew steadily brighter as he watched. He slowly rose to his knees, unsure what it was.

"Everyone at the ready," Major Stevenson ordered. "Something's happening."

The soldiers quickly fanned out and crouched watchfully, still hidden in the grass. Max knelt, rooted to the spot, his heart thumping louder as the glow grew brighter and brighter. Then the first flames sprang into view as they tore hungrily through the trees.

That much fire, and so fast . . .

Two massive trees began to lean in toward each other. Their groans echoed through the night while the flames devoured them. The trees swayed and finally collapsed against each other like two dying soldiers supporting each other's weight.

In that same moment, a large transport truck rocketed out of the forest beneath the temporary arch, rattling and steaming like it had been spat from the mouth of the devil himself. Then behind it, the huge trunks split, and the trees fell in a huge plume of ashes and sparks that completely blocked the road.

"Hold!" the major commanded, and lifted his hand. The entire unit watched breathlessly while the truck steadily slowed as it rolled toward them. Finally, with a loud screech of brakes, it rolled to a stop not far from their position. The truck sat there silently for a few moments, still smoking from the fire.

Then the front door creaked open. A man stepped down from the cab. Max couldn't make out his features because that side of the truck was cloaked in shadows opposite the forest fire.

"Major?" the man said.

"Jamie!" Max shouted. He dashed forward and threw his arms around the man's waist. "You made it!"

"Just by the skin of our teeth," Jamie said, and doubled over in a coughing fit. "Sorry," he continued when the fit had passed. "I think I inhaled too much smoke back there."

"I, for one, have had my fill of fire for one night," came Jack's voice. Max turned to see the big man climbing down from the back of the truck with his clothes smoking. "No offense, of course," he said, addressing one of the dragons, whose head peeked tentatively from inside the truck.

A girl about Max's age jumped down from the truck next and walked toward them. She was a little taller than him, and her golden hair and soot-blackened clothes still steamed slightly from the fire.

"Max," Jamie said, "I'd like you to meet my sister, Iris."

"Nice to meet . . ." he started to say before a large, scaly head loomed over her shoulder. "Is that your . . . dragon?"

Iris reached up to caress the creature's long neck. "It's okay, Galahad," she said. "We're safe now. Do you want to meet our new friend Max?"

Max hesitantly reached out his palm to lay it on Galahad's neck opposite Iris's hand. But just a few inches away, he paused, suddenly unsure. "You're sure it's okay?"

"Oh yes," Iris said. "He's very gentle."

Max took a deep breath and let his hand gently settle on the dragon's scales. They felt warm and smooth on his fingertips. "An actual, real live dragon," he breathed in wonder.

A soft rumble bubbled up from the dragon's throat that tickled his palm.

"He says it's nice to meet you," Iris translated.

Then with a sudden shudder and wheeze, the dragon quickly recoiled into the truck. Max saw the concerned look in Iris's eyes, but before he could ask what was wrong with Galahad, another girl came around the back of the truck and joined them. "And this is my friend Maud," Iris said. "She's Jack's sister."

"And she is also in quite a bit of trouble," Major Stevenson added, coming up behind them. Maud flinched at seeing him there, but her grandfather surprised her by reaching out to tousle her hair lovingly before pulling her into a tight hug. "But that can wait until we're all safely home."

When he released her, the major strode toward the front of the truck, where a few of the soldiers had gathered around a map spread across the vehicle's hood.

"It will be a race to the coast from here," Major Stevenson said. "The fire may have cut off the main road from the village, but it won't take long for the Germans to double back and find another way around."

Jamie nodded. "And now that we've made this personal, I don't think we can expect them to simply give up and let us escape."

"I think this Nazi truck we borrowed should be big enough to hold everyone," Jack said. "It'll be a tight fit with the dragons, but I think we can make it work."

The major stared toward the dragons. Max saw the man's face darken, and it looked like he was about to say something.

"There appears to be another road through here, sir," Jamie said, and traced his finger across the map. "What do you think?"

The major held his gaze on the dragons a few seconds longer before looking away to follow where Jamie was indicating. "It'll take us longer that way," Stevenson said after a moment, "but the Germans will be expecting us to take the shortest route to Dunkirk. This one may help us evade them longer. If Jamie is right, they're likely to pull in additional units to join the hunt."

Max's heart leapt at the mention of Dunkirk. And the thought of his grandmother there waiting for him. It seemed every time they got closer, the war had yet another thing to throw at them. And now they might have to go through the German army to get there.

"Everyone grab your gear and let's move out," the major ordered while he folded the map. "We don't have a second to lose if we're still going to make it out of this alive. Jamie, you already managed to escape a German camp, so I think that qualifies you to remain our driver."

Max stood watching everyone scramble to gather their things and climb aboard. A couple of soldiers took up positions hanging on to the outside of the truck to serve as lookouts. He waited awkwardly, unsure where his place was.

"Iris," Jamie said, "can you manage the dragons in back?"

She nodded and turned to Max. "Want to help me?"

His eyes went wide. "Can I?"

Jamie helped them both into the truck bed before quickly testing the tires and returning to his place behind the wheel. Max scooted to the very back next to Galahad and sat staring at the dragon with wonder.

"How old is he?" Max asked Iris.

"About the same age as us, I think," she replied. "Although dragons live a lot longer than humans."

"Okay, everyone on board?" Jamie asked, checking over his shoulder.

"A bunch of half-dead soldiers, three kids, a dog, and a couple dragons," Jack reported. "Gotta be one of the oddest units the military has ever seen, against possibly the best army in the world." He glanced around before finishing, "Let's go make a new chapter for the history books."

CHAPTER THIRTY-SEVEN

IRIS

France

Iris sympathized with the truck's groan of protest when Jamie shifted gears and eased it back into motion. With little sleep, an aching body, her clothes singed and torn, and food only a distant memory, she wondered how she was still moving. But they didn't have any choice. If they wanted to survive, rest wasn't an option.

As they drove away, she stared at the forest fire that still raged behind them until it disappeared from view. She hoped it would give them enough of a lead to beat the Germans to the coast. It had to.

Galahad shuddered violently once under her hand, and her heart thumped an extra beat with worry. His scales were almost too feverishly hot for her to touch. She squeezed his shoulder reassuringly. *Just a little longer now.*

Jack had gone back to working on the remaining chains still holding the dragons. A few of the other soldiers were helping him. He held his hammer unsteadily over one of the locks, trying to time his strike for a smooth patch of road. But the truck bounced violently just as he swung his hammer.

"Yeow!" Jack yelped, jerking his thumb toward his mouth.

"Jamie, I think you may have missed one or two potholes back there. Want to go back for a perfect score?"

"Just be glad the Germans were nice enough to lend us a ride. I only wish I could have seen their faces when they found out we'd fooled them with the fake mustard gas."

"Be careful what you wish for," Jack said. "The Jerries aren't likely to give up until they've caught us and strung us up."

"Jack's right," Iris said. "General Wyvern won't let the dragons get away that easily."

After a long time, one of the lookouts pounded on the roof of the truck. "Headlights incoming from the east," he called down.

Jamie slowed the truck to a stop and switched off its lights. From their position hidden back among the trees, the moonlight revealed a larger paved road a few yards ahead.

The major flicked his flashlight on briefly to check the map before switching it off again. "It looks like our route joins the main highway here. We'd better let whoever this is pass before we continue."

Soon a motorcycle with a sidecar attached drove past. Iris saw a large black swastika painted on its side and her heart skipped a beat. Germans. Then there was another motorcycle. And another. Behind those, several jeeps were followed by heavier artillery vehicles, then a long line of trucks like theirs. It seemed like the convoy went on and on as if it might never end. Soon a smaller group of German vehicles passed heading in the other direction as well.

"That's a lot of activity for this time of night," Major Stevenson said. "Something must be happening."

"Or they're looking for something," Jamie said. "Or someone."

He reached out and switched on a small radio attached to the dashboard. It crackled to life with what sounded like military chatter. "Anyone speak German?" he asked. "It would be good to know what our situation is before we make our next move."

Max leaned forward. "I can understand a little." He listened closer to the broadcast.

"Does any of it mention us?" Iris asked.

"I'm not getting everything they're saying," Max said, "but they did mention a small group of Tommies. That's their name for the British, right? It doesn't sound like they know where we are, but I did hear 'Dunkirk.'"

"So they likely expect we're headed that direction," the major said grimly, "which means speed is our best strategy now. Unfortunately, at the rate we're going on this route, we're not likely to get to the coast until tomorrow afternoon."

Jamie's head turned slowly back and forth, watching the German vehicles go by. "Maybe not," he said.

The major turned toward him. "Have something in mind?"

"Maybe," Jamie said, then, turning toward the back, he added, "Jack, think there's enough of that canvas tarp left to cover the back again? We need to make ourselves look like just any other German troop carrier."

"Help me out, mates," Jack said, gesturing to a few of the other soldiers. They started to pull the canvas tarp back into place over the truck bed.

"You're not seriously considering . . ." Iris said. She saw the canvas had a few holes in it big enough to see the stars through. Was it dark enough that the Germans wouldn't notice?

"It may be our best shot," Jamie said. "Like Max said, they're looking for a group of Tommies."

"Driving a stolen Nazi truck," Maud added.

"Max, did they say anything about that?" Jamie asked.

Max, who had continued to follow the broadcast in German, frowned and considered before answering: "I . . . no, I don't think so."

"So for all they know, we dumped the truck and found our own transportation, or are even on foot," Jamie said. Then, turning to the major, he added, "Sir, we're running out of time. At daybreak we lose our cover, and they'll spot us for sure."

The major looked thoughtful as he stared at the line of German vehicles. "It's a calculated risk, but I don't see that we have many other options. Okay, let's try it and pray our luck holds." He leaned out the window and motioned to the men who had been riding on the outside. "Everyone inside the truck. From this point on, we're a German troop carrier and we have to look the part."

Iris suddenly felt claustrophobic as Jack and the other soldiers finished pulling the tarp over the truck bed, closing them inside. What they were planning to do was risky, with a high likelihood that they could be discovered and captured. But she agreed that they didn't exactly have a lot of other options. If they were still out in the open when daylight arrived, they'd be spotted for sure.

When everyone was in place, they continued to wait in silence for what seemed like hours, though Iris guessed it was probably only a few more minutes. Iris thought her nerves, already feeling frayed and on edge, might finally snap and she'd go insane from waiting. Then at last, the line of German trucks heading toward

Dunkirk came to an end. Jamie shifted gears and swung out onto the road, joining the flow of traffic behind another truck that looked much like their own. Now all they could do was wait and hope they weren't discovered.

"I'd guess we're less than five miles from Dunkirk," the major said. "Let's stay with this convoy as long as possible and see if we can slip away unnoticed once we get close to the city. From there, unless there are any unforeseen problems, we should be able to connect with friendly forces and hitch a ride across the Channel."

They drove in tense silence for several minutes. Iris's gaze wandered from face to face, seeing the same strain she felt reflected in each. It felt like they were clinging to the barest lifeline of hope, with the next hour likely to determine their fate.

"Umm, possible problem ahead, sir," one of the lookouts said from the back of the truck.

Iris jerked her head toward the front. There was a problem already?

Jamie leaned a little out of his window. "A pair of headlights is moving this way but driving slowly. It looks like it's inspecting each vehicle."

"It's too late to change course," the major said. "If we make a break for it now, we're sure to be discovered."

Jamie straightened in the driver's seat and started counting down each truck in front of them as the inspection vehicle drew nearer and nearer. "Six. Five. Four."

Iris felt her chest tighten further with each number. When

Jamie reached *One*, she held her breath. A bright searchlight lit up the cab of the truck. Iris couldn't see what was happening outside, but she worried that even breathing might somehow give them away. The yellow glow seemed to crawl backward through the truck with agonizing slowness. Like it was probing into every corner. The light briefly caught the dragon Malory's shiny blue scales. For a second, an explosion of rainbows reflected across the inside of the canvas cover. Iris thought she should try to cover the dragon somehow, but she didn't dare move a muscle. Her heartbeat thumped in her ears. Could the German patrol hear it? Would Iris give them away?

Then at last the light was past them. She turned her head to watch a pair of red taillights continue onward into the night. She let herself take a long, slow breath.

After a few moments, Jamie was the first one to break the silence. "How is that even possible?" he breathed.

"What is it?" Jack asked.

"The driver," Jamie said, "I'd swear it was Wyvern."

"Then that bloke must be the devil himself," Jack said. "I thought for certain he'd been caught in the forest fire."

Jamie shook his head. "Hopefully I was wrong."

Iris returned to watching the red taillights growing smaller. And smaller. Just when she thought they were in the clear, Galahad shuddered again and let out a shriek of pain.

Iris's breath caught in her throat as she listened to the shriek's echo fade into the night. She glanced quickly at the dragon, then back at the vehicle in the distance. Its taillights were barely pinpricks now. Surely the driver was too far away to have heard Galahad's cry?

The lights suddenly glowed brighter. Over the strangled cry from her throat, she heard the loud revving of a motor. Then the vehicle swung violently around, and a pair of headlights began racing toward them.

CHAPTER THIRTY-EIGHT

MAX

France

"He's coming!" Max shouted. The yellow lights bore down on them faster and faster, looking to him like the glowing eyes of a demon.

"Turn off here!" Major Stevenson ordered. "Quickly! We might still be able to lose him in the outskirts of the city."

Jamie wrenched the steering wheel hard to the right. The truck bounced violently through a low ditch before crossing a patch of grass onto an adjoining road. As they did so, the radio on the dashboard burst into life.

"Don't need to understand German to know what that means," Jack said. "Our little game is up."

Behind them, the loud screeching of brakes and roaring of motors filled the night. Numerous pairs of headlights swung their way and bore down on them. Their truck careened around a bend in the road, temporarily blocking Max's view of their pursuers. The large outlines of buildings began to flash by. And in spite of their dire situation, Max felt a sense of elation bubbling up inside his chest. Because he realized that after all his traveling, he was finally here. He had made it to Dunkirk.

Grandmother!

If they could only outrun the Germans, very soon he would be able to fly into her arms. And he would be safe at last. Because they would both be on a ship heading for England. As they sped deeper into Dunkirk, the sky grew steadily lighter. Dawn was coming, Max realized. Its approach revealed his first view of the city. And with it, his spirits stuttered and fell.

Dunkirk was a shattered ruin.

Buildings stood broken and leaning at odd angles like jagged teeth. Destroyed vehicles, uprooted trees, and other debris littered both sides of the street. Occasionally, Max saw lifeless bodies lay sprawled among the rubble as well, but he avoided looking too closely at these, fearing he might see his grandmother's gentle face among them.

Nothing moved. For all Max knew, they might have been racing through an underworld city of the dead. His elation gave way to fear. There was little chance his grandmother still waited for him in this bleak landscape. The only small comfort he had was that the rubble disguised their exact route from the pursuing army. But he knew that wouldn't last long. There could be only so many ways to go. Instead of running into his grandmother's arms, he might very well be running straight toward the German army.

"There!" the major shouted, and pointed to a forlorn-looking sign indicating the way to the city's port.

The truck creaked wide to the left. Its right side momentarily left the pavement before slamming back down again. Max was thankful he hadn't eaten in a long time, or the ride might have made him lose whatever food he'd had in his stomach.

"The water should be just ahead," the major said. "Let's just hope our navy boys can provide us some cover fire while we—"

He didn't finish his sentence.

Max spun around to see what had happened, and his fear plummeted into despair. As they passed the remains of the city's tallest buildings, a sweeping view of the coastline opened up before them.

It was completely, utterly empty.

Not a single destroyer, barge, or ferry waited to evacuate them back to England. Only a few empty shells of ships that sat half sunken beneath the waves. Not a single living soul roamed the beach awaiting their arrival. Only more bodies scattered like forgotten toys among the sand.

Jamie braked to a stop at the top of a dune. Everyone wordlessly climbed down from the truck and trudged toward the water. Galahad, freed from his chains at last, shakily slid out of the truck bed and followed, leaning heavily against the dragon Malory on one side while Iris provided what support she could on the other.

"They've . . . left us," the major said.

They all stopped, huddled together in a small cluster staring out at the waves.

She's left me, Max thought, and immediately felt ashamed for thinking it. *No, she would never leave me.* Which only left . . .

He started to wobble a little until he felt a steadying hand on his shoulder. "I'm so sorry, Max." Out of the corner of his eye, Max saw Jamie kneel next to him, but the boy couldn't turn toward him. Not if he wanted to keep the flood of tears from bursting out in front of all these men. At his feet Plum whined, sensing the boy's deep sorrow.

"You understand it's not possible she's still here, right?" Jamie asked.

Max made a quick, almost imperceptible nod before dragging his forearm across his eyes. He knew he would have to somehow bury his pain and grieve for her later. Because if he and his friends didn't figure out some way to escape, there may not be a later. "What about us? We can't just give up, can we? You always seem to have a solution for every problem."

Jamie stared out across the empty landscape. "I'm afraid it would take nothing short of a miracle to save us this time. But we've got two dragons. They can at least get you, Iris, and Maud back home safely. The rest of us, well . . ."

"Absolutely not," chimed in Iris. "If you think I'm going to run away and let my brother get captured, then you're even more cracked in the head than Jack said you were."

"Ha!" Jack laughed. "It looks to me like it runs in the family." Then, turning to Maud, he asked, "Don't suppose there's any chance I can talk you into escaping with your dragon either?"

Maud crossed her arms. "I'm staying."

Jack stooped to pick up a wooden plank from the sand. "Well, then I suppose we'd all better get to work building a boat before we're out of—"

The ground beneath them started to vibrate. Max spun around in time to see what looked like an entire brigade of German vehicles begin to spill out of every street and boulevard leading to the shore. In the lead was the sleek car of General Wyvern. He drove to the edge of the sand and waited for the rest of his army to take up position around him. Countless German soldiers poured from their vehicles and stood with their rifles trained on the small group on the beach. Max felt his heart knock hard against his ribs at the sight of so many guns pointed in his direction.

At last the general's door creaked open and he slowly got out of his car. There was almost a spring to his step as he limped forward and stood at the crest of a dune looking down at the dragons.

"Forgive me, my little Valkyries," he said, addressing Iris and Maud, "if you found my hospitality not to your liking. I see you have made some new friends."

"Let them go!" Iris shouted. "We're the ones you want."

"Iris, what are you doing?" Jamie hissed. "I'm not about to hand you over to that man."

A thin smile spread across the general's face. "A noble offer indeed. But, alas, I no longer have need of your services. My scientists are quite capable of taking it from here."

Major Stevenson stepped forward. "Wyvern, I'm the senior officer here. I authorize releasing the dragons to your custody in exchange for our safe passage to England."

Iris spun toward the major like he had struck her. Jamie quickly grabbed her around the waist before she could spring at the officer.

General Wyvern chuckled, with no hint of humor in his eyes. Then, before Max knew what was happening, the general's hand darted to the pistol at his waist and he fired at Major Stevenson. With a cry of pain, the major crumpled to the sand, clutching his leg.

"Grandfather, no!" Maud gasped and ran to his side.

"Let me be perfectly clear," General Wyvern said. "This is not a negotiation. For, as you British say, I am the one who holds all the cards. I will accept nothing less than your complete surrender. Or else my soldiers will begin firing on my command."

Max's vision swam. He frantically looked around for any way to escape. Because he understood what surrender meant. They would all be killed. Maybe not right away but soon enough. And then the general would be free to do whatever he wanted with the dragons. He couldn't let that happen. There must be some way out.

Maybe one hundred yards away, the waves lapped lazily at the shore. Max couldn't swim, but he imagined himself as the hero Sebastian from his story, firing arrows in rapid succession and fending off the closing German army while his friends escaped through the water. But just as that thought came to him, he saw a swarm of dark shapes appear on the pink horizon. An entire fleet of German planes was headed straight for them, cutting off their only escape. It was truly over.

Plum began to growl low in her throat.

Then, as Max watched the approaching fleet, the first rays of the sun slid over the horizon. In the new day's light, something seemed strange about the planes. The way they glowed, yes, but that could be simply a trick of the light. No, it was something about the way they moved. It was their wings, he decided. They moved not like the wings of planes, but of . . .

"*Dragons!*" he cried.

CHAPTER THIRTY-NINE

IRIS

France

"Dragons!"

The shout echoed in Iris's head. At first, she thought it must be her imagination. Or maybe she had already been shot and her brain was slipping into a final hallucination before she died. When Galahad bellowed next to her with delight, she finally whirled around.

The sun rose like a giant ball of fire over the water. Its light seemed to burst across the sky like streaks of pink and orange fireworks. And in that light came dozens—no, at least a hundred—winged creatures, their bodies sleek and shimmering as if infused with magic. As if a host of twinkling stars had fallen from the sky and now streaked toward them.

Dragons.

Red dragons. Green dragons. Blue dragons. So many that they seemed to fill the sky. As they soared closer, their shrieks carried across the waves, and Iris thought it was the most beautiful sound she had ever heard.

Her heart thumped along to the beating of the wings, growing louder and louder as pure elation washed over her.

It was Galahad's lost herd. They had come at last.

The German army stood frozen in place; all faces now fixed on the sky. Even the towering general seemed to have been struck speechless.

Then the morning was shattered by an earsplitting shriek as the first of the dragons dove out of the sky. It was Belrath, the massive dragon king. His golden scales glowed in the light of the morning sun as he streaked downward like a deadly meteor toward the German army. A column of flame poured from his mouth and slammed into the earth with an intensity that shook the beach under Iris's feet hundreds of feet away. Behind him came dragons of all sizes and colors, filling the air with their shrieks and fire.

The neat ranks of the German army instantly dissolved into chaos. Most soldiers scattered out of the path of the dragons' charge. A brave few stood their ground and fired their rifles, but their bullets pinged harmlessly off the scales of the great beasts.

A giant purple dragon clutched a German tank in its claws and tossed it into the ocean as if it were no more than a child's toy. Another dragon tore a large transport truck in half while panicked soldiers spilled out in all directions. Other military vehicles exploded into flame from the dragons' fiery breath. The German soldiers fled for the cover of broken buildings, small pits hastily dug in the sand, and even toward the ocean—anywhere to escape the dragons' fury.

While Iris watched with awe as the chaos unfolded all around, a loud thump came from behind her.

"Did someone call for a ride?"

She spun around to see a grinning Tommy, on the back of an emerald green dragon.

"Took you long enough," Maud said, marching forward and punching him on the arm.

"Hey!" he said, rubbing his shoulder. "We came as fast as we could. Fortunately, when the dragons came looking for Iris, my dad sent them to the last place he'd seen her."

"And he let you come along?" Maud asked skeptically.

He shrugged. "I didn't exactly ask. But anyway, are we going to stand here talking all day, or do you want to go home?"

Iris looked around as more dragons thumped down in the sand. There were more than enough to get them all home to safety. "Everyone!" she shouted. "Find a dragon and let's fly before the Germans have a chance to regroup!" She saw Major Stevenson still lying in the sand holding his leg. For the briefest of seconds, she thought of leaving him there for almost killing Galahad. Twice. But then with a sigh, she said, "Maud, can you help your grandfather onto a dragon?"

"Way ahead of you," Maud called over her shoulder, already helping him to his feet.

"Max," Iris said when all the dragons had found riders, "do you feel like you can handle a dragon—" She turned around. But Max was no longer there. "Max!" she called, twisting to the right and left.

"I'll be right back!" he shouted.

Iris spun toward his voice and saw him dashing across the beach toward their stolen German transport with Plum at his heels. "Max! What are you doing?"

"I just need to get something first! I'll be right back!"

Iris glanced nervously around. The dragons had scattered the German soldiers, but she didn't see General Wyvern anywhere. She wouldn't feel completely safe until they were in the air on their way home. What was so important to Max that it was worth delaying their escape?

Galahad lay panting in the sand beside her, looking in no shape to fly. One of his large golden eyes slid open and rolled toward her. *Don't leave me*, he seemed to be pleading. Iris choked on a sob and fell to her knees at his side.

"Don't worry, I'll never leave you. I'll get you home. I promise."

Then she heard a low growl that turned the blood in her veins to ice. Her head jerked toward the noise. She gasped.

The general stalked across the beach toward them. With each step, he thrust his black cane into the sand and dragged himself forward with a grimace that looked as if he was in great pain.

Thump. His cane sank into the sand again.

"I will have my dragons," he said through gritted teeth.

Thump. Closer now.

A bolt of fury sizzled up through Iris's chest. She rose and moved toward the general, blocking his path. "These dragons belong to no one. You will *not* have them!"

Rage flashed in the man's eyes. He loomed over her, but Iris stood her ground even when he raised his cane, ready to strike her down.

Then, suddenly, the towering officer's eyes widened. With his cane frozen over his head, he staggered backward one step. Then another.

What was happening? Iris wondered. She whirled around and felt all the breath go out of her lungs.

As his eyes sparked with flames like Iris had never seen before, Galahad struggled to his feet. First one foot planted firmly in the sand, pushing himself up with great effort. Then another. And another, each time seeming to gain strength until he was standing on his own. For a few heartbeats, nothing happened. Finally, with a mighty roar and shake from his head to the tip of his tail, his dull brown scales seemed to explode off his body like shattering glass.

Iris threw up her arm to shield her eyes from the transformed creature before her. It was Galahad. Only, his new, brilliant red scales as they caught the morning sun blazed like he was on fire. Tears of joy and relief streamed down Iris's cheeks. It was the most beautiful thing she had ever seen.

Galahad shook his head as if waking from a dream, then turned to stare at the still-frozen general.

"No," the man said, staring wildly at Galahad. He started to back away slowly, then more quickly. "No! You are mine. Mine!"

Galahad roared again and unleashed a column of flame on the retreating officer. The man screamed as the fire blasted him backward. He managed to stagger a few paces before collapsing into the sand, where he lay face down, unmoving.

"Is he dead?" an awed voice asked nearby.

Iris turned to see Max returning toward them. She shook her head. "I—I don't know."

"I'm so sorry I put you in danger. I . . ." He held up a bow and arrow set. "These may be the last things I have from my mother and father, and I just couldn't leave them behind. But Galahad . . . I saw the whole thing and that was incredible!"

"Iris!" another voice called.

Iris looked over just as Maud and Malory landed on the beach nearby. With them was a small silver dragon. "We need to go!" Maud said. "I brought a ride for Max." She eyed Galahad with amazement. "Does Galahad feel up to flying?"

Iris stared at Galahad, still amazed by his transformation. "What do you think, Galahad?"

His roar of reply was healthy and strong.

"Go ahead," she told her friends. "We'll be right behind you."

She watched Max race away toward the silver dragon, then walked slowly toward Galahad. She tentatively let her fingertips slide over the shiny new scales. "I can hardly believe it. Maybe now everyone else will see you like I've always seen you."

Galahad rumbled low in his throat and nuzzled her neck.

"I know," she said, laughing through new tears. "You're still the same Galahad. And my best friend."

Galahad rumbled again. Then he crouched lower and looked out over the ocean where the rest of the dragons were already soaring toward home.

"You're right. We should go." She scrambled onto his back and felt the powerful spring of his back legs as they launched toward the sky. But they had barely gotten off the ground when something dragged them heavily toward one side. Galahad shrieked and beat his wings harder, lifting them clear of the ground. Iris automatically grabbed tighter to his neck to avoid tumbling off and looked down.

They were already twenty feet in the air and slowly rising.

But there below them, General Wyvern hung by one hand with his cane hooked around Galahad's rear leg.

A mad gleam filled the general's eyes. "I will have my dragons. Or no one will have them!"

Galahad flapped frantically. They reached eighty feet. A hundred. But it was clear that he wasn't going to be able to continue long with the added weight of the general. Far below, the ocean churned hungrily. Iris had to do something, or they would all plummet into the water and drown.

Suddenly, she saw Max on his silver dragon soaring toward them. Max was fumbling with his bow and arrow with his hands shaking, obviously doing his best to avoid looking down.

"Max, what are you doing?" she shouted.

"Trying to be brave!" he called back.

Iris craned her neck to look down at the general. Galahad wobbled sickeningly in the sky,

The huge general laughed at Max's bow. "Look at the little soldier," the man taunted. "Trying so hard to be brave while his hands tremble like a coward's."

Max slowly edged sideways on his dragon to take aim. Iris could see the terror in his eyes.

"Max, you'll fall!" she said. "You don't have to do this!"

"Yes, I do! He's the reason we had to abandon our home. He's the reason my grandmother is gone." Max's shaking hands steadied as he spoke. "And I . . . am . . . *not* . . . a coward!"

Twang!

The arrow shot off the bow. It streaked through the sky toward the general.

Clack.

It ricocheted off the officer's cane and fell harmlessly toward the water.

Max had missed!

The general cackled, watching the arrow spiral away. "I am a man of destiny! Fate is just beginning to write my chapter in history. No one can—"

CRRRRAAAACK!

He trailed off as the sound echoed through the air.

Iris ducked lower automatically, thinking maybe the German soldiers were shooting at them. But then her eyes found the general's cane. A split had formed across the black wood so that the two halves remained joined by barely more than a splinter.

Max hadn't missed after all!

Snap.

With the slightest sound, the walking stick broke in half. General Wyvern's eyes widened. Then he plunged toward the ocean.

Max and Iris watched him fall.

A few moments later, he disappeared beneath the waves.

It was over.

CHAPTER FORTY

MAX

England

The cool morning wind rumpled Max's hair from atop the silver dragon's back. Far below, the ocean's slate gray turned to sparkling blue as the sun climbed into the sky. In every direction, the air seemed to be filled with dragons of every size and color of the rainbow. Up ahead, Jamie rode a large golden dragon. And there was Jack to his left. And Iris and Maud trailed behind. All his new friends were safe at last.

"England!" came a cry from somewhere ahead.

"England!" "England!" The cry was taken up by several other voices as a long, glittering white cliff seemed to rise up from the waves to greet them.

Max knew he should be sharing in the elation the others felt. After so much time and through so much danger, they had survived. They were finally safe. But not even the fact that he was riding a dragon helped to shake the hollow feeling in his chest. It was as if his heart had simply crumbled and blown away in the wind, leaving only a dull, empty ache in its place. Because while all his friends were returning to their families and loved ones, Max was even more painfully aware that he had no one.

His parents were still missing. And his grandmother was gone.

"Hold on, Max!" Iris called as she surged past him astride Galahad's back.

The other dragons all banked along the tall white cliffs and Max's dragon joined them. Plum barked at their shadows racing along the cliff face, and everyone whooped and shouted in the sort of delight that can only be felt after a long, harrowing ordeal like they had all been through.

Iris laid her hand on Galahad's neck, and the dragon responded to her touch by dipping low toward the water. Max followed on his dragon, marveling at how the two seemed to be able to communicate without words. Then he gasped when a particularly high wave crashing against the cliff face sprayed them with icy water.

"Sorry!" Iris called, and giggled.

Max couldn't help but laugh too. "Where are we going?"

"To my village," she replied. "A lot of parents there are probably wondering where their kids are. It shouldn't be too much longer now."

They passed by small coastal towns and tiny villages. At each one, the locals stopped and stared into the sky with their faces transfixed in childlike wonder. Kids on the ground raced after them, pointing for their parents to look up at the parade of dragons. Max imagined their winged fleet was rather awe inspiring for those who had thought dragons were merely the stuff of fairy tales. And to be fair, up until a few days ago, he had been one of those people.

At last a small fishing village came into view with neat white and gray houses nestled into a harbor along the water's edge.

Iris angled toward it and started to fly over the village until they heard a shout behind them.

"Iris! Look!" Max said. It was Jamie. And he was pointing at the harbor, where a little blue-and-white sailboat with a bright yellow daffodil on its tattered sail limped toward the docks.

"Dad!" Iris shouted, and Galahad swung back around. The dragon landed with a crunch on the stony beach, and Max landed nearby on his dragon. Iris scrambled down from Galahad's back and ran toward where Jamie already stood at the water's edge. As the boat slid silently toward them through the morning mist, Max saw a tall man standing at the front of the boat. The man's left forearm was wrapped in a bloody, torn bandage, and his hair and beard were wild, as if they hadn't been combed in days. But his eyes were sharp and alert, and they immediately brimmed with tears when he saw Iris and Jamie waiting there. When the boat was almost to the shore, he threw a coil of rope to Jamie, who caught it and quickly tied it to a mooring while the boat bumped against the beach. Then with a quick stride and leap across the water, the man pulled Iris and Jamie toward him and hugged them fiercely against himself.

While he watched the little family locked in their embrace, Max suddenly felt sick to his stomach. He slid off his dragon's back and let Plum down to the ground before staggering a few steps away and doubling over. The hollow feeling in his chest had expanded until he could barely breathe.

No one was waiting desperately for his return. No one was waiting to throw their arms around him and welcome him home. In fact, he wasn't sure if he even had a home anymore or if it had been demolished by the German army like so many others.

"How in the world did you get here?" he heard Iris's father ask behind him. "And all the dragons? Where did they come from?"

"It's a long story," Iris said. "Maybe we should save it for later when we're all back around the living room fire with steaming cups of tea."

He laughed. "Fair enough. I can't tell you how relieved I was to sail in here and see your two faces." He paused. "And who do we have here?"

"This is our new friend, Max," Iris said. "He came all the way from Belgium."

At the sound of his name, Max straightened with a great effort and turned around. Iris's father studied him with a frown on his face. "Max, is it? From Belgium?"

"Yes, sir," Max said, wondering at the man's strange reaction. "Is—is there something wrong?"

Without answering, Iris's father climbed back aboard his sailboat and disappeared beneath the deck into the ship's hold. When he returned a minute later, he was carefully leading another person across the deck. Through the mist, Max saw it was a frail-looking, older woman wearing a shawl tied around her bowed head.

In the next moment, Max staggered backward as if he'd been struck. Then with a loud sob, he ran forward across the narrow strip of beach and splashed through the shallow water. His shoes came off in his rush, but he ignored them and scrambled over the edge of the ship and onto the deck.

The woman looked up at the noise of his approach and her face transformed. "Max?!" she cried in bewilderment, and threw her arms out to greet him. "My dearest Max!"

Max fell into her embrace, laughing and crying at the same time. "I—I thought you were . . ." But then words failed him, and he simply stood there with sobs racking his whole body, relishing her warm, familiar embrace.

"Where in the world did you find her?" Max heard Iris ask.

"The British abandoned their evacuation efforts and told me to clear off," her father answered, "but I refused to give up on your brother. As I wandered that godforsaken beach thinking I must be the last living soul left, along came this old bird who was the only one as stubborn as I was. She was half-delirious when I found her wandering the sand, repeating a single name over and over."

Max slowly pulled away and looked up into his grandmother's eyes.

With a tearstained face, she gazed at him and nodded. "Max."

"Well," Iris's father continued, "I figured I couldn't simply leave her out there at the mercy of the Germans, so I coaxed her onboard my ship to come to England before I returned to keep looking for Jamie." He paused and shook his head as he studied Max and his grandmother. "You know, they're already calling it the 'Miracle of Dunkirk.' And I guess whoever was handing out miracles wasn't quite finished yet."

Max smiled up at her, then turned to his new friends. His heart thumped in his chest, the hollow feeling now completely filled to overflowing. Not only had his little family been reunited, but he realized he had gained even more family along the way.

EPILOGUE

England, One month later

Iris sat in a sunny patch of grass in front of her house with Max and Maud. Nearby, Max's dog, Plum, raced barking back and forth between the dragons Galahad and Malory as they playfully tossed a ball between themselves just out of the dog's reach. It was one of those rare warm summer days that seemed to stumble accidentally into their lonely reach of the English coast, and they had decided to enjoy it while it lasted.

Malory tossed the ball in Galahad's direction. Before Plum could spin around, Galahad spat a small burst of flame that instantly incinerated the ball. It disappeared in a puff of smoke. Plum twisted back and forth between them in confusion.

"Galahad!" Iris laughed. "That's cheating!" Still laughing, she turned her head at the sound of a motor approaching in the distance. "Whoever could that be?"

The three children rose and brushed the loose grass off their clothes as a car appeared around the turn in the road and trundled to a stop. The driver's side door opened, and a tall, older man dressed in military uniform stepped out.

"Major Stevenson," Iris said, glancing quickly toward the dragons and back again.

"Ah, Iris," he replied. "Just the person I was hoping to find." He moved around the car with a slight limp in his step, supported by a cane.

Iris tensed as he approached and stopped in front of her.

He looked down at her and nodded solemnly. "I completely understand the scowl on your face—"

"No, sir," Iris interjected, embarrassed that her emotions had been so easily read. "I'm—"

"Now, now, it's quite alright," he said. "In fact, I don't blame you one bit. I was a pigheaded fool and tyrant, and it's a shame that it took getting shot in the leg to realize it. But during these last several weeks, I've had little to do but rest and think, which has helped me see the error of my ways."

"Sir?" Iris asked uncertainly.

The major gingerly got to one knee to be at eye level with Iris. "You see, when I was much younger than I am now, I had a sister named Emma who adored dragons—I think almost as much as you. Of course, back in those days the woods around here were full of the creatures. Emma would spend practically every waking minute playing among them. That is, until the day she died." He looked away, staring off into the distance. "It was a type of fever we'd never seen before, so of course the rumors started that it was somehow the dragons' fault. From there, the outrage fanned out of control until the relations between humans and dragons were beyond repair. I was young and hurting and looking for someone to blame. So I chose to believe the rumors, and my anger grew into a hatred for all dragons. I blamed them for Emma's death."

Here he paused and looked over at Galahad and Malory almost wistfully. "But seeing you and Maud with them, and finally witnessing for myself the gentle spirit of these creatures, I came to understand they couldn't possibly have been responsible for Emma's death." His eyes returned to Iris's. "Which is why I've brought you this." He reached inside the coat of his uniform and extracted a single folded sheet of paper, which he handed to Iris.

"What is it?" Maud asked, her eyebrows squeezing together quizzically.

Iris took the paper and unfolded it, then started to read.

"I still have a little pull at the higher levels of the British government," he said. "Which is how I've been able to have these woods declared—"

"A permanent sanctuary for dragons!" Iris blurted excitedly, and turned to wave the paper toward Galahad and Malory.

The major chuckled. "As well as, of course, the cave farther to the north that your brother has led me to understand has become their new home. But for any who choose to remain here"—he turned and bowed slightly toward Galahad and Malory—"they shall be welcome."

Iris ran toward Galahad and threw her arms around his neck. "Did you hear that? Isn't it wonderful? You can stay here for as long as you want!" She leaned back and looked up into his golden eyes. "That is, of course, well, if you want to. But if you'd rather . . ."

The dragon made a low rumble in his throat and leaned in to

nuzzle Iris's cheek. Behind her, the major cleared his throat. "There are . . . a few more matters of business."

Iris's heart sank. She had expected there might still be some consequences for her actions. After all, she had broken countless rules and even direct orders, as well as destroyed a barn in her efforts to rescue Galahad. However, when she turned around, the major was looking not at her but at Max.

Major Stevenson dipped a hand into his coat pocket and extracted a small piece of paper. "It's not quite what I was hoping for, my boy, but I expect you'll find it quite welcome nonetheless."

Max took the folded paper curiously, then opened it and read what was inside.

"Well, what is it?" Maud asked impatiently.

"It says . . ." he started, then stared up at the major as if he couldn't believe what he was reading.

The major smiled and nodded.

Max's whole face lit up. "It says my mother and father have escaped to Switzerland! They hope to come to England as soon as they're able!"

"I inquired with some acquaintances in the foreign service, and they were able to track them down. I had hoped to bring them to you myself, but the situation in Europe being what it is, this is the best I could manage for now."

"No, it's wonderful!" Max said, relief evident in his voice. He clutched the piece of paper tightly as if it was too good to be true.

"And now for Maud and Iris," the officer said. He reached through the open passenger side window of his car to retrieve something in the seat. When he straightened again, he held two small, flat boxes made of polished black wood. "There is one for each of you," he said, handing each girl a box.

Iris looked at Maud quizzically before unlatching her box. Inside lay a bronze cross on a crimson ribbon. She recognized it as the same type of cross that she had seen on the wall at Maud's house.

"It's a Victoria Cross," Major Stevenson explained. "Awarded for conspicuous bravery, or some daring or preeminent act of valor."

Maud reverently removed her cross from its box and placed it around her neck, where she stared down at it for several moments. When she lifted her head, her eyes were moist with tears.

"Your father would have been so proud of you," the major said. He sniffed and dabbed at his eyes with a handkerchief.

Iris's cross glinted in the sunlight as she turned it up to study its face. Beneath images of a crown and lion, she read the inscription out loud: "For Valor."

She looked up and found Maud watching her. They had defied the odds to stand up against the might of the German army, risking their own lives to save the ones they loved. The war was far from over, she knew, but they wouldn't stop fighting no matter what dark days lay ahead. As if sharing the same thought, the girls exchanged a silent nod.

No, they wouldn't ever stop fighting. Wouldn't ever stop believing that together they could conquer whatever challenges the future might hold.

Because they were women of valor.

ACKNOWLEDGMENTS

The story behind every story involves a broad cast of characters, including many who played pivotal roles in its creation without getting their moment in the limelight. I would like to acknowledge some of those here. First of all, a million thanks to my fabulous editor, Mallory Kass, for her ability to envision what this book could be, and suggesting a first line that inspired my imagination to see it, too. To Antonio Javier Caparo and Christopher Stengel for bringing my ideas to such vivid and fantastic life with a dust jacket that leaps off the page. Jalen Garcia-Hall expertly took the helm when needed and coordinated behind the scenes, while Lia Ferrone worked her magic to get my dragon book in front of readers everywhere. And to the many others at Scholastic who touched this book at various stages in its creation—Melissa Schirmer, Kristin Standley, Cassy Price—I am in your debt. A huge thanks to beta readers Stacy Alfano, Erin Bedell, Lesa Boutin, Cindy Christiansen, Julie DenOuden, Joshua Eisenman, Ben Gartner, Kristen Nadeau, Donna Rasmussen, Nicole Shabrou, Lauren Siefer, and Melissa Thom, who provided critical guidance and insights into the minds of young readers during the creation process. And last but certainly not least, I couldn't have done this at all without my family, who supplied generous amounts of encouragement, love, and time during the journey of creating this book.

ABOUT THE AUTHOR

Sam Subity loves writing stories that explore the magic and wonder of being a kid. He's still a little stunned every time he sees one of his books on a shelf in a bookstore or library, waiting for a reader to discover. When he's not writing, you might find him running the trails of northern California, where the endless winding miles past fog and ocean inspire tales of adventure and mystery. You can visit him online at samsubity.com.